NOT WITHOUT YOU

NOT WITHOUT YOU

JEAN BARRETT

FIVE STAR

A part of Gale, Cengage Learning

GALE
CENGAGE Learning·

Detroit • New York • San Francisco • New Haven, Conn • Waterville, Maine • London

GALE
CENGAGE Learning™

LIBRARY OF CONGRESS CATALOGING-IN-PUBLICATION DATA

Barrett, Jean.
    Not without you / Jean Barrett. — 1st ed.
        p. cm.
    ISBN-13: 978-1-59414-949-8 (hardcover)
    ISBN-10: 1-59414-949-6 (hardcover)
    1. Women television journalists—Fiction. 2. United States. Army—Officers—Fiction. 3. Americans—Iraq—Fiction. 4. Americans—Afghanistan—Fiction. I. Title.
    PS3552.A73435N67 2011
    813'.54—dc22   2010043414

First Edition. First Printing: February 2011.
Published in 2011 in conjunction with Tekno Books and Ed Gorman.

To my wife.
Not without you, Laura.

ACKNOWLEDGMENTS

No novelists work completely on their own. All of us depend on others to make our stories as accurate as possible, often through research, but sometimes, if we're lucky, by being able to consult individuals with firsthand knowledge. I am indebted to the following people for sharing their knowledge with me: Sergeant Chad Stellpflug, who told me about Iraq and the U.S. Army; Bill Bowman, whose experiences in Kosovo served me so well; Dr. Rory Johnson and R.N. Judy Scrimpsher, who patiently answered all my medical questions; Bill Herlache for giving me the names of Belgian immigrants and their culture in Wisconsin; engineer Ray Scrimpsher for his mechanical advice; Ann Lewis, who related much appreciated information on the subject of adoption; recruiting Sergeant Andrew Diedrick, who described army uniforms during the years this book covers; and the staff of the Decatur Public Library, who so generously helped me with my research. I am responsible for any errors that may occur.

CHAPTER ONE

PART ONE:
THE PERSIAN GULF WAR
SAUDI ARABIA AND IRAQ—1991

What's wrong with you?

Nothing, Kate tried to tell herself. This was just a normal reaction to all the shoppers flowing around her in the opulent, Riyadh mall. They were a shock after the harsh conditions she had experienced, in such sharp contrast to what she had left behind in Iraq less than forty-eight hours ago that they were making her a little nervous.

You just have to give yourself a chance to get used to this all over again, that's all. Because this is your reality now. And what happened back in Iraq between you and Efrem . . . well, maybe that was the illusion.

Was it? Kate wondered.

No! She refused to think it hadn't been every bit as real and vital as she wanted it to be. *Needed* it to be.

But the doubts, a product of the mistrust that had haunted her for so many years, persisted. They had been stalking her ever since her wrenching separation from Efrem.

Kate hadn't anticipated that parting. They had been together following their rescue, or at least near each other when they'd been returned to Saudi Arabia, where an army surgeon had examined them and pronounced both of them remarkably fit after their ordeal. She'd also been within hearing of his voice while they were questioned by military personnel.

It was afterwards, when it had been necessary for them to go off in different directions, when Efrem had been called back to his army unit to await orders and Kate had been flown to Riyadh, that anxiety had attacked her in earnest.

She'd managed somehow, like the professional war correspondent she was, to calmly handle the storm of media interviews in her hotel, including the one from her own TV news station. But all the while, deep inside hammering at her, was the awful fear that she would never see Efrem again.

Their parting had been hurried, accompanied by such confusion there had been no time for promises. And there were obstacles to any commitments, weren't there? So many obstacles. Chief among them was the one that waited back home for Efrem, but she couldn't bear to think about that.

There were other problems, of course, like the demands of their careers. The career that had once meant everything to Kate, but now . . .

She didn't know. Her only certainty had been how suddenly lost she'd felt without Efrem, as if some essential piece of her were missing. It was an alien emotion for someone who had always been so self-contained.

All this Kate had suffered and, angry with herself, had struggled to defeat without success. Then this morning had come that wonderful phone call in her hotel room and the sound of Efrem's rich, cheerful voice.

"I've finagled an overnight pass and the chance of a lift from my base here into Riyadh. Are you free for dinner this evening? And, if you're not, make yourself free because I need to see you."

Kate's heart had soared, and with her happiness came an urgent need for a special dress.

There was no lack of selections in the ultramodern mall. The shops were stocked with the latest fashions ranging from the current craze for finely embroidered fanny purses to genie pants.

Armed with credit cards, the oil-rich Saudis eagerly sought all the Western luxuries featured in the stylish boutiques. Kate found it ironic to watch the women covered from head to toe in their dark *abaayas* purchasing micromini skirts. She knew they couldn't possibly wear any of these form-fitting, revealing outfits in public, but they were probably acceptable in the privacy of their homes. Whatever the case, the women who swarmed through the mall wanted them.

And Kate, with funds wired to her from her station, was still searching for that perfect dress. But it eluded her as she wandered from shop to shop, still striving to convince herself that this, along with the bright lights and the hum of the mall, was the explanation for her nervous uncertainty.

It wasn't, of course. The truth was that the elation of Efrem's phone call had dimmed. The familiar, nagging doubts were gnawing at her again. This was the actual explanation, had been from her arrival in the mall.

"I need to see you," Efrem had said.

There could be any number of reasons for those decisive words, including a final goodbye. If this was his intention, if what they had come to mean to each other was no longer real or possible for him, Kate would somehow have to bear it no matter how cruel it would be. She was strong. Hadn't she managed to survive all the hardships they had shared?

She thought about those hardships. Was it actually possible that less than a week had passed since she had endured the first of them? But there had been so many events and intense emotions crowded into those days that they felt like a lifetime ago . . .

CHAPTER TWO

Six days earlier—Iraq

Much to Kate's relief, they finally untied her hands from behind her back. Just how many hours they had been lashed together at the wrists she had no way of knowing. A long time anyway. So long that her arms felt stiff and numb when she drew them slowly forward, holding them carefully down along the sides of her body.

The blindfold was still in place. Kate knew better than to try to remove it. She had learned at the very start that to attempt any action without permission, no matter how simple, resulted in stern objections.

She was in some kind of a building. That much she knew. It felt larger than the cramped bunker where they had held her last night. Whether this was good or bad remained to be seen. While she waited for instructions, she flexed her fingers in an effort to restore her circulation.

There was a rapid exchange of Arabic from her two captors behind her, not a word of which she understood. Then one of them issued a command, which she also didn't comprehend.

Impatient with her, he ordered a brusque, "In, in," which was probably one of the few English words he knew. It wasn't enough.

In? In where?

When she failed to comply, a hand came up against her back

and nudged her forward. Kate felt her way across a hard floor. As she waited for further direction, a metal door clanged shut behind her.

It was a chilling sound, with such a terrible finality about it she was instantly reminded of every old prison movie she'd seen. A cliché when it was fiction, but this was reality. A *harsh* reality, and it was happening to her!

No longer caring about the possible consequences, she lifted a hand and whipped the blindfold from her eyes. She was in a cell all right. Blinking in the gloom, she heard the sound of a key turning in a lock behind her.

Panic seized her with the full realization that she had just been sealed inside. Wheeling around, she faced a wall of iron bars that stretched across the front of the cell. On the other side of the bars stood the two Iraqi soldiers. They wore uniforms with green sweaters under tunics and matching pants tucked into heavy boots. They regarded her with faintly regretful expressions on their faces.

Except for those first moments after her capture, Kate had been docile, too terrified by her situation to challenge her guards. All that changed now with her sudden outrage.

Throwing herself against the bars of the door, she assaulted them with a righteous "I'm not a soldier! I'm a civilian! You can't treat me like this!"

Her effort was both absurd and a waste of time. They couldn't possibly understand what she was saying. Even if they could, they wouldn't defy orders by letting her out of the cell. Kate knew that, but she didn't care. Logic didn't count when she was both angry and scared, needing an emotional release.

They started to turn away. She slapped her hands against the bars and cried out to them.

"Don't you go and leave me here! There are rules about this! The Geneva Conventions!"

Kate had only a vague knowledge of what those rules were. Nor was she certain exactly to whom they applied. She was simply invoking them out of desperation.

Useless, of course. Paying no attention to her now, they retreated down the corridor toting their stubby AK-47s. She went on beating her hands against the bars and shouting after them, even after a door at the far end of the corridor closed behind them.

"Hey, take it easy."

The voice, deep and mellow, came out of nowhere. Or seemed to. Startled by the unexpected sound of it, Kate went instantly still.

"I can promise you, and believe me the advice comes from personal experience, that yelling at them will get you nothing but a sore throat. That's if you're lucky. And if you're not . . . well, you don't want to know."

She could tell this time that the quiet, masculine voice came from off to her left. There was a wall there, much too solid looking for any sound to clearly penetrate it, so presumably—

"You still there?" he said.

Where else would I be?

"Dumb question, huh? How about I ask instead if you're all right?"

That wasn't a sensible question either. She was far from being all right, although she supposed he was referring to her physical state.

The door to her cell was located on the extreme right side of the front wall. Moving away from it, Kate edged her way along the bars to the left side of the cell. "Who are you?" she asked him cautiously when she reached the solid side wall.

"Your friendly next-door neighbor. Welcome to the neighborhood, neighbor."

The bars were recessed just enough from the end of the dividing wall that she was prevented from seeing him. But his strong voice was so close now that she knew he must be standing only a few feet away from her, probably pressed against his own front wall of bars.

"How many others are in the neighborhood?" she asked him.

"As far as I've been able to tell, there are just the two cells. I figure they commandeered a small, local jail, and now it's full. You and I are it."

On one level his presence worried her because claiming to be a friend didn't mean he was one. But on another level she was glad to know she wasn't alone in this forbidding place.

He must have been thinking something along the same lines.

"I'm not going to say your arrival makes me happy," he said. "Putting it like that would be pretty selfish, but it was getting lonesome in here. You still haven't told me if you're okay."

"I'm not injured." *If you don't count some gruff handling from people who aren't happy I'm in their country.*

"That's good. So, are we going to get to some introductions here?"

Kate was still wary. He sounded like a fellow American, familiar and sympathetic, but at this point she was afraid to trust anyone. It could be he was just a bit *too* familiar and sympathetic.

"Maybe I shouldn't be talking to you at all."

"You always this suspicious?"

"After what's happened to me over the past twenty-four hours, I have every reason to be."

"Fair enough." He seemed to think about it before assuring her cheerfully, "Thing is, I'm one of the good guys."

"How do I know that? There must be a lot of Iraqis who speak perfect English, maybe even with American accents. You could have been planted next door in order to pump me for information."

"Why? You know any juicy military secrets?"

"What I know is this is an Islamic society."

"Meaning?"

"So why would they put a man and a woman side by side in the same jail?"

"Because this isn't like some of the other Arab countries. Iraq doesn't follow a strict practice of segregating men and women. The younger, modern women don't even cover themselves in public with those what-ya-call-it things."

"*Abaayas.*"

"Yeah, those."

If he was right, then she had neglected to do her homework. It was something she had always been meticulous about. But there had been no time for any careful research. Her assignment had happened too quickly.

"Just how do you know all that?" she asked him.

"Pentagon's got a thorough indoctrination program. Hey, maybe I'd better shut up. Could be you're the spy, some sultry, dark-eyed beauty just waiting for me to spill *my* guts."

Kate laughed. A laugh strictly without mirth. "I don't qualify as a femme fatale, even in my best moments. And, believe me, this isn't one of them. My hair hasn't seen a comb since they took my purse away from me."

She thought about her hair, how just before leaving the States she'd had its natural, light brown color enhanced with blonde highlights. That was after it was cut in a short, sassy style meant for easy care in the Middle East. Easy care? Oh, yeah, that was funny all right when it had to be a mass of snarls by now. No mirror either, which was just as well. She probably wouldn't want to see her face. Not after what the sun and grit of the desert must have done to it.

"When was that?"

"Yesterday." An eternity ago, she thought. "They did put me

in a great outfit." She looked down in disgust at her prison garb. "White sneakers that sort of fit and a yellow, baggy thing that doesn't. I'm swimming in it, with pants dragging down to the floor. Nice touch, though, with the big PW on a leather patch."

He chuckled. "I'm wearing the same thing, except the pants end somewhere above my ankles and my arms are hanging out of the sleeves. I guess they figure one size fits all. Goes with the whiskers getting long on my face. You haven't seen a comb, and I haven't seen a razor. How about that?"

It struck her that, considering the circumstances, this was a strange conversation to be having. He apparently didn't think so.

"You gotta admit this is reason enough for those introductions."

"Is it?"

"Come on," he coaxed, "talk to me."

But Kate was still reluctant. If he *was* the enemy, she didn't want to feed him any ammunition that could make her situation more difficult. Not that telling him who she was and how she had ended up being captured mattered when they already had that information. Besides, now that she'd had a chance to think about it, it didn't seem very likely that he could be anything but what he claimed to be, an American prisoner like her. All the same . . .

"Okay," he said when she remained silent, "then how about I start with telling you about me. You're gonna love it."

"I'm listening." How could she not when he had her curious about his identity? And if she was satisfied by what he had to say, then maybe, *just* maybe, she would provide him with the essentials about herself.

"That's better. Name's Efrem Chaudoir."

"Catchy."

17

"It's more impressive when you add the *lieutenant.*"

"What branch of the service would that be, Lieutenant?"

"U.S. Army. Want my service number?"

"I'd much rather hear how you managed to wind up in this place."

"Ah, now that's the interesting part . . ."

Kate turned her head to take inventory of her cell while she listened to him. Not that there was much to see. Dirty and dreary, the cell couldn't be more than ten feet in width and maybe six feet or so in depth.

Its solid walls had been coated in plaster, which was now stained and peeling, exposing the cinder blocks underneath. In one spot she could make out hash marks scratched into the plaster, evidence that some prisoner before her had tried to keep a record of the days. The cell contained nothing but a bench fixed to one wall and a metal cot with a thin, foam mattress and a single, folded blanket of rough, brown wool.

It was all so depressing that she had to control her urge to beat at the bars again.

". . . a search and rescue mission," he was saying. "One of our Apaches was shot down, and we flew out to recover the crew."

Kate knew that the Apaches were attack helicopters originating from inside Saudi Arabia where the international forces were massed near the Iraqi border. Though there had yet to be any ground offensive, the allies had been giving Iraq a pounding from the air since the start of the war, particularly key targets in Baghdad.

"Never made it," he went on. "Our Black Hawk went down under enemy fire. Pilot died along with the medic. I was lucky. I walked away from the crash without a scratch. But the other two soldiers under my command were injured, one of them pretty badly."

Kate's work had taught her the value of being a quick study with the people she interviewed. She had gotten pretty accurate at reading characters, but this man was proving elusive, maybe because she could only hear him, not see him.

A laid-back nature heavy on humor. More than a bit cocky. Nothing intense about him. That had been her impression of Lieutenant Efrem Chaudoir. Until now, when his husky voice went dark and sober.

"That's been the tough part. They separated us when we were captured. I keep hoping my men were taken to a hospital, that they're getting decent treatment. But they won't tell me anything. All I can do is worry and wonder."

She could hear the frustration in his voice, the anger and sense of helplessness. No, he wasn't an easy study.

"How long have you been here?" she asked him.

"This is my third day." His tone lightened again. "Your turn now."

"Why is it so important for you to know?"

"We're in this together, aren't we?"

Kate wasn't sure she wanted to think of it like that. It implied a kind of intimacy, and intimacy of any kind made her nervous. Which was maybe why she stood there twisting the blindfold in her hands. Until this moment, she hadn't been aware that she was still clutching it.

She threw the thing down on the cot, at the same time ridding herself of her indecision. Because he was right. It made no sense for her to withhold the essentials from him.

"CNA," she said.

"Come again?"

"Cable News America," she explained. "It's based in Washington, D.C. I'm on assignment for them in the Middle East."

"Okay, that's a start. How about a name to go with it?"

"Kate Groen."

"Hi, Kate. So, exactly what is it that you do for this CNA?"

"TV correspondent sent over to cover Desert Storm."

"Hey, impressive."

"Not yet. CNA isn't one of the big outfits, which is why you've never heard of it. But one day . . ."

"You'll be another Jane Pauley, huh?"

"If I'm good enough." And she meant to be.

"Why not? You have the right voice for a newscaster. How old are you?"

"Old enough."

Kate saw no reason to tell him she was twenty-three, which was a bit young to be an overseas newscaster, even for a small station like CNA. Revealing her age might suggest just how single-mindedly ambitious she'd been about her career, and that was something she had no intention of discussing with a stranger.

"How does a war correspondent end up being captured by the enemy?"

"By going where I wasn't supposed to go." Not without sanction anyway, she thought, remembering how Iraq was permitting Western reporters to cover the air strikes in Baghdad but was holding a news team captive in Kuwait. "It was a dumb risk, I know, but the station recalled the man I replaced because his coverage wasn't exciting enough."

"And you weren't going to make that same mistake, huh?" he said.

She'd have to watch herself with him, Kate thought. The guy was insightful. Enough so to have probably just figured out about that ambition of hers.

"I wanted some footage of enemy territory," she admitted. "My cameraman and I sneaked just far enough across the border to get it."

"No other crew?"

"A small station, remember? Anyway, Jerry was all I needed."

"Let me guess. You ran into an Iraqi patrol."

"Yeah, I messed up. I think when they grabbed me they thought I was military."

"Why is that?"

"I was wearing combat-style fatigues. You know, the camouflage stuff like our forces."

"Good for the camera?"

"The viewers back home seem to like it. Makes us more authentic somehow, I suppose."

"And you couldn't make the Iraqis understand you weren't military?"

"No, even though one of them spoke a passable English. All I got was his wanting to know who I was and what I was doing in his country and why were we bombing them when they're an innocent, peaceful people."

"Then what?"

"They held me in some bunker all night blindfolded and with my hands tied."

"Yep, they're big on blindfolds. Where was your cameraman all this time?"

Kate managed a brief, sorrowful "Jerry didn't make it."

Efrem didn't ask her to elaborate, and she was grateful for that. He was a soldier, after all, so maybe he understood about the loss of people who had come to matter to you and how you couldn't bear to talk about it.

"And after the bunker?" he wanted to know.

"They put me in a truck this morning, still blindfolded and my hands tied. What with stops along the way every time there was any sound of an aircraft overhead, it took nearly all day to get here."

And now that day was ending, Kate thought, turning her

head to see the fading light in the sky through the small, solitary, barred window high in the back wall.

"Where are we?" she asked him. "Do you know?"

"My guess, from the sounds I've been able to pick up from outside, is a small town. Maybe an oasis because I can see the tops of some date palms through my window."

"All I can see through mine is the sky."

A sky somewhere deep inside a country that couldn't understand why America was its enemy, where she was a prisoner and badly frightened. Did he sense that fear? Is that why he offered her a soothing "It'll be okay, Kate. The Iraqis will have figured out by now that you're not connected with the military, and our side must know you're missing. They're probably already working to negotiate your release."

She appreciated his confidence and wished she shared it. That she didn't have to keep remembering other Western reporters who had been held as hostages in the Middle East for months, even years, in awful places like this.

But it could be worse. You're not alone. You have Lieutenant Efrem Chaudoir close by.

Kate hung on to that knowledge, striving to draw strength from it. That wasn't easy when she wasn't used to depending on anyone but herself and her own resources. When, with her history being what it was, trusting another individual had always been a problem for her.

There was the rattling sound of something approaching out in the corridor.

"Our dinner," Efrem informed her as a trolley appeared through the gloom.

It was wheeled by an elderly, bearded man in a white caftan that Kate had learned back in Saudi Arabia was called a *thobe*. He was accompanied by a uniformed guard armed with the familiar rifle.

She hadn't seen him before. He wasn't one of the two escorts who had delivered her to the jail. Very young, she noticed. He had to be barely out of his teens, but he wore the black moustache that seemed to be a badge of adult male pride for so many Iraqi men.

The trolley stopped outside her cell. Kate watched the old man ladle water into an orange plastic cup which he placed on a small tray. The tray already bore a bowl of rice, a half slice of bread and a few dates.

"Chai," he told her, pouring a steaming liquid into a glass, which he added to the tray.

The young guard surprised her with a translation. "Tea," he said. "Hot and sweet. It's very good. You will like it. If you want more, you must tell him *bai chai.*"

"You speak English."

He surprised her again with a shy smile. "Some. Not as good as I'd like."

There was a slide at the bottom of her door. The old man opened it and pushed the tray inside. He also had a little smile for her, a sympathetic one. Then he and the young guard moved on with the trolley to Efrem's cell.

Kate picked up the tray and settled with it in her lap on the edge of the cot, which was situated lengthwise along the wall that divided the two cells. She eyed the meager fare with misgiving. Then, realizing it was all she was going to get and she'd better be grateful for it, she picked up the plastic spoon, stuck it in the bowl and tried the rice. It was a sticky mess without any flavor.

The bread was no better, stale and bland. The dates, however, were wonderful. And so was the tea when she tasted it.

By this time the guard and the old man had retreated with the trolley, leaving Efrem and Kate alone again.

"Not very appetizing, is it?" she called out to him.

Either his own cot, or his bench, had to be directly on the other side of the wall because he sounded very close when he answered her.

"That's what I thought the first time. Now I can't wait for the two meals a day they bring me."

He didn't add, "You will, too, Kate," but she felt he had to be thinking it. The conditions here were that bad then.

"The guard and the old man seemed friendly enough, anyway," she said.

"The guard's name is Jamil, and he's a gentle soul. Told me all about the girl back home he expects to marry. I think he's eager to improve his English. It's another guard, Tariz, you have to watch out for. Mean sucker."

"Because he doesn't like Americans?"

"No, he's just one of those guys who'd be nasty whatever his nationality or yours. Resents being stuck here in this backwater babysitting us. Jamil said Tariz wants to be back in Baghdad or at the front where the action is. I can relate to that."

"How many guards are there?"

"Just the two of them, not counting the old man who comes in with the food from the village."

"What about the two soldiers who brought me here?"

"Delivery boys. Probably went back to their outfit. That leaves only the four of us. Makes it real cozy."

The sky had darkened while they were eating. There were no fixtures in the cells. The only light came from a pair of bare, weak bulbs out in the corridor. Even those suddenly went out a moment later.

"What happened?" Kate wondered, alarmed by the almost total blackness.

"The electricity is never dependable," Efrem explained, "and even when it is, it gets shut down at night. Otherwise, the lights would make us a target from the air."

"What else do I need to know?"

"Just one thing. And believe me, Kate, it's the most vital of all."

"Which is?"

"The toilet. There isn't one. At least not as we know it. You gotta relieve yourself, you tell them you need to use the W.C. Not a bathroom or a latrine. They don't understand that, but for some reason they know the term water closet. Which is pretty funny because the only plumbing in there is a basin of scummy water and a soiled towel."

"You're too late," she told him grimly. "I've already been introduced. I had to use the place when I got here."

Kate shuddered at the memory of the fetid cubby and the hole in the floor over which she'd had to squat without benefit of a seat.

She had finished with her meal, including the rice and the bread. Unappealing though they were, she realized that Efrem was right and that before she was out of here—*if* she ever got out of here—she would be treasuring every morsel they allowed her.

"Will they come back to collect our trays?"

"Not until morning. Just set it over by the slide."

The clear, desert sky was spangled with so many stars that, narrow though her window was, it admitted enough starlight into the cell to enable Kate to find her way to the door where she placed the tray. She and Efrem were silent when she returned to the cot.

The night itself, however, was anything but quiet. She could hear the muffled sound of what had to be the guards' battery-powered radio issuing a stream of Arabic on the other side of a closed door. There was also the mewing of a cat somewhere close by.

"The cat's an advantage," Efrem said. "Might be overrun

with mice without him."

Or worse, Kate thought, imagining the horror of rats.

It wasn't the fear of rats, though, that had her shivering as she huddled there on the cot. She had been told that summers in this part of the world were unbearably hot. What she hadn't expected was how cold, even gray and damp, the winters could be. And this was February. The rawness of the night had already seeped into her cell.

Reaching for the blanket, she wrapped it around her and stretched out on the cot. All talked out, exhausted by the long day and with nothing else to do in the darkness, she decided to try to get some sleep.

Impossible. The blanket was inadequate. She couldn't get warm enough to fall asleep. The sound of her squeaking cot as she squirmed on it in discomfort alerted Efrem. He mistook her restlessness for despondency.

"Hang on, Kate," he spoke to her softly, the creak of his own cot as he shifted his weight an indication that he, too, must have settled down for the night, early though it still was. "You gotta believe it's going to turn out all right. It's the only way we'll survive this. Okay?"

The man was plainly an optimist. Well, that was probably something good to be in a situation like this. Even if that quality wasn't always inherent in her own nature, she couldn't help smiling at his effort to reassure her.

She didn't correct his misunderstanding about her restlessness. All she did was respond with a simple, "Okay."

Something must have worked, maybe just the comforting timbre of his deep voice because, in spite of the cold, she managed to drift off.

"Kate! *Kate!*"

The insistent, urgent sound of Efrem calling out to her

repeatedly finally penetrated her sleep. Coming awake, she struggled up to a sitting position on the cot, trembling in the blackness, disoriented.

"What?" she croaked. "What is it?"

"You were crying out. That must have been some hell of a nightmare you were having. It's a wonder the guards didn't hear you and come running."

She remembered the dream now. It had been bad. Very bad.

"You want to tell me about it?"

"No."

"Might help if you do."

Maybe he was right. Maybe she needed to get it out. "It was Jerry. I was reliving what happened to Jerry."

"Your cameraman, huh?"

"They shot him. He resisted when they took his video equipment away from him. He wanted it back, and they thought he was trying to attack them. One of them who was just a nervous kid killed him on the spot. He never had a chance."

She could still hear the crack of the assault rifle, still see the look of utter surprise on Jerry's face just before he collapsed.

"Yeah, that stinks all right. I wish there was something I could do besides tell you how sorry I am."

"Thank you, but nothing you could do or say would be enough because it's my fault he died. It wouldn't have happened if it hadn't been for my blind, stupid ambition. I had to take us in there to get that footage. And for what? To serve my career. All for my damn career."

"You're being too hard on yourself. This is a war, Kate, and stuff like this . . . well, it just happens in war."

"You don't understand."

"About guilt? Oh, yeah, I do."

His men, she thought. She had forgotten how worried he was about his two men who had been injured when the Black Hawk

27

went down. As their officer, he would feel responsible for them. That was only natural. But now it sounded as though he was also blaming himself for what had happened to them, even though he wasn't to blame.

"Yes, I guess you do understand that."

"You gonna be all right, Kate?"

"Sure, I'm all right," she said, deciding that his warm voice was as good as a pair of arms around her.

She was startled by the analogy almost the instant it occurred to her. What on earth had prompted the image of—yes, admit it—*his* arms holding her? The need for a simple human comfort? Okay, that was understandable. But anything beyond that . . . no, that was not to be considered.

There was a long silence between them. Then she asked him something she had been wondering about.

"Efrem, have they questioned you yet? I don't mean things like your name, rank and service number. I mean, *really* questioned you."

"In any detail? No."

"Me either. Why do you suppose that is?"

He paused for a moment before telling her, "I think we're waiting. The guards, too."

"For what?"

Again he hesitated. "I'm guessing a visit from a senior officer. Someone experienced in interrogation."

"Oh."

She tried not to sound anxious. She knew he didn't want to worry her, and that's why he'd been reluctant to tell her. But she *was* anxious. Because, as casually as he'd phrased it, there had been a somber undertone in his voice. An ominous something that said to her: This can't be good.

CHAPTER THREE

It was strange, Kate thought, how much her senses had shifted from sights to sounds. How, locked away like this, she had to depend on those sounds to keep her informed.

It was sound that awakened her early the next morning. A distant wailing somewhere outside her cell. She was puzzled about it until she remembered she had heard it back in Saudi Arabia. The cry of the muezzin calling the faithful to prayer in the local mosque.

There was something else she could hear. A huffing in the next cell that told her Efrem must also be awake. There was something rhythmic about the mysterious noise.

"What on earth are you doing?" she called out to him from her cot.

"Morning," he responded.

She understood the huffing then. It was his labored breathing coming from the vicinity of the floor. Had he collapsed?

"What's wrong?" she asked him anxiously.

"Nothing. Just doing some exercises."

She decided he must be on the floor lifting and lowering himself in a series of pushups.

"How can you be so ambitious at this hour?" she grumbled, blinking at the first rays of the sun that managed to find their way into her cell. "And why?"

"Because it's important to keep fit."

"I haven't read the prison manual on that one, but I'll take your word for it."

"That mean you're ready to join me?"

"If you're inviting me for a cup of coffee," she said, sitting up on the cot, "the answer is yes. If you're talking about calisthenics, you can forget it."

"You always this grouchy in the morning?"

"Are you always this cheerful? What are you doing now?"

She could tell he was on his feet but still breathing hard.

"Running in place. Come on, Kate, it's good for you."

She eyed the dirty floor with distaste. "No pushups, thank you. And I'll pass on the running in place."

"You never exercised back home?"

"Sure I did. Every day."

That wasn't altogether the truth. She'd made an effort in her apartment in D.C. to perform a regular, daily routine of stretching exercises, but her busy schedule hadn't always permitted it.

"Well, then?" he urged.

There was no schedule now. There was nothing but time. Why not? "I'm on my feet, master," she reported.

"Doing what?"

"Bending over and touching my toes."

"That's a start."

For the next fifteen minutes or so Kate committed her body to a series of exercises, none of which were anything as strenuous as what she heard in the next cell. But she tried to tell herself they were beneficial when, finally surrendering, she sank back down on the edge of the cot.

"What now?" she asked when she finally recovered her wind.

"We wait for the first of our two meals a day," he answered her. She could tell by the squeaking of his cot that he, too, had seated himself. "You get a chance to use the W.C.?"

"I took the opportunity when Jamil came by in the middle of the night to check on us with a flashlight."

"I got there myself on another check."

"That's good."

They were quiet after that. Kate stirred restlessly on the cot. She wasn't used to being idle. She had spent most of her life being anything but, particularly these last few years when it seemed she'd always been on the run. How was she going to endure long hours of empty waiting? Waiting for meals, waiting to be taken to the W.C.

There was something else they were waiting for. The interrogator Efrem had talked about last night. But it was better not to think about that.

"It's hard, isn't it?" Efrem called out to her.

"What is?"

"Not having anything to do."

Uncanny. Had he read her mind? Or was it only natural that, with both of them being inactive like this, he should be sharing the same thought?

"Yes, it is," she agreed.

"They say that boredom is one of the worst things inmates in prison have to bear."

"I've heard that, too. I'm considering a walk, even if it is in a circle."

"I have a better idea. Let's tell each other some stories."

"You want us to swap tales, like around the campfire?"

"I'm not big on fiction. I like biographies."

"Who did you have in mind? Abraham Lincoln?"

"I already know his story. I don't know yours, though."

"You heard it yesterday."

"That was just the latest chapter. What about all the rest?"

"Efrem, I don't think—"

"All right, I'll tell you mine, and if you're not asleep by the end of it, maybe I can convince you to share yours."

"This had better be entertaining if you want me to stay

awake," she warned him with a laugh.

"It's more than that. It's fascinating. What do you know about Belgians?"

"I beg your pardon?"

"See, you're already hooked. That's my ancestry on both sides, Kate. Belgian."

"Come to think of it, I don't remember having met anyone of Belgian descent before."

"That's because not that many Belgians emigrated to America. At least that's what I've been told, and that a lot of them ended up in Wisconsin. Mostly concentrated on the southern half of the Door Peninsula, which is where I come from. That's near Green Bay."

"Belgian, huh? I guess that explains your surname, Chaudoir."

"Oh, yeah, there are Chaudoirs all over the peninsula. That and Herlaches and Martines and Bouches and Jossarts."

"And what did these people do after they settled there?"

"Built solid farmhouses of brick and stone with bull's-eye windows in the gables and sometimes, if they were really devout, roadside chapels."

Kate tried to picture such a rural scene, all those houses with bull's-eye windows and the big, loving families that they sheltered. But it was an existence that was totally alien to her. She wondered how deeply Efrem missed it.

"So you're a farm boy when you're not fighting wars."

"Uh-uh. Pop gave up the dairy business before I was born, leased out the land to a neighbor and started a cabinet-making operation in the barn. I worked with him for a couple of years alongside my two brothers after my own aspirations crashed and burned."

"What were you hoping for?"

"A career in professional baseball. I went to college on a

baseball scholarship. One of the majors picked me up after I graduated and put me on one of their farm teams. I was good but not good enough. Got dropped after two years."

"I'm sorry."

"So was I. That's when I went into Pop's business, but after a few years I knew that wasn't for me either. Ended up joining the army."

"And have you found the right career for you?"

"I think so."

"But you're not sure."

"I'm gonna have to be sure pretty soon. Hell, I'm twenty-eight years old. It's time I made a decision about my future. Your turn, Kate."

Efrem's abrupt switch from his life to her own jolted her. She wasn't sure she wanted to talk about her background. There were too many hazards there.

"Come on," he insisted. "You didn't fall asleep, so you owe me your story."

"It isn't very interesting. For one thing, I don't have a genealogy like yours. I don't know much about my ancestors or where the name Groen originated. Somebody once told me it's probably German."

"Didn't your parents ever talk to you about the family history?"

"I don't think it mattered to them one way or another. They only cared about the here and now."

"No grandparents to tell you? Uncles, aunts?"

"Afraid not. My grandparents were either deceased by the time I came along or lived on the other side of the country, and both my mother and my father were only children, like me."

Kate was aware of how that must sound. That, unlike Efrem, she hadn't known the warmth and closeness of a big family. Well, it was true. She supposed her parents had loved her, but

33

she couldn't remember them ever expressing it. The only clear memory she had of her childhood was how busy they had both been with their careers. And still were.

"Maybe the kind of existence you had," she went on wistfully, "takes a rural setting. We're as different in that as we are in families. I've never known anything but an urban environment."

"Where was that?"

"Before D.C.? Baltimore."

"Your folks still there?"

"They are. They're both lawyers."

"They share a practice?"

"They never did, and now they don't even share lives. They were divorced a couple of years ago."

"Tough."

"I was on my own by then and living in D.C., so it didn't much matter. And that's it, my whole story."

"You're right. It isn't very interesting."

"That's blunt."

"Oh, I don't mean your life was dull, Kate. I just think . . ."

"What?"

"That maybe you've left something out of that story. The vital part that says who you are now and why."

He surprised her with how perceptive he was. She could have told him he was right. How what had happened to her as a young, vulnerable teenager had played a very strong role in shaping her into the woman she was today. How that very painful episode had taught her to be very careful about where she placed her trust, including with her parents.

But Kate had no intention of sharing any of this with Efrem. She had resolutely put that part of her life behind her, and she meant to keep it there, where it couldn't hurt her.

Her media career made that possible. It was the one thing of real value she *had* learned from her parents. That a relentless pursuit of success could deaden regrets, make everything but your goal unimportant. Most of the time, anyway.

"You're wrong," she said. "The only vital stories I have to tell aren't mine. They belong to the people I cover in the news. Are we done?"

"Not yet. You haven't told me whether you've got anyone special waiting for you back home."

"How special are we talking about? If you mean friends, I do have a few of those that I value."

"I was thinking more like a boyfriend."

"No one who's declared himself. Anyway, if you're going to chase stories around the globe, like I want to do, then it's better not to have attachments like that."

"Not even a cat?"

She laughed at the idea. "Afraid not."

Kate decided that, except for an uncomfortable moment or two, she was enjoying their conversation, strange though it was when they had yet to even glimpse each other. Maybe it was because he was easy to talk to.

"So how about you?" she asked him. "You have anyone special waiting for you back home?"

He was silent.

"Hey, you still there?"

There was another pause before he answered her. "I'm married, Kate," he said solemnly. "I have a wife back in Wisconsin."

"Oh."

Now why hadn't he told her before this, when he was letting her know all about his family? And why should she find his disclosure so disappointing? It was absurd. Even more ridiculous than her fleeting image last night of his arms around her. A man she had never seen, a man she had known less than twenty-four hours.

It's our circumstances, she told herself firmly. It's the kind of situation that does crazy things to your emotions.

"You must be missing her."

"You'd think so, wouldn't you?"

"What's wrong?"

"The marriage. I wish I could say it's solid. It isn't. We were having problems even before I joined the army. And that didn't help. Jackie didn't like it. She would have been content to have me stay at home and go on working with my father, even though I was getting nowhere."

"Do you have children?"

"No, and that's a good thing. Because when I was shipped over here . . . well, I think we both knew our marriage probably wasn't going to survive the separation."

"I'm sorry, Efrem."

She tried to be genuinely sympathetic about his troubled marriage, but the truth was that his wife didn't seem very real to her. Their lives before now and the people they had left behind felt remote in this place, another world without any true substance.

The only reality was the here and now and what circumstances were forcing them to share. But their connection, and how it was deepening, worried her, even frightened her a little as she huddled there on the cot, hugging herself against the morning chill.

It was the other guard, the one called Tariz, who accompanied the old man when their morning meal finally arrived on the clattering trolley.

This was the first time Kate had encountered Tariz, and she didn't like what she saw. He had a sour expression on his broad face, a look of speculation in his vigilant, black eyes.

Tariz watched in silence as the old man prepared her tray

and pushed it through the slide before rolling the trolley on to Efrem's cell. As hungry as Kate was, she hesitated to collect her tray, waiting for Tariz to join the old man who was already delivering Efrem's tray to him. But the guard remained there just outside her cell, eyeing her with an interest that made her uneasy. The command he finally uttered was in Arabic, of course, but she understood the gesture of his hand motioning for her to fetch the tray.

With a wary reluctance, Kate left her cot and crossed the cell. When she bent down and rose with the tray in her hands, she hoped Tariz would be satisfied and go, but he went on standing there.

That's when she made a serious mistake. Unable to resist the lure of the food, she looked down at the tray, checking its contents. It didn't offer much. No tea this morning, just a cup of water. A few of the wonderful dates, a slice of bread, and a dish of what seemed to be stewed tomatoes mixed in with the familiar rice.

It was only a brief glance, but that's all it took for Tariz to catch her by surprise. Before she could back away, his hand shot through the bars and closed around her arm.

She managed to hang on to the precious tray while trying to free herself, but his grip was like a manacle.

"Let me go," she ordered him, making an effort to remain calm.

He had to have understood what she was demanding, but he didn't release her. There was a little smile now on his wet mouth. Kate didn't have to know Arabic. His meaning was clear when he leaned forward and began to murmur something to her. In any language it had to be obscene. At the same time, his other hand stretched through the bars in an effort to fondle her.

Efrem, who must have been aware by now of what was happening, came fiercely to her rescue, shouting angrily at the guard from his cell.

"Turn her loose, you bastard! You hear me? Take your hands off of her, or—"

"Efrem, no!"

Kate's plea came too late. Although Tariz freed her, it was only so he could turn a cold rage on Efrem. The guard wasn't armed with a rifle, but he did have a pistol. Whipping the semi-automatic out of his belt, he shoved the bewildered old man out of the way in order to position himself in front of Efrem's cell.

Kate pressed her face against the bars, watching in horror as Tariz raised the pistol, directing it at the figure she couldn't see but whom she knew was there only a few feet away, a helpless target unable to defend himself.

"Please!" she cried out. "Oh, please don't!"

Tariz paid no attention to her. His gaze was fixed on his objective, his mouth twisted in a sneer.

"Go on, you coward," she heard Efrem challenge the guard. "I can't stop you, so just get it over with and shoot me, why don't you?"

Oh, why did Efrem have to go and further antagonize him? Why didn't he just shut up?

She saw Tariz brace himself to fire and died her own death as she waited for the explosion. To her immense relief, what she heard instead was the pounding of boots racing along the corridor. Jamil, who must have heard the commotion in the guardroom, was suddenly, blessedly there.

The young guard clamped his hand on Tariz's arm. Tariz tried to fling him away, but Jamil held on. Kate listened to the heated exchange that followed between the two men. She couldn't begin to comprehend their rapid Arabic, but the essential meaning of their dialogue wasn't lost on her. Jamil was arguing with his fellow guard not to shoot the prisoner.

In the end, uttering an oath of frustrated fury, Tariz tucked the pistol back in his belt and stormed away down the corridor. When he was gone, Jamil gazed at the two prisoners in their cells, his expression registering his unhappiness with the incident.

"Foolish, foolish," he scolded, and Kate wasn't sure whether he was blaming them or the volatile Tariz.

In any case, neither Kate nor Efrem made any effort to justify themselves. Jamil muttered something to the old man, turned away and went off along the corridor. The old man followed him with the trolley.

When they were alone again, Efrem spoke to her, his voice husky with concern. "You okay, Kate?"

"Yes," she murmured, sagging weakly against the bars. Then, recovering herself, she came fully, rigidly erect. "No," she said, changing her mind, "I'm not okay at all! What I am is angry with you! You almost got yourself killed! And I won't have you on my conscience like Jerry! I *won't!* Do you understand me?"

"I understand. Do you have your tray?"

"What?"

"Were you able to keep your tray, or did he make you drop it?"

"No, I'm still holding it, but what has that got to do with—"

"Then let's sit down and eat because whatever almost happened didn't, and right now the food is important."

She lost the will to go on fighting with him, maybe because she realized he was right, except she didn't see how she could swallow anything when she was still shaken by the ugly scene with Tariz. But once she'd seated herself with the tray in her lap, she realized just how hungry she was. She began to eat.

They were silent for a few minutes while they concentrated on their food. Then Kate asked him, "What do you suppose Jamil said to Tariz to convince him not to shoot you?"

"Who knows. But if I had to guess, I'd say Jamil told him the interrogator wouldn't be at all pleased with him when he got here and learned that he'd killed the prisoner before he could be questioned."

"That's what I was thinking. I'm also thinking this tomato and rice stuff is a real mess."

"Try the bread. It's almost fresh today."

"Not bad," she agreed, after biting into her slice.

"Kate?"

His voice had turned serious again.

"What is it?"

"About Tariz. I want you to be very careful there. Stay away from the bars whenever he's in here, and don't ever let him take you to the W.C. Always get Jamil to escort you. He's probably already figured he'll need to do that. Do you follow what I'm saying?"

Kate understood only too well what he meant. If Tariz ever got her alone, she could end up a victim of rape, and there would be little she could do to prevent it. The possibility made her shudder, but she didn't want Efrem to know that.

"I'll be all right," she assured him, stressing her independence. "I've been taking care of myself for a long time now."

"I sort of got that."

Damn him. She was still upset with him for risking his life to protect her. She didn't want to admit to herself she was also deeply moved by his reckless heroics. But she knew she was and that maybe she wasn't so independent after all.

Kate didn't know how long she had been asleep on her cot, but judging from the light slanting through the small, single window, she guessed it must be sometime around mid afternoon, which meant she'd been asleep for about an hour or so. Without her watch that had been taken away from her that first night in the bunker, it was impossible to tell for certain.

Efrem had encouraged her nap. There was nothing else to do but talk or sleep, and since she'd been all talked out, she had obeyed his suggestion and drifted off on her cot.

But the nap left her feeling groggy, and that's why it took her several moments before she began to sense that something was wrong. It was so quiet, much too quiet. An absolute stillness in which nothing stirred.

Lifting her head from the cot, she called out a soft, "Efrem, are you there?"

She got no reply. Nor was there any sound of movement from the next cell. That's when she panicked. Sitting up on the cot, she was suddenly convinced Efrem was gone. That he had been removed from his cell and wasn't coming back. Something terrible must have happened to him!

She was frantic at the thought of being all alone now, of having lost him. She understood then just how much he mattered. What was she going to do without him?

"Efrem, where are you?"

Her wild cry was answered by a low, "I'm here."

She went limp with relief. "Thank God. I thought Tariz might have—Why didn't you answer me?"

"Sorry."

Brief though his response was, she could detect the puzzling change in his voice. A weary monotone without any trace of his familiar animation.

Kate got off the cot and went to the bars. "What is it? Are you sick?"

"No."

"Something must have happened. Talk to me."

For a moment she got no reply. Then she heard a heavy sigh of resignation and the groan of his cot as he got to his feet. He must have approached the bars on his side because his voice sounded very close when he spoke to her.

"I asked to use the W.C. while you were asleep."

"Was it Tariz who took you there? Did he—"

"No, it was Jamil who went with me. He knew how worried I was about my men. The two soldiers who were separated from me when we were captured."

"I remember."

"Jamil had heard something, and he managed to whisper it to me."

"It was bad, wasn't it?"

"Yeah," Efrem said bleakly. "The one who was more seriously injured didn't make it, even though both of them had been taken to a hospital to be treated."

"Oh, Efrem, I'm so very sorry."

"Boomer. That's what the guys called him. He was just a kid with a big grin and everything to live for, and now—"

Efrem's voice broke. When he was able to speak again, the flatness was gone. There was emotion again, the heat of anger and helplessness.

"It stinks! I shouldn't have been separated from them. If I'd been with them—"

"There would have been nothing you could have done for the boy but watch him die."

It was pointless to tell him this, of course. He would know it himself, just as she had known when her cameraman died. But logic had no meaning when you were stricken by a death for which you felt in some measure responsible, even when you weren't responsible.

Any further expression of sympathy would be hollow, but Kate longed to comfort him, understood how much he needed some form of comfort. That's why, without examining her action, she reached out to him, stretching her hand through the bars in the direction of his cell.

For a minute nothing happened. Her hand just hung there.

And then, with what she sensed was a slow uncertainty, his hand came into contact with hers. That was all it was at first, just a meeting of their hands, an acceptance of her effort to console him.

Seconds later, it went beyond that. Strong fingers suddenly curled around hers, clinging to her as tightly as a lover's embrace, flesh to warm flesh.

It was a magical moment, but so charged with emotion that it shocked Kate. She felt both confused and scared by its intensity. In the end, she was unable to bear the powerful union any longer and tugged her hand away from his. He let her go. She was relieved and disappointed at the same time by the absence of their connection.

Feeling the need to defuse the moment, she searched her mind for something to distract them. An idea came to her.

"Why don't we play a game?" she suggested.

"You want to play a game when—"

"I know. It sounds callous when you've just learned something so awful, but maybe it will help. Anyway, shouldn't we try to keep our minds active? Isn't that just as important as physical exercise?"

He hesitated, then agreed to her proposal. "Okay, let's play a game. What did you have in mind?"

"I'm an old movie junkie, and if you're any fan of them yourself . . ."

"Enough to be up to a challenge. So, how does this work?"

"It's very simple. We take turns giving clues for the plots of movies, only the movies we choose have to be familiar enough to recognize. The first clue is free. If you can't guess the title from it, then you're given more clues, but each one after the free clue costs you a point. The one who ends up with the fewest points is the winner."

"I've never heard of this game."

"That's because I've just made it up. Shall I go first?"

"Let's hear what you've got."

"A spinster and a lout go downriver on a leaky old boat to—"

"The African Queen."

"You didn't even let me finish the clue."

"Didn't have to. I figured it was your kind of movie. A feisty, headstrong woman ready to do battle. Nothing personal, you understand. Am I right?"

Was that a note of amusement she heard in his voice? She was sure it was. "Yes," she conceded. "Your turn."

"Let me think." There was a pause. "All right, I've got it. The hero has this extraordinary talent. He's got the promise of a great career ahead of him, until an irresistible woman ruins him."

"I don't know. Give me another clue."

"Robert Redford played the hero."

"Are you sure this isn't some obscure film no one ever heard of?"

"It was a big hit, very popular. If you want a third clue, it's gonna cost you another point."

"Just give me the clue."

"His extraordinary talent was baseball."

"Now why am I not surprised by that? Look, I don't know, so why don't you just tell me?"

"I think if a player gives up, it should cost him three points."

"Where did that come from?"

"Hey, if you can make up the game, then it's only fair I get a say in the rules. The movie is *The Natural.* Your turn."

"All right, you can have that rule." She was beginning to regret her inspiration, even if it had taught her something else about Efrem Chaudoir. He could be exasperating.

"Let's see." Kate searched her mind for another title. "Oh, I know. This is also one of my favorites. Here's the free clue. The heroine goes searching in the jungle for her missing sister. The sister has a valuable ruby that the bad guys are after. The hero helps the heroine find her sister and the ruby."

Efrem was unable to guess the title, even after she fed him several more clues.

"You've got me. What is it?"

"Romancing the Stone."

"Romancing the—That's not the plot of that movie. You've got it all screwed up. The stone wasn't a ruby, it was an emerald. And the sister didn't have it, and she wasn't missing in any jungle."

"It is the plot, and you're being a bad sport."

"Just because I expect something like an accurate storyline?"

It was not an issue that deserved a hot quarrel, with both of them rapidly talking over each other, but that's exactly what did result. At some point Kate realized she was still arguing, and Efrem wasn't. He was laughing. That's when she started to laugh along with him.

"Listen to us," he said. "Fighting like a couple of kids over a dumb game."

"I know. Ridiculous, isn't it?"

But it had also felt good, removing them for a little while from the hard reality of their situation. And the laughter it produced was a release both of them needed.

They weren't laughing now, however. They were both suddenly silent. Kate could *feel* it. Their sober, risky awareness of each other.

"What's happening with us, Kate?"

"Nothing. It's just our circumstances. We don't have anyone else to turn to but each other. That's all it is. It isn't real. It *can't* be."

Efrem wasn't so sure about that. He'd felt some pretty strong emotions when their hands were linked. Emotions that were . . . well, yes, actually vital.

Kate spent the rest of that long day trying to convince herself she was right. That she and Efrem had formed a bond purely out of necessity. That they could never be anything but friends. She reminded herself over and over he was married, that to feel anything beyond that was absurd when they had known each other less than two days.

All this and more she told herself. And all the while she struggled, and failed, to shut out something else. Something that insisted it didn't matter she had known him less than two full days, had yet to see his face. Because he was already familiar to her, and whether they were either talking or silent for long stretches wasn't important. It was enough just to know he was there.

CHAPTER FOUR

Efrem didn't like it. It had to be mid morning, maybe even later than that, and they had yet to be fed their first meal of the day. Something was up. He was afraid to give it a name, but he could guess what it might be.

Kate spoke to him from her cell. "I can hear you pacing in there. Is anything wrong?"

This was the beginning of her third day. She hadn't been here long enough to realize the schedule for POW meals in this place never varied. Until now.

He didn't want to worry her. "Just getting some exercise."

"You already went through that ritual hours ago."

"I know, but my legs needed stretching."

He would have preferred to go on pacing, but that might start to make her wonder again. Instead, he went and sat on the hard bench. Hunched forward, he dangled his hands between his legs and thought about Kate.

Her third day. Was that all it was? It felt as though he had known her a lot longer than that. As though—yeah, as though she had always been in his life. He felt that close to her.

"I'm hungry," she complained. "What's holding up our breakfast?"

"It'll get here."

But it wasn't the trolley that finally arrived in the corridor.

Efrem went to the bars when he heard the sound of approaching boots. Both of the guards appeared with their rifles. The old man wasn't with them. No, this wasn't the usual routine.

There was nothing to learn from the expression on Tariz's face. It was never anything but hostile. But Efrem had never known the kind Jamil to look this solemn.

He expected the two guards to come to his cell. But, without sparing him so much as a glance, they went straight to Kate's cell instead. Efrem began to grow alarmed.

"What do you want with her?" he demanded, pressing his face against the bars.

They ignored him. Jamil unlocked Kate's door, and both men went into her cell. Efrem heard the mutter of their voices, but he couldn't understand anything that was being said in there. He was frantic.

A moment later Jamil and Tariz led Kate out of the cell. The two men blocked Efrem's view of her, giving him only a quick glimpse of her, mostly from behind. They didn't pass his cell. They took her out the other end of the corridor.

"If you hurt her," he shouted after them, "if you so much as touch her . . ."

They were gone before he could finish his useless threat, the door closing behind them. Efrem slammed his fist against the bars in helpless frustration.

He went on standing there against the bars. There was nothing he could do but wait. And worry.

What was happening? Where had they taken her? But he knew, didn't he? Or at least strongly suspected it. It was what had been bothering him ever since he'd realized how late their meals were.

The interrogator had arrived. That was the explanation for why the familiar routine had been interrupted. The interrogator had arrived, and Kate was with him in an interview room. Or what would pass for an interview room in this place.

Didn't they realize by now that Kate wasn't connected with

the military and had nothing worthwhile to tell them? Okay, so that probably didn't make a difference. They'd question anyone they captured. What Efrem didn't understand was why the interrogator wasn't questioning him first when, as an American army officer, he would be more likely to know something of value.

Or maybe he did understand. Maybe this was a form of psychology. Leave him behind to fret so that when they got around to him, as he knew they would, he would be more vulnerable when he was interrogated.

If that was the intention, it was working. He was out of his mind with the fear that gnawed at him. Not for himself, for Kate. He tried to keep himself from thinking about the horror stories of POWs subjected to torture when they refused to provide their captors with information. Tried to tell himself nothing like that would happen to Kate. If only he could be with her now . . .

Was she scared? She hadn't seemed frightened when they'd removed her from her cell. But, hell, how could he know what she'd been feeling when she hadn't spoken, when his glimpse of her had amounted to almost nothing?

Efrem was left with an impression of a slender, petite figure and a head of short, light brown hair streaked with blonde. That was all.

He wanted to know more about her. A lot more. Not just what she looked like either. There was one thing he was pretty sure of. Kate had been deeply hurt sometime in her past and was distrustful. He had sensed that almost from the start. Which probably meant she had no use for a man in her life, a man who could complicate her career.

Hell, what was he thinking? That he wanted to be in her life? That was crazy. If nothing else, there was the little matter of his marriage. He wasn't able to forget that.

Efrem used all of this rationale. Made a massive effort to tell himself that, when all of this was over and they were out of here, no longer dependent on each other, he wouldn't feel this way about Kate.

But in the end none of the arguments worked. Whether it made sense or not, all that mattered to him was his certainty that, if anything happened to her, if she failed to come back, it would tear his guts out.

Efrem must have been at the back of his cell when the guards returned Kate to what she was beginning to think of as no better than a cage. She heard him spring to his feet, but by the time he reached the bars she was already locked in again.

"Are you okay?" he called out to her. "Tell me you're okay. I've been going nuts with worry in here."

She thought it was a rash thing for him to admit in the presence of Jamil, who understood enough English to realize it was something that could be used against him. Jamil was decent enough that he might not communicate this to the interrogator, but Kate waited until both guards had left the corridor before she answered Efrem.

"I'm fine," she assured him.

"You wouldn't lie to me, would you?"

"I'm not that noble, Efrem."

"They didn't touch you then?"

"There was nothing physical about it." This time, she thought, knowing it wouldn't be her last session with the interrogator.

"What happened? Where did they take you?"

"I think you've probably guessed that already. I had the privilege of meeting the interrogator in an interview room. He speaks perfect English. His name is Colonel Pahlavi."

"And he questioned you."

"Actually, he didn't."

"He must have wanted something." Efrem sounded disbelieving.

Kate was reluctant to tell him, fearing his reaction.

"Are you going to tell me, or do I have to plead with you to get it?"

"Yes, he wanted something."

Kate's memory took her back to that cramped, dismal little room where she was seated on a hard chair facing a scarred desk. Colonel Pahlavi was behind that desk. He was a handsome man, probably somewhere in his late forties. But there was both a sadness and a weariness about him, as if he'd seen too much war, questioned too many prisoners. His manner was sympathetic enough when he leaned toward her, even genuine, but that didn't mean he wasn't capable of something less humane if circumstances made it necessary.

She could still hear his quiet, patient voice, could see the portrait of a smiling Saddam Hussein on the wall behind him, could—

"Kate, I want to know," Efrem said.

Kate realized he wouldn't give up until he'd gotten it out of her. "I'm being asked to make a video denouncing the United States for its bombing of Iraq. The colonel told me it would be in my best interests to comply with his request. Very persuasive is the colonel."

"Meaning he threatened you with consequences if you refused."

"Not exactly, but it was implied."

"What did you tell him?"

"That I wasn't interested, and giving me a chance to think about it wouldn't work because I wasn't going to change my mind."

There was silence from the other cell. Then, in an emphatic voice, Efrem said, "Let him know you've reconsidered, that you'll make the video."

"I can't believe my ears. I thought you'd tell me 'good girl,' and that you're proud of me."

"I *am* proud of you, but this man probably has strict orders to obtain results whether he likes it or not. What do you think will happen to you if you hold out on him? Damn it, this stubborn courage of yours isn't worth the sacrifice."

She smiled wryly. "I see. Very sensible. And, of course, that's what you'd do if they asked you to make such a video. You'd agree to save your skin."

"Damn right I would."

"You're lying."

"All right, but it's different with me. I'm military. You're not."

"What's that supposed to mean? That you have to remain loyal to the flag and I don't?"

"Listen to me, Kate. Everyone back home knows that hostages are forced to make these videos. No one takes them seriously or blames the hostages."

"This isn't going to work, Lieutenant. I'm not going to make that video."

She should have been furious with him for urging her to issue a statement on behalf of the enemy that would end up being broadcast on every TV news station in America, including her own. But she wasn't angry because she understood what Efrem was doing. He was trying to safeguard her. He cared about her, didn't want her hurt. She would have done the same if it had been him. Whether it was right or not, he mattered that much to her.

"I don't like this," he muttered.

"Yes, no breakfast," she said, seizing an opportunity to change the subject. "And I'm as hungry as you are. It looks like we're not going to get any meal."

"Kate, please—"

"It's probably deliberate," she went on swiftly. "Maybe they're planning to starve us into submission."

She was afraid. Not to miss a meal certainly. She was afraid for Efrem. Colonel Pahlavi wasn't finished with them. She knew that. Knew he was saving Efrem and that eventually, maybe when they could no longer stand the suspense, he would get around to him.

It was probably less than an hour later, though it seemed much longer than that to Kate, when they came for Efrem. Longing to look into his face, she strained against the bars as the two guards removed him from his cell. Efrem tried to meet Kate's gaze, but Tariz blocked their views of each other.

All she got was a teasing glimpse of him from behind as they led him away in a direction that didn't pass her cell. It was enough to show her a head of dark, tousled hair and a rangy figure with an easy gait. Then he was gone, and she was left alone, sick with worry.

She went on standing there in the awful silence for a long time. Then, realizing she was trembling, that her legs were suddenly too shaky to support her, she went and sat down on the bench.

There was a trail of ants on the floor. By now she was so used to the conditions in this place that she didn't let their presence bother her. She watched the ants without thinking about them, her mind on nothing but Efrem.

She had a feeling—no, more than a feeling, a conviction—that he wouldn't receive anything like her lenient treatment from Colonel Pahlavi. There would be no patience with Efrem if he resisted, and she knew he would. Knew that the colonel wouldn't hesitate to order something severe.

The images of what they might be doing to him swarmed through her mind. There was only one thing worse than those cruel images. The possibility that Efrem would be taken out and shot. That she would never see him again. And if that happened, if she lost him—

Kate couldn't bear it.

She was at the bars again, clutching them tightly, when they came back with Efrem. Jamil and Tariz were on either side of him, hauling him down the corridor and past her cell.

Efrem's head was hanging down toward the floor, his limp body supported by the two guards, his legs dragging behind him. He was either unconscious or too dazed to support himself.

She had only a quick glimpse of his lowered face, but it was enough to see that he was battered and bloodied. Her heart turned over in her chest at the sight of him.

"What have you done to him?" she cried out.

Tariz ignored her outrage, but Jamil flashed her an earnest look of apology. Then they went on by her with their burden. She could hear them dumping Efrem on the cot in his cell. Relocking the cell door, they vanished along the other side.

Kate was out of her mind. Unable to go to Efrem, there was no way she could help him. Nothing she could do to ease his suffering. She wasn't even certain he was still alive.

"Efrem," she called out to him softly.

He didn't answer her. Not so much as a groan.

"Dear God, let him be alive."

"Prayers aren't necessary. I'm still here."

His voice was thick and raspy, as if delivered through swollen lips, but it was unbelievably cheerful. Cheerful as it hadn't been when he'd learned one of his men had died, even though he must have endured a savage beating.

"Don't try to talk," she urged him.

"Hell, why not? Talk is all we've got, and I need to talk."

"You're hurting. I can hear it."

"Nah, I'm not that bad. Just let me get . . ." The sound of his creaking cot told her he was carefully shifting himself into a less painful position. "That's better. Good thing you can't see me, Kate. I can't see me either, but something tells me my face isn't a pretty sight."

He was letting her know he was still capable of his wisecracks, and he wanted her to joke about it too. It was his way of not being defeated by their captors. Kate made an effort to oblige him, though her voice was unsteady when she answered him.

"Just as long as nothing has happened to that grin I love."

"How do you know what my grin is like? You've never seen it."

"I can tell."

"Yeah?" There was a pause. "So you love my grin, huh?"

"Don't get cocky about it, Lieutenant."

"Never."

But she could hear he was pleased. Her reckless admission about his grin had been a mistake, though. Now he would know how she felt about him. Did she really mind that? She wasn't sure. It was all getting so tricky.

"Stop talking," she said. "You need to rest."

"Come on, you know you want to hear about all the fun I had with Colonel Pahlavi."

"Later."

He paid no attention to her request. Even though she knew it had to be difficult for him to go on talking, he began to relate in his happy-go-lucky tone all that had happened in that hateful interview room.

"The colonel had some questions for me. Hey, can you believe it, Kate? We actually rate a colonel. Bothered to come all this way just to meet us. Heck, I was real impressed. Told him so, too. You'd think he would have been happy with that."

"And he wasn't."

"Afraid not. And just because I couldn't answer his questions."

"*Wouldn't,* don't you mean?"

"Now how am I supposed to know all the details about our forces? Stuff like their number and how they're deployed and what weapons we've got. I'm just a lowly lieutenant. Think the top brass is going to share things like that with me? Danged unreasonable of the colonel to expect it, don't you think?"

"What I think is that, even if he'd asked you how many buttons are on your dress uniform, you wouldn't have told him. How badly did they beat you, Efrem?"

"It was just Tariz. Jamil wasn't there. Let's just say that the guy enjoyed it, and I didn't. Neither did the colonel. He got up and turned his back on us so he wouldn't have to watch it. I'm thinking that underneath it all he's probably a decent man who hates his job. So, okay, maybe I *would* have enjoyed it if I'd had a chance to fight back. But roped to that chair like I was . . ."

Kate clenched her hands in impotent anger, picturing the vicious, all too willing Tariz pounding on Efrem with his heavy fists, taking pleasure in punishing him for his defiance.

"The man is an animal!"

"Could have been worse," Efrem said, as casually as if he'd been smacked for being naughty. "They could have used a Talk Man on me. I've heard about those."

"What's a Talk Man?"

"A cute little device."

A creaking told her he'd paused to ease himself into a new position on the cot. She heard him suck in his breath against what she guessed was a fresh jolt of pain. She, too, felt that pain.

"They wrap this wire affair over a POW's ears and around his jaw," he continued a few seconds later. "The wire gets connected to a car battery, and every time the prisoner decides not to answer a question he gets a shot of juice. Cute toy, huh?"

Kate shuddered over the image, wondering why Efrem had chosen to describe the Talk Man to her. Why he'd been so ready to have her listen to everything that had happened to him in that room. It would have been more in character for him to shield her against any mention of torture.

And then she suddenly knew why. It was deliberate. If, by telling her what had been inflicted on him, he could frighten her into making that video for Colonel Pahlavi, it would save her from a similar abuse.

Nice try, Efrem. And why do you have to be so damn wonderful that you make me want to cry?

What was she going to do about him? What was she going to do about *them?*

If there was an answer to that question, she was saved from having to acknowledge it by the arrival of Jamil. He carried a jug and two plastic cups. When he arrived at their cells, he shook his head and put a finger to his lips, meaning for them to be quiet about his presence.

Kate understood. What he was doing was forbidden and would get him in a lot of trouble if either Tariz or Colonel Pahlavi learned of it. She silently blessed him for his kindness.

Jamil quickly filled the cups with water from the jug. Then, opening the slides, he pushed the cups as far as he could reach into their cells. Indicating in a hurried whisper he would sneak back later to retrieve the cups, he swiftly departed with the jug.

When he was gone, Kate spoke to Efrem. "Jamil brought us water."

"Yeah, I got that."

"Can you manage to reach it?"

"I'd crawl on my hands and knees for just a sip of it."

It maddened her that she couldn't bring the water to him, help him to drink it. She had to stand there and listen to him struggle up from the cot, shuffle slowly across the floor and make another effort to bring the cup to his mouth. He must have succeeded because she heard him eagerly gulping the contents of the cup.

"Man," he panted, "that was better than beer."

"Better pass your cup to me if you're finished with it. I'll hide both of them under my cot in case Tariz comes along to check on us before Jamil gets back to collect them."

The cup, when empty and turned on its side, was able to fit through the bars. Efrem stretched out his arm and passed the cup to her.

"Now you get back to that cot and try to sleep," she ordered him. "I don't want to hear another word out of you until . . . well, I just don't want to hear another word."

It was evident to her just how sore his body was when he didn't try to argue with her about it.

They'd had nothing to either eat or drink since last night. Kate herself was as dry as the desert outside, but she didn't touch her own cup of water until she was satisfied that Efrem was back on his cot. Only then did she bend down and lift the cup to her mouth.

When she'd eased the worst of her thirst, she took both of the cups back to her cot. She sat there, swallowing the rest of the water and listening. A few moments later she heard Efrem snoring softly from the next cell.

The sound brought her a measure of relief. But not for long. She knew that Colonel Pahlavi wasn't finished with Efrem. That, sooner or later, they would come for him again. He would be subjected to further questions, further torture when he refused to answer them. She was determined to prevent that.

Kate thought about her intention as she went on sitting there, waiting for Jamil to retrieve the cups that were stashed under the cot. Any act of pure, unselfish sacrifice was alien to her. It was more typical of her to seize whatever opportunities came along in order to advance her career. To examine her motive this time wasn't necessary, she supposed. She knew what she wanted to do and why. And for now that was enough.

Kate grew anxious as the long minutes passed and Jamil failed to reappear. There was the risk of Efrem waking up and demanding answers before she had a chance to execute her plan. There was also the possibility, God forbid, that Colonel Pahlavi would send for him again.

Her relief was considerable when Jamil finally arrived in the corridor. Grabbing up the cups, she hurried to the bars and spoke to him in an undertone.

"The lieutenant is asleep. We don't have to disturb him, do we?"

The guard looked puzzled for a few seconds. Then, comprehending, he shook his head.

"That's good." She passed the cups to him before going on earnestly, "Jamil, I need you to go to Colonel Pahlavi. Tell him I'm ready to do what he asked. Do you understand?"

"Yes, I understand."

"Will you do this for me?"

"I'll tell him."

Jamil departed. More tense moments passed before he returned. He was accompanied by Tariz, who unlocked her cell door. There was no word exchanged. The two guards led her out of the cell and along the corridor. As far as Kate knew, Efrem never stirred.

It didn't take long, less than an hour probably before she was back in her cell. Refusing to reproach herself, to feel anything like even a modicum of regret, she went and sat down on the bench again. It was done, and if there were consequences for her action, she would deal with them later.

"Kate?"

He was awake. "I'm here."

"You weren't a few minutes ago."

"No. How are you feeling?"

"Never mind that." She heard him sit up on his cot. "They took you to see Pahlavi again, didn't they?"

"Yes, but it's all right. I made the video for him."

"Why? What made you change your mind?"

"You wanted me to agree to it, didn't you?"

"Yeah."

"Well, then."

"So telling you what happened to me worked, huh? You didn't want them to do to you what they did to me."

"That's right. I did it because I didn't want to suffer the same punishment."

"And I'm supposed to believe that, am I? The hell I do. I can tell from your voice that wasn't your reason. You went and made a deal with Pahlavi because of me, didn't you? Told him you'd make his video if he promised not to have Tariz beat me again."

She should have known he was too intuitive to be deceived. "What difference does it make why I did it?"

"It makes a difference to me," he said angrily. "It was one thing to do the video to save yourself from harm but another to do it for my sake."

"Would that be a male ego at work?"

"Aw, Kate . . ."

"What?"

"It's more than that," he said, his anger giving way to something softer. "A lot more. It's me willing to do anything to see you're not hurt, and you wanting to do the same for me. There's a reason for that."

"Of course, there is. We're all we have, so we've got to turn to each other. You said it yourself the other day. That if we're going to survive this thing, we need to count on one another as well as ourselves."

"It was true then, and it is now," he admitted. "But something else has been added to the mix since then."

"I can't imagine what."

"You know what." His voice turned husky with earnestness. "Oh, sure, I know all the arguments for why it can't be real. Only it is real, and once we get out of here—"

"Let's not discuss any futures together," she pleaded with him. "Because you and I can't happen."

"Don't be scared of it, Kate. Be happy that we've found each other. I am."

She didn't answer him and was thankful when he didn't press her any further. They fell silent. Before this, whenever they were all talked out and didn't speak for long stretches at a time, it had been okay. It was enough to know he was there only a few feet away. But now that he had put into words the feelings she'd been battling, the silence was no longer comforting for her.

She was relieved when a meal finally arrived for them. Apparently, now that Colonel Pahlavi had his video, he was willing to have them fed again. By the standards of the place, what the old man placed on Kate's tray was practically a banquet. Something that resembled pita bread, jelly, a hard boiled egg and a generous glass of the sweet chai.

"How are you feeling now?" she asked Efrem when they had eaten.

"Doing okay. A good night's sleep and I'll be even better."

The old man didn't wait for morning this time but came back for the trays. It was getting dark outside when they were permitted separate visits to the W.C., after which Kate heard Efrem crawl onto his cot again. A moment later the sound of even breathing in the next cell told her he was asleep.

Kate didn't sleep. Huddled on her cot, arms locked around

her knees drawn up to her chest, she rocked slowly in the blackness of the night, unable to silence her thoughts.

Efrem and her. Was he right about them? Had she, against all reason, actually fallen for him? Was it possible when the sum total of their relationship had been no more than conversation? And even though they had never even seen each other's faces?

That wasn't true though, was it? They had shared much more than that. An intimate bonding. She couldn't deny it. Nor could she forget the warm, wondrous sensation of his hand linked with hers. Brief though the connection was, it had generated powerful emotions.

There had been no other physical contact, so it made no sense for her to feel this adulterous guilt over something that was innocent really. Yes, but her longing for him wasn't innocent.

Kate had always considered herself a sensible woman. However, when it came to this, wanting a man who was married, maybe she wasn't so sensible after all.

Anyway, what did it ultimately matter? Genuine or not, what she and Efrem were experiencing couldn't survive. Once they were out of here and back to the reality of their lives—and, please, God, let that happen—this thing between them would go away. How could it last and flourish when there was nothing of any real substance to support it?

But since when, a tiny, insistent voice mocked her, did feelings so strong they chewed you up inside care about that?

CHAPTER FIVE

She felt a hand on her shoulder shaking her, heard a familiar voice calling to her.

"Kate, wake up," he insisted. "I need you to wake up."

Surfacing from her deep sleep to a foggy consciousness, she opened her eyes to the early morning light spreading through her cell. It revealed a tall stranger bending over her cot.

Only he couldn't be a stranger because she had recognized his voice. She was startled by both Efrem's presence and his appearance. He looked like a desperado with his unruly dark hair, the stubble on his chin, the mean bruise on one cheek and a small cut on the other.

"I know," he said. "I'm a mess." He grinned down at her, flashing perfect, white teeth that would be the pride of any dentist.

Kate's bewilderment was suspended by a sudden fascination for what, until now, she had only glimpsed for a second at a horizontal angle. She looked behind the whiskers and the wounds to the wonderful face that was underneath. It wasn't a handsome face, she realized. Its features were somehow a bit too much out of balance to be defined as handsome. But you could quickly forget that when it was such a strong, masculine face, lean and square-jawed and with expressive black eyes, even with one of them swollen half shut.

"I'm a mess," he repeated in that voice that, with her full attention now, was so familiar and precious to her. "But you—

you're beautiful."

It was an absurd thing for him to say when Kate knew she was anything but beautiful with her tangled hair and rumpled, grimy prison garb. When even looking her best, she could never qualify as a beauty. And yet in this moment, his eager, searching gaze made her feel more than she was. It had her glowing inside.

"Blue," he observed softly. "A sweet blue. Why did I know your eyes just had to be blue?"

His hand slowly reached down, as if intending to circle her eyes with gentle strokes. The hand passed into a beam of sunlight slanting through the window, rupturing the spell as it revealed the lighter skin on his finger where his wedding band would have been before one of his captors removed it.

The circle of pale skin was a rude reminder to Kate that Efrem wasn't hers, that he belonged to another woman. The warm glow was extinguished. In its place was a dull ache that was beneficial in at least one respect. It had her instantly alert to the reality of the situation.

Shoving herself to a sitting position on the cot, she gazed up at him in astonishment. "What's happened? How did you manage to get out of your cell and into mine?"

Sobered by her demand, his hand withdrawn now from any contact, Efrem jerked a thumb toward the wall of bars. She glanced swiftly in that direction to see her cell door wide open.

"Both my door and yours were unlocked. Don't ask me when or why. All I know is that they've cleared out, the colonel probably yesterday after he got his video and Jamil and Tariz sometime in the night or early this morning."

Kate listened and was aware then of the total silence in the building. There was no sound from the town outside either. Where was the muezzin calling the faithful to prayer in the mosque?

"Are you sure they've gone?"

"Oh, yeah, I checked the whole place. We're alone here all right."

"Efrem—" Flinging the blanket aside, she swung her legs to the floor. "—this doesn't make any sense. Where could they have gone?"

"Dunno, but if I was to make a stab at it . . ."

"What?"

"I might guess that our forces have crossed the border and that the ground offensive is finally underway. If that is the explanation, then maybe both guards were needed at the front."

"But to leave us completely on our own here—"

"What else could they do if they went off to fight? They sure wouldn't want to burden themselves with a couple of POWs. As for the mystery of the unlocked cell doors . . . well, I'm not even going to try to explain that one."

Even though what Efrem said had logic, Kate was still baffled by all of it.

"Look," he went on, "let's not waste time questioning it. Let's just see it as the opportunity it is. This is our chance to get out of here."

"Escape? Where? How?"

"I've been thinking about that. If our forces *have* crossed the border, and if we can avoid the Iraqis, with any luck we'll manage eventually to meet up with our army."

"Efrem, that's crazy. We don't have a vehicle."

"Yeah, I know, and there isn't much likelihood of getting our hands on one. We'll have to go on foot."

"Across that desert?" Kate surged to her feet, confronting him. "You *are* out of your mind!"

"Okay, it's a risk. A big one. But what would you have us do? Remain here and just wait to be recaptured? Or, worse, shot by the enemy?"

"We could be shot out on the desert."

"Kate, it's my duty as a soldier to make every effort to escape, but if you want to stay behind, I'm not going to leave you here on your own. We're sticking together where I can try to keep you safe."

Deeply moved by his promise to stay with her, she thought about it for a second. "No, you're right. The desert is a better choice."

"That's a relief. My only worry is whether you feel fit enough for a trek like this."

"*Me?* It's you we should be worried about after what they did to you yesterday."

"I'm a fast healer. All I needed was a night of sleep."

Gazing at his long-limbed, athletic body, Kate was prepared to believe that his recovery was as rapid as he claimed. And maybe not so amazing, considering the rigorous training of an army that conditioned its men and women to face the worst.

If she needed any further evidence of that, Efrem provided it with his energetic decisiveness.

"We're losing time," he urged. "We need to go."

She followed him out of the cell, hurrying to keep up as he strode along the corridor ahead of her with his fluid gait, a long-legged figure who wore his body like a man comfortable with himself.

Something occurred to her as they reached the door at the end of the corridor. "How can we possibly cross that desert without food and water?"

He had anticipated her. "Thought about that," he said over his shoulder as he opened the door and led the way along a short passage. "Could be we can find some essentials in here."

They turned into what Kate assumed from the bunk beds against one wall was the guardroom.

"Let's start looking," he said.

Their rapid search of cupboards and a pair of desks produced nothing useful. They moved on to a door whose lock was so old that, with repeated kicks of his foot, Efrem was able to batter it into submission. What the door revealed when it was finally open was a supply closet.

There were open shelves on the walls, most of them empty. But along one of them were arranged small, plastic bottles of water. There was also a trove of pocket-sized packages.

Efrem tore two of the packages open. "Field rations. Dates in this one and some kind of crackers in the other. Somebody upstairs is looking out for us."

Although they satisfied their thirst with one of the bottles of water, there was no time to eat. Kate was aware of the minutes hurrying by as they loaded rations and water into a pair of ancient knapsacks abandoned in a corner. There was the risk of being discovered before they could flee into the desert.

"Don't take anymore than you can comfortably carry," Efrem cautioned. "These are going to be heavy enough before too many miles."

"Do you suppose there's a first aid kit somewhere?" she wondered, eyeing the gash on Efrem's cheek as they emerged from the closet.

"A weapon would be more useful. Not that they'd leave anything like that behind."

"We ought to clean and dress that cut of yours."

"Don't fuss. Fast healer, remember?"

"You won't be bragging about that if you get an infection out on the desert."

"If it was going to get infected, it would have happened by now in a place like this."

He had a point. And maybe he wasn't exaggerating about being a fast healer. She had already noticed his swollen lip from yesterday was no longer visible. Realizing in any case that she was going to get nowhere with this stubborn man, she dropped the argument.

Knapsacks strapped to their backs, they made necessary visits to the W.C. before seeking the door to the street.

"Let me check first," Efrem said, carefully opening the door when they located it.

Kate waited nervously while he slipped outside. Within seconds he was back.

"All clear."

An understatement if ever there was one, Kate decided when she joined him in the street. There was a total, eerie silence in the town. Nor did they glimpse a solitary soul as they set off along the street. There wasn't so much as a barking dog to challenge them. The whole place was totally deserted.

"Where is everyone?" Kate asked in a hushed voice.

"I'd say my guess about the ground offensive being underway was right."

"Meaning the townspeople must have evacuated to get out of the way of an enemy invasion. Are you sure we're headed in the right direction?"

"I have a pretty good sense of direction," Efrem assured her. "Besides, it's early enough that the sun is still behind us in the east, which means we're going west where we want to go."

Kate took his word for it. She was already lost in the narrow, winding streets where the squat buildings, most of them cinder block but some mud brick from an earlier era, all looked the same to her.

Though they were cautious in their progress, their assumption that the town was entirely empty proved to be a mistake. At least one of its citizens hadn't fled. He was suddenly there in front of them when they rounded a corner.

All three of them came to an abrupt halt, Kate gasping at the unexpected encounter. She recognized him almost immediately. It was the bearded old man who had delivered the meals to their cells. She feared he would shout an alarm or back away in haste, but all he did was stare at them soberly.

Then, in a low voice, pointing first at himself and then at them, he spoke what must have been the only English words he knew. "John Wayne."

Efrem was baffled. "What in the name of all that's weird is he trying to tell us?"

Kate understood. "Don't you see? There's probably not that many places on the globe that haven't seen at least one American John Wayne movie."

"A sort of common denominator, huh?"

"I think so. He wants us to know he's a friend. I hope."

She smiled at the old man, and to her relief he smiled back, revealing gaps where teeth were missing. "Yusef," he said slowly, pointing to himself again.

"He's introducing himself." Kate indicated herself in return and then Efrem, giving him their own names. "Kate, Efrem."

Yusef nodded once more, then spent several seconds gazing at their prison garb before shaking his head in disapproval.

It was Efrem this time who translated. "He's either letting us know we're not supposed to be out of our cells or that we're making a big mistake trying to escape in these outfits. I'm betting on the second one, and he's right. This bright yellow screams POW."

Yusef beckoned for them to follow him.

"Should we?" Kate wondered.

"Let's chance it. Maybe he's offering us a solution."

This turned out to be exactly what the old man intended when he led them down an alley and into a small building that was presumably his home. Several minutes later he was pressing garments on them that he lifted from a battered wardrobe, a striped burnoose for Efrem and a long robe that belted at the waist for Kate.

Their need for the clothing was too necessary for them to refuse Yusef's generosity, though Kate felt guilty accepting the gifts when she knew that the people of this community had to be so poor that, parting with any garments, even those as old and worn as these, was a sacrifice.

When they had clad themselves in the outfits that effectively hid the yellow prison garb underneath, and with the hood of the burnoose covering Efrem's head and a cloth that fastened under the chin concealing all but Kate's face, Yusef stood back to inspect their transformation. He nodded his approval, letting them know with gestures that, unless they were directly approached, they could safely pass as an Iraqi couple.

The old man's assistance should have ended there. It didn't. With more gestures, he insisted on escorting them to the edge of the town where he pointed out the dirt road that traveled southwest in the direction of the Saudi border.

Shaking their hands, receiving their gratitude with a solemn dignity, he parted from them with an earnest, *"Mashallab."*

Kate recognized it as an Arabic blessing that she promised herself she would never forget.

She had known that crossing the seemingly endless, barren terrain that was the Al-Hajara Desert, which stretched from Iraq into Saudi Arabia, wouldn't be easy. Certainly not on foot. But until now, tramping mile after mile over the hard-packed, rocky sand, she hadn't appreciated just how difficult a trek it was.

The road had dwindled into nothing but a rough track, and in places they seemed to lose it altogether. On these occasions, it was necessary to search for it, losing time before they were able to pick up the thread of it again. And always there were the snakes and the lizards and the scorpions to watch out for and avoid.

There was one advantage anyway. Shortly after leaving the

town, a place whose name they never did learn, the sky became overcast. The cloud cover shielded them from a scorching, desert sun that would have been merciless. However, this was winter, so it also meant a drop in temperature. Kate was glad for the robe that Yusef had provided. It meant an extra layer against the chill.

Knowing how concerned Efrem was about her, she was careful not to complain. But there was no way to hide her weariness from him.

"Let's rest again," he suggested.

Kate shook her head. "We've already had too many rest stops. I'm for going on."

Efrem didn't argue with her, but after that she was aware of him watching her for signs of exhaustion. It made her nervous. She made an effort to distract him.

"This is unreal. Where are the troops? Where's all the fighting?"

Except for a deserted watchtower, they had encountered no sign of human life in the vast no-man's-land through which they trudged. There had been aircraft overhead from time to time, but they'd been too high to try to signal, and it might not have been theirs anyway.

"If there is action," Efrem answered her, "it's at the front, wherever that might be."

Kate had to be satisfied with that.

She made no objection when he called a halt sometime around midday. Dropping with relief at the side of the road, they slung the knapsacks off their shoulders and drank from their bottles of water. The dates and the crackers in their sealed packages made a welcome lunch.

"I'm not sure these are crackers," Efrem said. "Could be they're some kind of hard, pressed bread. They taste of cheese, don't they?"

"Or sand."

The fine dust had been a source of aggravation from the beginning of their trek. It seemed to invade everything, their clothing, their hair and now their food. Kate could even feel the stuff seeping into her pores.

"What I wouldn't give to be clean again. *Really* clean."

Efrem's response was a simple "Amen."

Fed and rested, at least reasonably so, they went on again. The morning had been uneventful. The afternoon was not.

It was an hour or so after their noon break that Efrem brought them to a stop, holding up his hand with a sharp "Listen!"

"What is it?"

"The sound of an engine. Something's coming."

Kate could hear it now too. She could also see a cloud of dust in the distance announcing the approach of a vehicle. Friend or enemy, Efrem was willing to take no risk.

"We've got to get off the road before they can spot us."

There was a sand revetment nearby thrown up by the Iraqis. The shallow hollow contained some kind of abandoned, burned-out vehicle. Why it had been fired and by whom didn't matter. The blackened shell offered a place to hide. They climbed into it quickly and crouched low. As the vehicle out on the road sped by in the direction he and Kate had come from, Efrem lifted his head just far enough to peer out a blank window frame.

"An armored truck," he informed her. "Iraqi, and they're in a hurry."

"Are they in retreat?"

"Maybe."

Efrem was ready to believe it when, a few hours later, as they tramped along the road, Kate muttered, "What's that awful odor? It smells like burning oil. A lot of it."

"It is. Look over there."

Kate gazed in the direction he indicated. Far off to the south, plumes of smoke darkened the sky. "That's Kuwait somewhere down there, isn't it?"

"Yeah. Could be the Iraqis *are* in retreat, and they're firing the oil wells behind them."

It made sense, Kate thought. Because if the Iraqis were being forced out of the tiny country their army had invaded and occupied, they probably would try to destroy Kuwait's one source of wealth—its rich oil fields.

She and Efrem became certain of that as the stench of the burning oil that poisoned the air became unbearable. There was relief only when the wind finally shifted, carrying the worst of the fumes away from them.

If our troops are on the move, Kate wondered, then where are they? Why aren't we seeing or hearing some sign of them? There was no answer to that. Anyway, all that mattered, all that she really cared about, was that Efrem was beside her.

Nightfall overtook them on the road. Efrem knew that it would be madness to try to travel any farther. They could so easily lose the road altogether in the dark and become hopelessly lost out on the desert.

He found a dry *wadi* that was deep enough to shelter them against the temperature that fell rapidly in the desert after sundown. He didn't like it, but they would have to spend the night here.

There was just enough light left in the sky to let them make another meal out of the dates and crackers, which they washed down with their bottles of water.

Efrem was worried about their rations, the water in particular. They had seemed plentiful enough when they'd started out, but they'd diminished throughout the day. The supply would last them through another full day, but after that . . .

How far have we come? Efrem asked himself. It felt like a

long way, but something told him that the distance they had yet to cover would be considerable.

Kate. He was anxious about Kate. Her courage had never wavered. He admired her for that. But would her strength sustain her? He knew how fatigued she was. Maybe a night of rest was all she needed.

Except that didn't look too likely, he thought, gazing down at her tenderly. Even with all they'd been through, she still looked beautiful to him. Beautiful, but cold. Huddled there, with knees drawn up to her breasts, she shivered as she hugged herself.

"It's frigid," she said, aware of him eyeing her.

No, this wasn't a state conducive to sleep.

"Here," he said, shifting himself against her side. He put his arm around her, drawing her tightly against his body. "Better?"

"Much," she sighed, snuggling willingly into the warmth he offered.

This was what he had wanted from that first day. To hold her in his arms, make her safe. Damn, but she felt good. Every bit as soft and good as he had dreamed of.

"Look," she whispered, nodding toward the south.

He gazed in the direction where Kuwait lay. The horizon there was lurid with the red glow of the burning oil wells.

"Maybe that's what hell is like," he said.

"Yes," she agreed.

But Efrem wasn't interested in hell. At this moment all he cared about was Kate. He thought how, in spite of bars and the solid wall that had separated them back in their cells, a highly charged, emotional closeness had developed between them. That emotion had deepened with each passing mile throughout the endless day. Efrem was conscious of it now. He sensed that Kate was aware of it, too, simmering between them.

Needing more than just to hold her, he removed his arm so that he could turn her around to face him. He longed to see her, but it was too dark now for that. What he couldn't manage with sight, however, he achieved with touch.

Understanding his desire as his hands reached out to her face, Kate lifted her head to accommodate him. His fingers slowly, gently explored the contours of her features, learning them like a blind man eager to assure himself of her reality.

Arched eyebrows, silky smooth cheeks, small nose where he detected a slight bump, full mouth. He traced them all, cherished each of them, but they still weren't enough. With big hands framing her face on either side, he yearned for that full mouth under his.

Kate must have felt his breath, realized what he intended when he lowered his head. "This is wrong," she murmured.

"Why?" he demanded.

"For one thing, I'm filthy and I probably smell like—"

"So do I. I don't care. It doesn't matter."

"No, I guess it doesn't. None of it matters."

Because in that moment, he thought, there was no one else but the two of them alone together and needing each other, and that was enough. No, it was everything. He knew Kate understood this when she surrendered her mouth to his.

Despite the frequent rest stops he had forced on her throughout the morning of their second day on the road, Efrem could see that Kate's strength had been sapped by their arduous journey. Each step was an effort for her now.

When she stumbled over a rough spot in the road, he caught her as she started to sink to her knees. She laughed weakly while he steadied her.

"Look at me, staggering like a drunk. I'm not going to make it, am I? But you can. You can go on without me, and if you get through—"

"The hell with that," he said angrily. "Nobody's abandoning

anybody." He looked around. "There's another wadi over there. It must be about noon. Come on, time for another break."

Arm around her waist, he supported her into the wadi where she collapsed on the sand. The sky had cleared in the night. The sun was hot, baking the desert, baking them.

They ate the last of their rations, but they still had water. The water was even more vital today without any shade, but how long would it last?

When they had eaten, Kate curled up and closed her eyes. Efrem left her sleeping and went up on the lip of the wadi, hoping to see some sign of the coalition forces. There had been no sight or sound of either friend or enemy all morning.

There was nothing now as he scanned the desert in all directions, but he wasn't alone. Unless he was seeing a mirage, that was a camel out there. What was a camel doing here all on its own? He seemed to recall hearing that Bedouin nomads used this desert, so perhaps the camel had somehow wandered away from their camp.

If he could manage to catch the beast, Kate would no longer have to walk. On the other hand, he had also heard that camels could have nasty dispositions, so maybe this one wouldn't even let Kate mount it. But it was worth a try.

Efrem crept slowly toward the camel, but the animal was too wary to have anything to do with him. Every time he closed in on the thing, it loped away a safe distance. In the end, he had to give up the chase.

He was trotting back to the wadi when he heard Kate calling for him frantically. Heart in his throat, he reached the wadi to find her on her feet.

She met him with a hoarse, "I woke up, and you were gone! I didn't know what to think!"

She was trembling. Efrem didn't hesitate to fold her into his arms. His hands stroked her back with a soothing "It's all right, sweetheart. Nothing is wrong."

He explained about the camel while he went on holding her, remembering the kiss they had shared last night in another wadi. How deep and intense it had been, fired with emotion.

He wanted to kiss her again, tell her just how much she meant to him. That he had fallen in love with her. But before he could seek her mouth with his own, Kate disengaged herself from his arms.

"I'm ashamed of myself," she apologized, her voice steady now. "It was stupid of me to go and panic like that. Look, I'm rested and ready to go on."

Any declaration of his feelings for her would have to wait, Efrem realized. He saw the wisdom in that, but it didn't help his frustration.

They returned to the road where she made a stalwart effort to continue their journey. But Efrem couldn't stop worrying about her. Whatever their pace, he knew that sooner or later she would be too weak to go on. He fiercely promised himself he wouldn't leave her when that happened. Never. If necessary, he would carry her.

They must have traveled a couple of miles down the road when a helicopter swooped down out of nowhere, buzzing them just overhead.

"It's one of ours!" Efrem yelled. "An Apache!"

Kate shared his excitement. "They had to have seen us! Do you think—"

"Yeah, they'll report sighting us. This could be it, Kate. The rescue we've been praying for."

The helicopter zoomed away and didn't reappear. They were alone again. Another half hour passed as they pressed onward, their hopes dimming. With these outfits we're wearing, Efrem thought, the chopper probably figured we're Iraqi civilians or

Bedouin nomads. Maybe not worth bothering about. If that was the case—

Kate broke in on his thoughts with a tense "Listen! Do you hear it?"

He did. A low roar that had the familiar sound to him of a considerable force on the move. They halted, peering anxiously down the road, waiting.

Moments later, out of the clouds of dust raised by its advance, emerged a mass that sorted itself out as a fleet of approaching tanks accompanied by armored humvees.

Efrem recognized the tanks. "Kate, they're M-1s. *U.S.* M-1s."

Behind the tanks and the humvees, taking form in the shimmering waves of heat that rose from the desert floor, laden with field gear and rifles, streamed American marines in battle dress.

They aren't army, Efrem thought with a grin, but what the hell.

CHAPTER SIX

He was late. Kate tried not to be nervous as she waited for him in the lobby of the Riyadh hotel. But she couldn't seem to shake the concern that had gnawed at her all day, the fear that this dinner with Efrem might be the last meal they ever shared.

Things were so different since their rescue. What if one of those differences was his feelings for her? Assuming, that is, he still had them, since she had never permitted him to actually express how he felt about her. Or what if, now that they were safe and plugged back into the lives they had left behind from before they were captured, Efrem could see only the barriers preventing any possible future for them.

Kate herself hadn't changed. If anything, her feelings for him had deepened into a love she could no longer deny.

She tried to convince herself this dinner date was not intended to be a goodbye. Made herself remember how fervently he had kissed her that night in the wadi. It hadn't been the kiss of a man reckless with his emotions. Nor had anything else he had communicated in their days together, verbal as well as physical, been anything but serious. No, she couldn't have mistaken his feelings, so maybe . . .

It was no use. Kate couldn't stop worrying.

She glanced in the direction of the reception desk where she had already asked the attendant if there had been a phone call for her. There hadn't. No point in asking again. They would page her if Efrem phoned.

She'd parked herself in a chair where she had a clear view of the front entrance to the hotel. There were a few American soldiers out on the street, but none of them was Efrem. She continued to wait, restless, making an effort not to squirm.

It was several minutes later when he strode into the lobby, and then she didn't know him. Not right away. He had altered so vastly from the Efrem she remembered that it was like seeing a stranger. A tall, good-looking stranger, clean and freshly shaven, trim in his dress green uniform.

Removing his billed cap, he scanned the lobby. She rose from her chair to make herself more visible to him. Her appearance had also changed considerably, so maybe he wouldn't immediately recognize her.

Kate had finally found the special dress she'd sought in the mall this afternoon, a simple, black sheath that hugged her curves without revealing any of the flaws of her figure. The hotel catered to Western guests so she'd managed, too, to have her hair done in its salon.

When Efrem's gaze finally did land on her, she could see even from yards away how his eyes widened in pleasure. The provocative dress was a success anyway, she thought, watching him as his long legs carried him swiftly across the lobby to where she waited anxiously.

"Tell me I'm not imagining it," he greeted her with a lusty growl. "That the sexy female standing in front of me is real."

Kate laughed in relief. "If she seems sexy, it's probably because she's the first woman you've seen in days who wasn't covered with either a veil or grime."

"Naw, that's not it. She just happens to be naturally gorgeous, even in a grungy POW outfit."

"Thank you, and you're late."

"Sorry about that. There was a delay with the plane."

"You're forgiven, but only because I like your compliments."

He smiled at her broadly.

He might have exaggerated his admiration of her, Kate thought, but not his claim back in Iraq about being a fast healer. She saw that the bruise on his cheek had faded to almost nothing, that the cut on his other cheek and the swollen eye were hardly noticeable.

"I'm starved," he said. "One of the guys on the plane told me that the restaurant upstairs is great, but if you'd like to go somewhere else . . ."

"Here is fine."

It's going to be all right, Kate told herself as she and Efrem headed for the elevator. He might have changed externally, but inside he's the same Efrem.

Her joy in that realization lasted all the way to the top floor of the hotel where the dining room, with high windows on all sides, overlooked the city below. They were seated at a table with a sweeping view of Riyadh, whose countless bright lights and modern buildings were in sharp contrast to the immense desert that surrounded it.

The service was smooth and efficient; the meal they ordered flawlessly prepared. It consisted of richly seasoned, generous slices of lamb accompanied by a selection of exotically flavored vegetables.

Together with the elegant setting, it should have been a perfect dinner, everything Kate could have wished the evening to be. But even before the platters were delivered to their table, she felt the relief she had embraced in the lobby ebbing away. Something was wrong.

It was evident in their sudden awkwardness with each other, in the way they both picked at their dinners. After the meager fare they had endured in Iraq, they should have been ravenous for a feast like this. Where was the appetite Efrem had claimed in the lobby? It seemed to have fled, along with his eager, cocky admiration of her. He was as disinterested now in his food as Kate was in hers.

Something was wrong. She became increasingly convinced of that as their conversation dwindled to what amounted to polite talk.

"You been overwhelmed by the news media?" he asked her.

"Afraid so."

"Me, too. How the hell did we end up as heroes?"

It was a rhetorical question. She didn't feel the need to respond to it.

Even when things were at their worst, we were always at ease with each other, Kate thought. Now we're like strangers. She was afraid to tell herself why, but a sick, sinking dread had settled in her stomach.

There was a lengthy pause. Efrem ended it with a casual "You talk to your people back home?"

She nodded. "I spoke with both of my parents and my boss at the station. How about you?"

"Yeah, there were calls from my family."

Did that include his wife? she wondered. She didn't have the courage to ask, but it would have been odd if they hadn't talked. She waited for him to tell her and considered it a bad sign that he didn't.

There was another pause. It struck Kate that it was unlike those intervals in their cells when they hadn't talked. Those had never been uncomfortable silences. This one was.

"I almost forgot," Efrem said, as if snatching at a topic for the mere sake of conversation. Any topic, as long as it filled the void. "I learned the explanation for the mystery of why our cell doors were left unlocked that morning."

"What is it?" she asked him, pretending to care.

"You've probably heard that the Iraqis were surrendering in hordes." Kate had. "No combat for me. I was put to work checking the lists of POWs. Guess who was on one of them."

She was a war correspondent, she reminded herself. She was supposed to be interested. She tried. "Tell me," she urged him.

"Jamil. I managed to go and see him in the POW camp. Turns out what I guessed was true. Jamil and Tariz *were* ordered to report immediately to the front when the ground war began. Their instruction was to leave both prisoners locked in their cells where they would be collected in a few hours for transportation to another area. Only Jamil didn't trust that promise. He was afraid we'd be forgotten there, so just before he and Tariz left, he sneaked back to the cells and unlocked our doors."

"That sounds like something Jamil would do." She was glad, after all, that Efrem had told her.

"Yeah, he gave us the chance to save ourselves. I made sure to thank him for that."

"I'm glad you did, Efrem."

They had finished their dinners, or at least as much as they were in the mood for. She could see he was restless now, impatient to leave the dining room.

"Look, there's something I've got to say, and I don't want to say it here. So, unless you mind skipping dessert and coffee . . ."

"I don't at all."

Dessert and coffee wouldn't change what she knew was coming. He was going to tell her they couldn't meet again. So, yes, why not just get it over with?

They would part in the lobby, she thought as they went down in the elevator a few minutes later. There would be a quick and final goodbye, and somehow she would survive the heartache.

It didn't happen that way. "This is no place to talk," he said when they reached the lobby. "Too public." Looking around, he spotted a glass door. "That looks like some kind of a garden out there. Will you be cold if we go out there for a bit?"

She wished he hadn't suggested the garden. Why delay the

inevitable? For that matter, when she had first sensed something was wrong, why hadn't she just asked him about it?

Stop kidding yourself. You know why all right. And it isn't because you're a coward. It's because you want to squeeze in as much precious time as you can with him before you have to let him go.

In the end that was why Kate permitted him to take her into the garden where they were alone in an oasis of lush vegetation, a goldfish pool, and the soft light of lanterns. It was a setting out of *Arabian Nights,* which Kate supposed would have been appropriate if she hadn't been too apprehensive to appreciate it.

"What are your plans now that the fighting is all but over?" Efrem asked as they strolled along the network of paths.

"CNA has forgiven me for making that video for the Iraqis, which won't be aired now anyway. The station has asked me to stay on for another week or so to cover the end of the war."

"Will you?"

"I suppose so. They've sent out another cameraman. How about you?"

He was silent for a few seconds. When he finally spoke, there was a somber tone in his voice. "Kate, I got my orders today. I'm being shipped back home."

"When?"

"Tomorrow on an early flight. That's why I was able to wrangle an overnight pass. Told my c.o. I had personal business in Riyadh before I left."

So soon. This was it then. He was going to tell her goodbye now. She didn't want him to see her misery, didn't want that image to be his last memory of her. She tried to look and sound happy for him. "You'll be reunited with your family."

"That's what I was told. That they'll be there to meet me when we land at Andrews."

And, troubled marriage or not, she thought, his wife was still his wife. She would probably be with them. The night air was suddenly very sharp. Too sharp for the dress she wore. She shivered, and Efrem noticed it.

"You're cold."

She tried to object when he removed the jacket of his uniform. But he insisted on placing it around her shoulders.

It was still warm from his body, and it bore traces of his masculine aroma blended with his aftershave, making the garment too personal and far too intimate. A mistake, she thought even as she relished the feel and scent of it.

To neutralize the temptation, Kate made herself ask him what she didn't want to know but had to know. "Efrem, you haven't told me whether you and your wife talked."

"Yeah, we spoke. It wasn't a long conversation. Jackie said she had something important to tell me but that it could wait until I got home."

A lump lodged itself under Kate's heart, dull and heavy. "What do you suppose it is?"

"I don't have to suppose. I know. I could hear it in her strained voice. You remember my telling you our marriage was pretty rocky and that I didn't expect it to survive our separation? Well, it hasn't. Jackie's going to ask me for a divorce, only that isn't something you want to announce over the phone to a soldier who's just been a prisoner of war."

Kate tried to grasp what he was saying, but she suddenly felt too lightheaded to understand the significance of his words.

"I've been wanting all evening to tell you," he said, his speech rapid now. "Only I was too damned scared of how you'd take it to just come out with it. But I don't care now. You've got to hear it. Kate, I'm going to be a free man because if Jackie doesn't ask for a divorce I will."

The bleakness that had tormented her throughout the long day and into the evening lifted like storm clouds parting to reveal the face of the sun.

"I'm going to be a free man," he rushed on, "and I want us to be together. If you haven't realized it by now, I've fallen in love with you. The kind of love that makes a man desperate."

They had stopped on the path and were turned facing each other. She could see by the light of a lantern the pleading expression on his face.

"Kate, you're killing me here. What are you thinking?"

She managed to find her voice, hoarse though it was. "That," she said slowly, "a woman in love can be as desperate as any man."

"Are you saying—"

"Yes, I am saying it. I love you, Efrem Chaudoir, and what are you waiting for?"

"Absolutely nothing."

Swiftly closing the gap that divided them, he slid his arms around her, drawing her tightly against his solid length. Her lips were already parted for him, ready to receive his kiss when his mouth angled across hers.

Delirious with joy, Kate inhaled the flavor of him, his scent together with his clean taste. Celebrated the mingling of their breaths. Welcomed his tongue sliding against hers as he deepened their kiss, expressing his ardor for her.

When his mouth finally lifted from hers, he rested his forehead against her brow with a contented "This is what I've been wanting all evening. To have you in my arms where you belong."

"Me, too."

His jacket had slipped from her shoulders in the heat of their kiss. She hadn't missed it. She was anything but cold. His protective instinct, however, had him scooping the jacket up from the path where it had landed and settling it again around her shoulders.

His hands lingered on her lovingly. "I'll be there waiting

when you come home," he promised her earnestly. "All you have to do is let me know the time and the place. By then I should be on my way to being free for us."

His reminder of his marriage jolted her out of her rush of happiness. "Efrem, your wife . . . I don't want to be responsible for breaking up a marriage."

"Haven't you been listening to me? You're not breaking up anything because there is no real marriage between Jackie and me. All we've done for months now is go through the motions, and she knows that."

Wanting to believe he and his wife would have divorced in any case, Kate managed to silence her guilt.

"And, Kate?"

"Yes?"

"I haven't forgotten your difficulty with trust. I'm going to be there for you, helping you to work through it. I need you to believe that. Need you to know that I want to take care of you."

No one had ever promised her this, had ever imagined that the strong, independent Kate Groen might need to be taken care of. And maybe she didn't need to be, but it was wonderful to hear it.

As for her old problem with trust, where Efrem was concerned she had already shed the last traces of her resistance. Someday she would explain to him the origin of that mistrust because she wanted to keep no secrets from him. But this wasn't the time for that. They wouldn't see each other again for days, possibly even weeks, and she wanted something more than explanations on their last night together.

"When do you have to report?" she asked him.

"First thing in the morning at the airfield here. One of the guys I rode down with has my gear with him. He booked a room for the night at another hotel. Said I was welcome to bunk in with him."

Kate thought about their kiss and how, when he had pressed himself against her, she had felt the hard ridge of his arousal.

"Now why would you want to do that when I have a big room right here?"

He grinned at her. "Yeah? Twin beds?"

She shook her head. "Afraid not. There's just one bed, but it's very roomy."

"I guess we can manage."

That wide bed could have been a narrow cot for all that it mattered, when, with their clothing hastily removed and discarded, they came together on it.

Kneeling face to face, they gazed into each other's eyes. If it was true that the eyes were the windows of the soul, and at this moment Kate was ready to swear they were, then she must be looking into Efrem's soul, just as he was looking into hers. The wonder of it had her glowing inside.

Gathering her against him, he molded his body to hers with a raspy-voiced "Can you feel it? How you were made for me?" He buried his nose in her hair. "You even smell right, all sweet and warm."

He began to kiss her again. Deep, feverish kisses that dazed her, filled her with such longing she was unable to keep herself from collapsing on the bed.

"Yeah, I came prepared," he said as she watched him sheathe his hard length. "A guy can always hope."

"So can a woman," she whispered when her arms wrapped around him as he settled himself between her thighs.

He entered her slowly, gently. The feel of him inside her was pure bliss. Equally intense was the rapture of his long, measured strokes as they rocked together in rhythm with each other. She was consumed by the rich euphoria of her climax, followed almost immediately by his.

Afterwards, his arm snugging her against his side, he breathed a contented sigh. "That jail where they held us might have been a rotten place," he said softly, "but I found something wonderful there, and now I don't want to ever let her go."

"You have to. For a little while, anyway."

"But until then . . ."

He couldn't get enough of her. Nor could Kate of him. They spent the night in each other's arms. He made her soar again and again. Alternately, they dozed, still holding one another.

"I can rest on the plane," he apologized a few hours before daybreak. "But what about you? Can you sleep in after I'm gone?"

She shook her head. "Afraid not. I've got an interview with a general in the morning. But it doesn't matter."

And it didn't, Kate realized. The career that had meant everything to her was no longer the most important thing in her world. She wouldn't have thought that possible only days ago, but that had been before the miracle of Efrem Chaudoir.

Of course, their careers still meant something, and that might make problems for them. It wouldn't be easy for a TV war correspondent, who could be sent anywhere, and a soldier, who could be stationed anywhere, to be together. But other couples managed to work out the conflicts of their careers, didn't they?

Efrem refused to worry about it when she expressed her concern to him. "Whatever happens, wherever we are," he said, "we'll always manage to find each other. All you have to remember is, not just that I love you but, how *much* I love you. The kind of love, sweetheart, that never lets go."

Kate clung to that solemn pledge when it was time for them to part as the first light of day streaked the sky over Riyadh.

"I don't want you seeing me off at the airfield," he told her while dressing in his uniform. "I want to remember you like this, all flushed and sleepy-eyed from our lovemaking. You got the number for contacting me?"

"Tucked safely right here in my pocket."

She went in her robe to the door with him where he kissed her good-bye. It was a quick, bittersweet kiss. After she made herself release him, she stepped into the corridor to watch him stride toward the elevator.

At the corner, where the hall rounded to the elevator, he turned and tossed her a little salute. "See you soon," he called to her with a cheerful certainty. And then he was gone.

Chapter Seven

In The Years Between Saudi Arabia and Kosovo

Washington, D.C.

Waiters bearing trays of drinks and hors d'oeuvres circulated through the elegant ballroom of the Saxony Hotel, serving the equally elegant crowd gathered there.

Kate presumed all of these people had the kind of money that would permit them to contribute generously to the cause the reception was for. Whatever that cause was. She didn't know and wasn't in a mood to care.

"Dara, do you know any of these people?"

"Um, not exactly." The tiny redhead at Kate's side went on searching the crowd.

"Then what are we doing here?"

"It's a party, isn't it? You need a party. We both need a party. And with my boss and his wife not being able to use them, the invitations were just going to go to waste, so why not—Oh, look, there is someone over there I recognize! Hang on. I'll be right back."

Dara sprinted off to the other side of the ballroom, leaving Kate behind. She idly scanned the gathering. Her heart stopped when her gaze came to rest on a tall, dark-haired man in an army uniform.

Efrem.

The officer turned to accept a drink from a passing server. It was not Efrem. Nothing like him.

Damn it, would this ache ever go away? It had been over a year since she had lost him, and she was still grieving, still seeing him everywhere. Why couldn't she accept the finality of their parting? Put him behind her and get on with her life?

Dara came back, squeezing through bodies, a slim man with fair, thinning hair trailing behind her.

"Kate, this is Gordon May. Gordon, meet my friend, Kate Groen."

They shook hands. He had gray eyes behind a pair of wire-rimmed glasses. *Kind,* gray eyes and a small mouth that looked like it smiled a lot. It was smiling now.

"Are you having fun, Kate?"

Before she could answer him, Dara squealed another discovery. "Ooo, Arnie from the office. I've gotta say hi to him."

The redhead hurried away, deserting Kate again.

"A real dynamo, isn't she?" Gordon said.

"She means well, but she does tend to exhaust people. How did you come to know Dara?"

"Damned if I know. But we must have met somewhere since she seems to know me." He tipped his head to one side, observing her for a moment. "You aren't having fun, are you?"

"Well, it's not my kind of scene."

"Mine either," he confessed.

Kate laughed. "I got dragged here. What's your excuse?"

Gordon chuckled. "I kind of have to be here since I promoted this fundraiser. That's my job, public relations."

"I guess I shouldn't admit I don't know, but funds for what?"

"The restoration of a Lee mansion in Alexandria." He leaned toward her to whisper confidentially, "What this crowd doesn't know is that the place once served as a brothel for some of

Washington's influential citizens." Kate had to chuckle over this interesting bit of information. "Look, would you like to get some air? I could use a stroll outside."

"Uh, wouldn't you be missed?"

"Not at this point. Besides, I have two of my people here. They'll handle it. I promise you I'm harmless."

Given her history, why she immediately trusted him Kate would never know. Maybe it was those kind eyes. They seemed to offer an uncomplicated empathy, something she badly needed.

Spring in Washington was the one season you could count on to be agreeable. It was just that this evening, with a gentle breeze off the Potomac and blossoms scenting the air.

Kate and her companion walked in silence for a block. Then, while waiting to cross the street, he turned to her with an abrupt "You're not very happy, are you, Kate Groen?"

She could have denied it. Why didn't she? Why, instead, did she find herself seated a few moments later on a park bench beside Gordon May relating her story to him? There was an explanation, of course. It wasn't just because he was a stranger and therefore safe in an impersonal way. Unlike friends like Dara Weinstein, Gordon listened to her patiently and without judgment.

Kate told him everything, starting with her capture in Iraq and how she and Efrem fell in love and how there had been the promise of a future together. Sharing with Gordon the outcome of that intense love was the tough part. The awful sting of it was still in her heart, the memory still fresh in her mind.

When she arrived back in the States from Saudi Arabia, Efrem was there to meet her after she came through customs at Dulles International. One look at the bleak expression on his face told Kate at once that something was wrong. *Terribly* wrong.

"What is it? What's happened? You never mentioned anything when I called from Riyadh."

"Kate, it isn't something I could tell you on the phone. Look, let's find a quiet corner somewhere."

"Tell me," she demanded the instant they were seated across from each other in a coffee shop booth.

His voice was as bleak as his expression as he leaned toward her. "What Jackie had to tell me when I got home . . . I was all wrong about that. It wasn't the request for a divorce that I expected. She—she's pregnant."

"A baby," Kate said numbly, amazed that she could even find her voice after his jolting news. "Yours?"

"Yes."

The misery in his gaze mirrored the pain that radiated from deep in the center of her. She understood without needing to hear it. "It's over, isn't it? You're staying with her."

"What else can I do?" he appealed to her. "Jackie needs me. Kate, she isn't strong and independent like you, with a career to sustain her. She's counting on me to stay with her and make our marriage work for the sake of the baby."

"Yes," she agreed, knowing he was already gone even before they parted. Knowing, too, that something vital had just died inside her.

Kate wondered now as she finished her story whether she would spend the rest of her life striving to recover that vital something and failing. It was a dismal prospect.

She was relieved when Gordon offered no word of sympathy. It was enough just to have told him. All he said was a light, "You know what I think you need? I think you need me to take you to dinner tomorrow night."

And that's how she found Gordon May and learned in the months that followed to bless his presence in her life.

Fort Benning, Georgia

Efrem hated these weekly, Saturday night dances in the officers' club. The same crowd, the same tired conversations in a setting that was too warm and too loud.

But Jackie looked forward to these affairs, and he always obliged her. He'd done his best to please her since their reconciliation. Sometimes his efforts worked, and sometimes they didn't. Still, he kept on trying. A sense of guilt probably.

"Hey, Chaudoir, over here. We've saved you places."

It was Howie McNabb who shouted to him from across the room. McNabb was a captain, like he was now himself. Efrem didn't particularly like him. The man was a loudmouth. But Jackie was a friend of McNabb's wife, Donna. They always sat with them and another couple.

Efrem could see that Howie was already half drunk as they approached the table. It was going to be a long evening.

Jackie wasted no time in exchanging the usual gossip with Donna. It seldom varied. What officer on the base seemed too interested in what other officer's wife, and was it true that . . .

Efrem sat nursing his beer and wishing he was home with his daughter. The conversation at the table didn't interest him. Not, anyway, until it turned to the six o'clock news.

It was Ward Johnson, an African-American lieutenant Efrem played golf with, who raised the subject. "Anyone see the CNA coverage of that latest mess down in Peru? Those rebels never seem to give up. Wonder if we'll end up getting involved in it."

"The reporter on the scene seemed to think it's a possibility," Ward's wife said. "I like that Kate Groen. She knows her stuff."

Efrem was instantly alert. And cautious. With good reason.

Howie leaned toward him, licking his lips like a dog eyeing a choice piece of steak. "You knew her back in the Gulf War, didn't you, Chaudoir?"

Efrem knew Howie had to be already aware of that. Their capture and recovery had been all over the media at the time. The man was just digging. Well, he wasn't going to get anything.

"Briefly. We were held in the same jail, happened to escape at the same time."

"And?"

"Nothing. She went her way afterwards; I went mine."

Efrem could feel Jackie gazing at him. He pushed back from the table. "I'm going to check in with the babysitter."

Jackie stopped him as he started to rise from his chair. "Nell is just fine. You worry too much about her."

He needed to get away from the table and nosey Howie. "You're right. The sitter is reliable, and Nell is okay. So let's do what we came here to do." He held his hand out to her.

Jackie complied. She loved to dance even more than she loved to socialize with their friends.

They joined the other couples on the floor. The music was soft this time, but there was no conversation between them.

Efrem looked down on the woman in his arms, thinking she deserved a better husband than him. Jackie was a conscientious, loving mother. She was also a desirable woman, with her dark hair and distinctive green eyes. Those green eyes were on him now, speculative, wondering.

She waited until they circled the floor before she asked him. "Just how well did you know Kate Groen, Efrem?"

He had never told her about Kate, and he wasn't going to tell her now. He might be a cheating bastard, but there was one thing in his favor. He wouldn't hurt Jackie.

"You've never asked that before."

"I didn't think I had a reason to."

"You don't now," he assured her.

Add that to your record, Chaudoir. That you're also a liar.

Three years, he thought. It had been three years ago when he and Kate had walked away from each other at Dulles. There had been no contact between them since. But he had never stopped loving her, never stopped longing for her. He knew he always would. She was a part of him, an *essential* part he had sacrificed. And missing that part was the hell he lived with every day.

Washington, D.C.

Kate was home between assignments. After her headline-making ordeal in Africa, the station wanted her to take some time off, rest before they sent her out again. She didn't want to rest. She wanted to keep busy, her mind active, which was why she was at her desk this morning checking the research on her next story to make sure it was accurate.

The newsroom at CNA was never silent. There was always noise and movement. Kate had trained herself long ago to shut them out. But this time she sensed a difference in the stir, a wave of curiosity that rolled across the room to her desk.

Looking up from her work, she saw heads swiveling in her direction as the object of all that attention came straight toward her with purpose in his long-legged stride. Kate felt herself grow rigid, the breath sticking in her throat.

She didn't have to wonder how he had gotten past the receptionist outside. He had always been impressive in that army green uniform, would be whatever he wore. The receptionist wouldn't have hesitated to admit him. Not if he had flashed his irresistible grin at her.

Efrem wasn't grinning now. The expression on his strong face was a sober one as he approached her desk, cap in hand. It had been almost five years since she had last seen him, and by now she should be immune to all that potent masculinity. She wasn't. It hurt just to look at him.

They didn't speak when he reached her desk. They just gazed at each other for a minute, he with apparent ease, she with concern. What was he doing here?

"Ask me to sit," he said in that familiar, rich voice.

Before she could issue an invitation, he snagged a chair from the empty desk next to hers, turned it around and straddled it facing her.

Kate glanced around. She was relieved to see that, curiosity satisfied for the moment, the other occupants of the newsroom had gone back to their jobs. Her gaze focused again on Efrem. She voiced what she had asked herself seconds ago.

"What are you doing here, Efrem?"

"I'm in town with my c.o. for meetings at the Pentagon."

"And you thought you'd just stop by to—what? Say hello?"

She'd meant to sound casual about it, but it came out as a challenge.

He leaned toward her, the cap in his hand dangling over the back of the chair. "I've been worried about you, Kate. That business in Rwanda, the insurgents holding you and the other news teams hostage like that. Hell, they threatened to kill all of you. I needed to know you're okay."

"If you've been following the story, you'd know we were released without being harmed. And if you hadn't heard, you could have phoned the station. They would have told you."

She hadn't forgotten the way his voice deepened whenever he was seriously emotional about something. It deepened now. "I had to see for myself."

Was it just an excuse? Or did he still care that much? She didn't want him to care.

"As you can see, I'm fine."

"Yeah."

Both of his hands were busy now with the cap. She watched his long fingers rotating it slowly. The wedding band that had been taken from him in Iraq had been replaced with a new one. Not that she needed the sight of it to remind her he was married. And a father.

"Is your wife in Washington with you, Efrem?"

He shook his head. "She's back home with Nell."

"You had a daughter? She must be quite a young lady by now."

"Nell is great."

There was no missing the pride and love in his voice. "I'm glad she's in your life, Efrem."

His dark eyes searched her face, looking for—No, she didn't know. Didn't want to know. Whatever it was, she was afraid of it. Afraid of the sorrow she could now see in those eyes.

His hands had stopped turning the cap. He seemed to have made up his mind. "Look, Kate, if you're free, I'd like to take you to lunch. Maybe we could do some catching up."

She had no intention of going to lunch with him, or anywhere else with him. What was he thinking? That, if nothing else, they could still be friends? Or did he have something else in mind? Either way, she wouldn't risk it.

She considered letting him know about Gordon. She didn't. Doing that might sound smug, as if telling him, "I have someone else in my life now. I don't need you." And she didn't want to hurt him.

All she said was a gentle but firm, "I've moved on, Efrem."

He understood her message. "Yeah, I don't know what I was thinking." He got to his feet, settling the cap on his head with a decisive "I won't bother you again, Kate."

She watched him turn and leave, willing herself not to let either his visit or his abrupt departure matter. Over time, and with Gordon's help, she had taught herself not to care. But she knew the moment Efrem was gone that she hadn't cured herself. She still cared. Far too much.

Washington, D.C.

Kate stood in the kitchen of the Georgetown apartment she and Gordon shared, phone to her ear as she listened to Hank Bushati pitch his latest proposal to her. Hank was an editor at *The Washington View*. He was also a good friend who gave her whatever freelance assignments his staff reporters were, for one reason or another, unable to cover. Kate was grateful for that.

"Before I tell you what I want," he said, "you should know that you'll be going to Kosovo for this."

"Kosovo! Hank, that's out of the question. Come on, you know I quit CNA just because I could no longer take covering hot spots all over the globe. And now you want to send me to another one." Only partly true. She'd also left Cable News America because she wanted to stay close to home where she could spend more time with Gordon.

"Kosovo isn't a hot spot. The Balkans are quiet now."

"Uh-huh. Then what are all the rumors about the Serbs getting ready to violate the latest peace accord?"

"Just that, rumors. *Exaggerated* ones. You might at least listen to what I'm after."

"That I am willing to do."

Hank began to describe the story he wanted, a familiar enthusiasm in his gravelly voice. "There's this village up north in the highlands of Kosovo. It's called Reva. I'd like you to move in with the people there, get to know them."

Kate stretched the cord of the wall phone far enough to permit her to look around the doorway to check on Gordon in the living room. He was lying on the sofa where she had left him, eyes closed.

"How did you come to choose this Reva?"

"I have a connection with the village. My grandparents emigrated to America from Reva. What I'd like is a feature that tells us how its people—they're Muslim Albanians—survived the war and what life is like for them now that the Balkans are at peace again. The kind of personal stuff that you're so good at, Kate. Interested?"

"Maybe. What does it pay?"

Hank named an impressive sum, the kind of money she and Gordon needed.

"Let me think about it, and I'll get back to you."

She wanted to discuss it with Gordon before she decided. He was awake and sitting up on the sofa when she went into the living room. She refrained from asking him how he was feeling. He hated it when she was anxious about him.

"Hank Bushati called."

"What did he want?"

Kate told him about Hank's proposal. "The thing is, it means going out of the country for a bit."

"Kate, I've told you before not to worry about me. I'll be fine as long as I follow my doctor's orders, and my assistants are there to see that I do. If you want this assignment, then take it."

She nodded, glancing around the living room with its Georgian fireplace and classic paneling. She would be reluctant to give it up, but they needed to think about moving to another place. Georgetown was too expensive a location.

It was after she called Hank back and told him she would go to Reva and do his story that Kate remembered something. Macedonia was just next door to Kosovo, and Efrem was stationed there on a NATO base.

Dara Weinstein worked at the Pentagon, where she had access to the military files. She never failed to keep Kate informed of Efrem's current posting. Kate had repeatedly told Dara she was going to be fired if her superiors ever learned she was passing that kind of information.

She also told her friend she wasn't interested in where Efrem Chaudoir was stationed, but she was lying. Dara must have realized Efrem was like a vice to her because she went on feeding Kate what she secretly yearned to know.

Macedonia. Kosovo. They were small countries where

distances weren't great, but it was absurd for Kate to be concerned. There was no reason why she and Efrem should ever encounter each other. Besides, she hadn't forgotten his promise of three years ago in the CNA newsroom.

I won't bother you again, Kate.

So it was all right. No risk of any temptation. She would be perfectly safe on her side of the border.

CHAPTER EIGHT

PART TWO:
THE BALKAN CONFLICT
KOSOVO—1999

Kate could have asked herself how she had ever ended up in this terrible mess, but it didn't pay to think about that. She was here, and that was that. Anyway, the nightmare would soon be over. That is, if everything worked out as scheduled. She could only pray that it would.

Here was a derelict, stone-walled barn in the central highlands of war-torn Kosovo. Stationed in the open doorway of the crumbling structure, Kate watched anxiously for some sign of the promised rescue plane. But there was no sight or sound of an approaching craft. Nor did anything stir out in the valley that the barn overlooked from its lonely position against the lower side of a mountain.

For that matter, there was nothing but silence behind her. There should have been the lively chatter of young voices, maybe the noise of scuffling in the hay or at least a rustling that would be the evidence of a normal, restless impatience.

But this wasn't a normal situation, she reminded herself. Not with the Serbian paramilitary on the rampage, determined to eliminate every Muslim Albanian in the province.

Kate turned her head to check on her charges. There were fourteen of them ranging in ages from seven to twelve, six girls and eight boys huddled together on the floor.

Making an effort to let them know everything was going to be all right, Kate smiled at them encouragingly. The children did not smile back. She didn't blame them. They had nothing to smile about. How could they believe anything was ever going to be all right again when the only world they had known was gone?

Unable to bear the sight of those grave, tired faces gazing at her wordlessly through the gloom of the barn, she went back to her vigil in the doorway. The March sky was cold and overcast, suggesting the possibility of snow before nightfall. The late afternoon light was already weakening in the valley. If the plane didn't arrive soon—

There! That was it at last, the drone of an aircraft somewhere above the clouds.

Kate watched tensely. A moment later the plane descended through the cover. With a vast relief, she waited as it winged in over the mountains, circling for a landing in the abandoned field across the road below the barn.

As it sank toward the edge of the field, she was able to see it was painted in the familiar camouflage colors of a small, military transport. A prop plane, she noticed, and not a jet. Well, the field probably wasn't long enough to accommodate a jet in this narrow valley tucked between the mountains. A helicopter might have been the best choice, but apparently one large enough to contain all fifteen of them along with the crew wasn't available.

Kate turned again toward the children, calling for her translator who rose to her feet among their midst.

"Halise," she instructed the girl, "tell the children you must all wait here in the barn while I go down to meet the plane."

Kate needed to make certain the situation was safe before she would allow her charges to emerge from the shelter where all of them had been hiding.

"Yes, miss."

Halise began to address the others in their Albanian dialect.

Kate was grateful for the intelligent ten year-old Halise. She was the only one among the children who, having spent two years in America, spoke a fluent English.

Satisfied that her message was being conveyed, Kate left the barn and began to descend the slope toward the road. The plane was down and bumping along the rough field as she passed the charred foundations of the house, framed now by dry weeds, that had once been occupied by the farmers who had presumably fled the region.

The ground was so uneven that, before she could pick her way over it and reach the road, the plane had rolled to a stop. She paused to watch a door in the side of the craft open, permitting a tall figure inside to swing himself to the ground.

She saw that he wore the battle dress of a soldier with a thick, leather jacket for warmth and a baseball-style cap perched at an angle on his head.

Kate started forward again as the solitary figure with his erect, military bearing advanced toward her across the field. He was nearing the road that divided them when she came to a halt. There was no mistaking that long-legged, confident gait.

She had hoped Efrem wouldn't be on the plane, even though she had found it necessary to name her connection to him when she'd called the NATO base in Macedonia for their help in removing the children to safety. But she should have known that, promise or not, he wouldn't fail to be here. That her pulse would still quicken at the sight of his lean-hipped, strong-shouldered body, triggering all the unwanted memories of what they had once meant to each other. Memories that were still poignant, however hard she had worked to bury them.

Sharply reminding herself of their present situation, Kate knew her emotional turmoil would have to wait. It was imperative they get the children on that plane and out of here.

She was conscious then that the craft was already positioning itself to be ready for a takeoff. Efrem was still coming toward her, his arm raised in greeting. He never reached the road, for at that moment there was the alarming burst of a rocket that seemed to originate from somewhere high in the wooded hills on the far side of the valley.

The Serbian paramilitary!

The thought, more conviction than speculation, barely registered in Kate's mind before the shell found its target. The plane that was to be the means of their salvation suffered a direct hit. The roar of the explosion echoed across the valley.

Efrem, who had come to a standstill, shouted for her to go back. Then, without further pause, he swung around and raced toward the crippled plane.

Too late, Kate realized as she watched the scene in horror. He's too late to help the crew. The plane was already raging with fire.

Dear God, the children!

Galvanized into action, she turned and sped toward the barn.

When she reached the structure, breathless from her rapid ascent, the children were crowded into the open doorway. The younger ones and a few of the older girls were whimpering with fright. The others had stoical expressions on their faces.

This is what war did to children, Kate thought angrily. Made them eventually immune to all the unspeakable acts committed in senseless hate.

She herded them back into the interior of the barn, away from the sight down on the field. Enlisting the help of Halise and the older boys, she made an effort to calm and comfort the little ones. There was no time to permit herself to wonder what was happening with Efrem and the plane. She had to concentrate on the children, try to decide what she was going to do with them now.

There was an enemy force concealed somewhere out there. They were equipped with artillery that could destroy this barn, and if Efrem didn't turn up, if he wasn't driven back by the intense heat in his rescue attempt and, unthinkable though it was, perished in those flames . . .

But to her relief he did appear moments later, joining them in the barn. Although she anxiously searched his face, the light was too dim now to read his expression. All she needed, however, was a slight shake of his head to tell her that none of the crew had survived. Kate fought back tears of deep sorrow.

"I had to come, Kate," he said, his voice husky, earnest. "Whatever our history, whatever you didn't want, I had to be here for you."

Shaken by the loss of the plane's crew, all she could manage was a simple nod. Nothing else was possible when their plight was a serious one that had to be remedied immediately. Efrem drew her off to one side where they conferred in hurried whispers.

"The barn is no longer a safe refuge," he said. "Whoever blew up the plane—"

"The Serbian paramilitary probably."

"Yeah, we had a report they were in this area. The light is going so it isn't likely they'll try to advance into the valley tonight, but first thing in the morning . . ."

"They musn't find us here. We have to go before it's too dark to move out."

"Where?" Efrem asked her. "Can you think of any safe place we can hide these kids until we can find help?"

"The caves, miss."

Neither of them had been aware that the alert Halise had drifted away from the others, edging close enough to them to overhear their exchange.

Efrem gazed down at the thin girl with her lank hair beneath a knit cap. "What do you mean, sweetheart? What caves?"

"Up the mountain."

Kate explained it to him. "We passed this series of caves along the trail down to the barn. Thank you, Halise. That was very smart of you to remember them."

"Is any of them large enough to fit all of us?" Efrem asked.

"I don't know," Kate said. "We didn't take the time to investigate them. But I don't see that we have any other choice."

"We don't," Efrem agreed. "All right, let's move out."

Kate rounded up the children and hurried them out the back door of the barn. The shrubbery was thick here, so if an enemy was observing the barn from the other side of the valley they wouldn't see its occupants fleeing. Without any clearing that might betray them, the path went directly through the high shrubbery into the cover of the pine forest on the side of the mountain.

Kate led the way, with Efrem bringing up the rear. She had Halise remind the children to be careful not to leave any footprints in the scattered, crusty patches of snow that hadn't melted in the last thaw. This had been the rule from the beginning of their trek on foot, but it was more vital than ever now not to leave any tracks that would be an evidence of their route.

If the children were confused and wondering what was going to happen to them now, and they had to be, they neither asked questions nor objected. Trusting Kate, they followed her silently up the twisting path. She worried about them. They must be exhausted after a long day of tramping over these mountains, and this climb was a steep one. She was struggling herself, and the failing light didn't make it any easier, particularly down here among all these pines.

Kate was puffing by the time the trail leveled off near the top of the mountain, where the caves were located in the vertical face of a limestone ridge. Efrem was bearing the youngest child piggyback when he caught up with them.

"He was all tuckered out," he explained, easing the small boy from his shoulders and placing him on the ground where the others were resting.

His act brought a lump to Kate's throat, but she didn't comment on it. The twilight had deepened, which made it necessary not to waste time finding the right cave for them. She and Efrem quickly examined several of them before selecting the largest cave with the smallest visible opening.

Efrem used a penlight from one of his pockets to make sure the spacious interior of the cave was dry and not inhabited by any animal. Before they lost the last murky light of the day, Kate instructed the children through Halise to gather up armfuls of the plentiful pine needles for their beds.

It was dark by the time she had settled the children for the night. She and Efrem seated themselves at the mouth of the cave, where she willed herself not to think of the potential complications of his presence. Things that were far too emotional to bear examination. It was better to just be grateful he was here to help her.

Maybe Efrem agreed with that. Maybe that's why, as they kept a vigil, he addressed her with a safe subject.

"The kids going to be able to sleep back there?" he asked in a low voice.

"Probably like babies after all we've been through."

"It's getting colder, though."

"The ethnic Albanians are a hardy people used to the harsh winters here. Besides, if you hadn't noticed, all of the children are wearing thick, quilted coats. They'll be warm enough. You'll see."

"What about you, Kate?"

"Me? I'm okay. I've got wool slacks and a bulky turtleneck

sweater under this parka."

Efrem's concern for her triggered an image of how his solid body had kept her warm in that Iraqi wadi eight years ago. It wasn't a safe image.

She pushed it away with a quick "I'm more worried about how I'm going to feed the children. You wouldn't happen to have any candy bars in those pockets of yours, would you?"

"I wish I did. How long has it been since all of you last ate?"

"We finished off the remains of what we had around noon."

"Then you and the kids must be pretty hungry. We'll have to see what we can do about that come morning."

"At least water isn't a problem. There are springs everywhere in these mountains. We've been drinking from them all day. I can only hope they were safe."

He had no response to that. Since it was too dark now for them to see each other, she hadn't a clue what he might be thinking. It was better that way. Knowing his mind could be risky if it involved anything that was remotely intimate.

That they had been thrown together again might be unavoidable, but she meant to keep their situation as impersonal as possible. And that included no treacherous reminiscing because even after all the years since Iraq and Saudi Arabia, her wound was still tender, making her feel vulnerable.

The silence between them had no sounds to alleviate it. Nothing stirred out in the night, which hopefully meant they were secure here in the cave. She should have left it at that. Silence was easier, less uncomfortable, but there were things she needed to know.

"We're in a bad fix, aren't we?" she asked him softly.

"It's not good. We don't really know what's out there or who we can trust."

Kate didn't need Efrem to expand on that to understand what he meant. She realized only too quickly they could be caught between two hostile forces, the Serbs who were determined to rid the province of the Muslim Albanians and the guerillas of the Kosovo Liberation Army, who were fighting the Serbs.

"No one knows for sure who's in control of an area at any given time," he said. "Could be either the Serbs or the KLA because they're also roaming these mountains."

Kate's meticulous research had taught her before coming to Kosovo that the mountains they were talking about, the Interior Highlands, formed the central spine of the province, running from the north to the south where they joined the higher Sar Moutains along the border of Kosovo and Macedonia.

"And if we run into the wrong force . . ."

"Yeah, a bad scene," he said, his voice grim.

"Won't NATO know it has a plane down?"

"They will, and they'll try to mount a search and recovery operation from the air. But hanging around this dangerous area waiting for another plane or a chopper would be asking for more trouble."

"So what's our option?" she asked him anxiously.

"Way I see it, only one. We've got to find some way to transport these kids into Macedonia."

"How about arranging another rendezvous with NATO? A safer one this time."

"Sounds good. Except for one little problem. How do we contact them? All I've got on me is a small two-way that was meant for communicating with the crew on the plane. It's only got a range of a couple of miles. What about you?"

"I have an international cell phone here in my bag," she said, adding regretfully, "but I haven't been getting any signal on it since I contacted your base yesterday."

"Could be the whole network is down."

"Now I wish I'd bought a satellite phone."

"I had one," he said dryly. "*Had* being the operative word here. The copilot borrowed it. He was thinking about getting one for himself and wanted to examine it. Big mistake. It went up with the plane."

"Efrem, this is all a real mess. What are we going to do?"

"Nothing tonight. But in the morning I'll try to find a working line telephone in one of the villages."

There was another silence between them. It lasted for only a moment before Efrem asked her, "How did you know about the NATO base, Kate?"

"It's my business to know, remember?"

"Yeah, general things like the existence of the base and that our planes have been bombing key targets in Serbia in an effort to stop the genocide in Kosovo. But not specific stuff like me being on that base. They told me after your appeal came in, asking for NATO's help in removing your kids to one of the refugee camps in either Albania or Macedonia, that you said Major Efrem Chaudoir would vouch for you."

"I had to use your name, Efrem. It was the only way I could convince them to believe me."

"Still doesn't explain how you knew I was there."

She had been afraid of this. Afraid he might conclude she had kept track of him through the years, knew he was a major now and where he was currently stationed. And if she had bothered to learn all this, then he must somehow still matter to her.

Kate couldn't involve Dara Weinstein. All she could give him was an inadequate "It might be a cliché, Efrem, but it's still true. Reporters don't reveal their sources."

"I get it. You don't want to talk about it."

She silently thanked him for not pursuing the subject, for not taking them into any raw territory.

"Then how about explaining the mystery of what you're doing here in Kosovo and how you came to have these kids. I'm guessing it has something to do with your work as a war correspondent."

"You'd be wrong in guessing that. I'm no longer with CNA. I've been away from the TV scene for a couple of years now."

"Huh. I've wondered why I wasn't seeing you on the screen anymore."

So, in turn, he had been following her career, tuning in to her reports. She wouldn't ask him about that, though.

"Ironic, isn't it?" she observed with a wry little laugh. "I was the one who was so certain about my direction, and you . . . well, you weren't sure about sticking with the army. Now here we are, you making a career of the service and me having walked away from what I once wanted so badly."

"What happened, Kate?"

You happened, she thought. The career that was supposed to ease the anguish of losing you wasn't enough. Except she couldn't tell Efrem that. Instead, she gave him another explanation, one which was also very true, although it didn't include Gordon.

"Too many hot spots around the globe. I thought I was tough enough for all the atrocities I was sent to cover, and in the beginning I was. Eventually, though, I just couldn't take it anymore."

"What have you been doing since then?"

"Another kind of reporting strictly in the States. Freelancing for newspapers, mostly *The Washington View*."

"This isn't the States, Kate."

"Ah, yes, Kosovo." Her legs were starting to go numb from sitting cross-legged for too long on her blanket of pine needles. She paused to shift them into an easier position before resuming. "We can blame Hank Bushati."

"Poor Hank. Who is he, and what's he got to do with you being in Kosovo?"

She explained about Hank and the story he'd sent her to Reva to write. "The children back there come from Reva."

"Peace again in the Balkans, huh? Too bad none of us, including your editor, realized the Serbs had no intention of honoring the peace accord."

"Yes, by launching another brutal offensive that I got caught right in the middle of. Now *that's* irony."

"It's been bad for you, hasn't it, Kate?" he said, the concern strong in his voice.

"Not near as bad as it's been for the children."

I didn't want to come over here, Efrem. Even though there weren't supposed to be any horrors of war this time, I didn't want to come. But I needed the money, you see. I needed it for Gordon, who's been there for me all these years helping me to recover from you. Only I can't tell you about that because it would hurt both of us too much.

"You want to tell me the rest?"

"No, but I suppose you should hear it. Reva is pretty isolated. We had no idea the paramilitary was conducting raids again when I went on that field trip yesterday morning with Enver Kastrioti and his kids."

"Uh, who—"

"Enver was the village school teacher. He spoke excellent English and had a lot of insights about the village and its people, which made him pretty valuable to me."

If Efrem noticed her use of the past tense, he didn't remark on it. But he did remember the name then. "Enver Kastrioti. You mentioned him in your appeal about airlifting the kids out of Kosovo."

"I did, yes."

"But there weren't any other details in the report I received. Just that it was urgent the kids be removed. You want to supply what I'm missing?"

Kate didn't, but he had a right to know. "There was the field trip with Enver's class and three picnic baskets. He took us into the mountains on foot to the ruins of this Roman temple where we ate our lunch and Enver had his history lesson. Then we hiked back to the village, only—"

She broke off there, hating to relive the episode. Efrem waited silently for her to go on.

"This isn't easy," she croaked, "but here it is. Enver knew something was wrong before we even reached the village, and I could feel it myself. It was too quiet down there." An eerie silence, Kate remembered with a shudder. "Enver went down to investigate while I waited up in the woods with the children. When he came back—" Her voice cracked again.

"You don't have to tell me the rest, Kate."

"Idiotic of me to go all emotional like this after the things I saw in places like Africa. I'm all right now," she insisted, recovering her self-control.

"Your school teacher found something pretty nasty, huh?"

"The worst. He took me aside and told me the paramilitary had been there, looted the houses and massacred everyone in the village. Not a single soul survived the slaughter."

Efrem muttered a savage curse.

Kate, herself, wanted to wail in rage. Instead, she made herself continue her tale, this time as steadily as possible. "We couldn't bring ourselves to tell the children, but we knew they sensed it. They're ethnic Albanian. Even the youngest have memories no child should ever have."

"And?"

"Enver said we had to get out of the region and bring the children to safety, that the regular soldiers would come to the village and finish what the paramilitary started. They'd bury the bodies and torch every house, and if they found us there . . ."

"This is when you made the call to NATO?"

"Yes, and arranged a rendezvous with the plane for the next day in the field by the barn. Enver knew the place, you see."

"It must have been too late by then for you to head for the barn."

"It was, and also too far. We spent the night out in the hills sleeping in the open. I don't recommend it, either then or now."

Before Efrem could agree with her, Kate was startled by a short, sharp barking out in the darkness.

"Nothing to be alarmed about," he assured her. "It's just a fox."

"How can you be sure?" she asked, fearing a sneak attack in the night.

"Kate, I'm a country boy, remember? I know a fox when I hear one. You were telling me?" he prompted her.

"We spent the night in the hills and early this morning started for the rendezvous."

"And your school teacher?"

"He never made it." Kate's voice went flat now, without emotion. It was the only way she could finish her story. "He sacrificed himself. That's what it amounted to. He insisted on going ahead of us to make sure the trail was safe. It wasn't. The path cut through a corner of an Albanian cemetery. The cemetery was mined."

It wasn't necessary for her to tell Efrem that Enver Kastrioti had stepped on one of those buried mines and was dead by the time she got to him. He would realize this had been the outcome.

"I think he knew something might happen to him. That's why he had me memorize the route to the barn." Kate shook her head in a frustration that had been her constant, dark companion all through Africa, the Mideast, South America and now the Balkans. "What kind of people go and mine a cemetery? Kill a good, innocent man?"

116

Efrem had no answer for her. Not that she expected one. Soldier or not, how could he understand this kind of evil any better than she did?

"Kate," he murmured.

That's all he said, just her name. But he managed to express in that single word a wealth of feeling—understanding for what she'd endured, sympathy and a soft something she had no intention of trying to define.

Kate was ready to accept a verbal comfort from him, but certainly not a physical one. She stiffened when, reaching out to her, he laid his warm hand over hers.

"No," she whispered.

He withdrew his hand, but she wasn't satisfied with that. The situation had suddenly become too latently intimate, something she feared she might not be able to handle. She got quickly to her feet.

"I think I heard one of the children stirring back there."

"I didn't hear anything."

"I'm going to check on them. Can I borrow your light?"

She could hear him groping in one of his pockets for the penlight, which he pressed into her hand. Kate switched it on and moved into the depth of the cave, shading the beam with her hand so that its glow wouldn't disturb her young charges. All fourteen of them were curled up on their beds of pine needles and sleeping the solid sleep of exhaustion.

Returning to the mouth of the cave, she returned Efrem's penlight to him. She settled again on the floor of the cave, this time putting what she hoped was a secure distance between herself and the man at her side.

"Kate," he said, his husky voice sounding a warning to her, "there are some things I'd like to say about you and me. *Need* to say."

She was ready for that. She blocked him with a swift,

emphatic "Let's not do this, Major. Look, it's been a long day. I'd like to get some sleep, if you don't mind taking the rest of the first watch. Call me when you're ready to be relieved."

To her relief, he left it at that. Stretching out on the pine needles, she turned her back to him. In spite of her need, she didn't know if she could sleep. Not when their lengthy conversation had been so intense, not when he was still too close to her in the narrow mouth of the cave.

Far too aware of Efrem's stalwart presence, her mind churned with a mixture of emotions. Sorrow for what they had once shared and lost, concern over possible temptations she might not have the strength to withstand. It was only by thinking of Gordon that at last, overcome with fatigue, she managed to drift off.

CHAPTER NINE

The first signs of daybreak were sifting through the canopy of pines outside when Kate, stiff from her long vigil, got to her feet. Working her sore muscles, she looked down at Efrem. He had stretched out and promptly gone to sleep after she'd replaced him for the last watch of the night.

There was just enough light to distinguish his face as she gazed at him on his bed of dry needles. Although the early morning pale glow was an improvement over the dimness of yesterday's twilight, it was still difficult to tell whether he had altered in the three years since she had last seen him.

Not much, she decided after leaning down for a closer look. There were some new lines around his mouth and the corners of his eyes, but that was to be expected. He must be what now? In his mid thirties, she figured, contrasting this against her own age of thirty-one. Otherwise, those chiseled features were the same. Still as purely masculine and appealing as ever, and made even more so by the stubble on his jaw.

A warning went off in her mind.

Temptation, Kate. The temptation you were worried about.

This was dangerous, as unwise as the portions of their conversation last night that had awakened a recollection of how they had talked in their cells back in Iraq. And now here she was trapped with him again in another war zone and risking feelings that ought to stay buried and forgotten.

Turning her gaze away from his face, she peered toward the

119

back of the cave. The children were apparently still sleeping. There was no sound from any of them. She could leave them for a few minutes. *Needed* to leave in order to get away from the sight of Efrem.

Venturing out of the cave and into the open, where the gray shadows were beginning to recede, Kate saw there had been a dusting of snow in the night. She was thankful there was no more than that. They had enough to worry about, chiefly the danger of the paramilitary, without a heavy snow to impede them.

Where was the paramilitary this morning? she wondered. Unlike the regular Serbian army, which was ruthless enough, they could be a vicious and unpredictable force. There was no way to guess their intentions. But as there had been no sign of them since yesterday, she could only hope they'd decided the occupants of the barn weren't worth hunting for and had moved on.

The early morning was brittle, but she didn't feel the cold. Maybe because of her thick clothing. Or maybe just because her body over the last two days had adjusted to these temperatures. Whatever the explanation, she felt warm enough to exercise her legs by strolling a short distance along the trail.

Alert for any sound or movement that might mean trouble, she went only as far as the end of the ridge. This was the route she and the children had traveled yesterday, but she didn't remember the narrow path there on her left branching off the main trail. It seemed to wind down the back side of the mountain.

As she stood there contemplating it, with her breath smoking in the frosty air and the aroma of the pines strong in the stillness, she heard the trickle of water. Its source couldn't be more than a few yards down the path. Another spring, she hoped. That meant water for them.

By the time Kate turned back to the cave, daybreak had advanced far enough she could see the sky. A good sign, she thought, promising a day without the cloud cover that had been their dreary companion since leaving Reva.

Her mood wasn't shared by Efrem. He was on his feet and outside when she reached the cave. "Where have you been," he challenged her sharply, "and why didn't you get me up?"

"Good morning."

Her calm greeting cooled his anger. "Sorry," he muttered. "I was worried when I woke up and didn't find you here."

"I was careful. I only went far enough to find water for us, and we're not the only ones awake."

She nodded toward the mouth of the cave behind him where the children were crowded at the opening, staring at them silently.

It was one of the older boys who told them through Halise that he thought the path Kate had discovered was a route to a village located in another valley down the back side of the mountain. However, he wasn't certain of that.

"I'll have to chance it," Efrem said. "I've got to try to find a working phone somewhere, and we need food. I hate leaving you and the kids, but I think you're better off here where you can hide in the cave."

Kate had no argument with his plan.

The sun was up and already melting the powder of snow when he parted from her outside the cave a few minutes later.

"I know you have to go as far as the spring," he said, "but other than that, stick close to the cave."

She assured him they would.

"It may take me several hours, but I'll be back," he promised her. "And, uh, take care of yourself, will you?"

She could detect more than concern in his eyes. There was

an expression there she could only describe as yearning. Was it? Better not to know, she decided, relieved when he finally turned away from her and headed quickly along the trail.

After Efrem was gone, she rounded up the children, explaining with Halise's help that they were going for water. She made certain all of them had their collapsible plastic cups in their pockets before they set off. The cups were all that remained from the picnic baskets, which they had abandoned yesterday after finishing the last of the food in them.

The light snow that had fallen in the night was entirely gone by the time they reached the spring. Kate was glad of that. With no snow and the trail hard and stony as it was, they would leave no obvious footprints for an enemy to track. Providing any enemy turned up in the area, and she prayed none would.

While waiting for the children to fill their cups at the spring, she gazed at the path that descended through the pines. She thought about Efrem somewhere on that path below them, his tall figure hurrying down the mountain.

It was not altogether the same figure she had known back in Iraq, or even on his brief visit to the CNA newsroom. She'd observed the change outside the cave just before he departed. Although he was still as fit as the athlete he'd once been, his body had matured, lost something of that youthful lankiness.

And unless she was mistaken, there was another difference in Efrem. He seemed a bit . . . well, hard-edged would be the word for it. Nothing that had actually manifested itself, just something she sensed in him. But then their grim situation could be the reason for that.

Why do you keep thinking about him? What does it matter how he's changed?

She had Gordon to think about now. He needed her as she'd once needed him to survive Efrem. Patient, gentle Gordon had seen her at her worst. And hadn't he helped her to not just overcome that worst but to be a better, stronger woman, one more compassionate and tolerant? She liked to think so.

Halise tugging at her sleeve jolted her out of her reverie. "It's your turn now, miss."

It was on their way back to the cave, after all had satisfied their thirst, that Kate surrendered to another image of Efrem. It was when the first rays of the sun had slanted through the pines that she'd noticed he was no longer wearing the wedding band that had once caused her so much heartache.

Well, he'd once told her his marriage wasn't a strong one. It wasn't surprising if, at some point, he and his wife had divorced. Not that it mattered to Kate. She wouldn't let it matter.

After going off into the shrubbery one by one to relieve themselves, Kate and her charges seated themselves in the sun outside the cave to wait for Efrem's return.

They're hungry, she thought, gazing around at the silent children who should have been complaining and weren't. That's why they had no energy to do anything but sit and gaze vacantly into space.

But she knew, looking into the pinched faces that were too old for their years, this wasn't the real explanation for why they weren't laughing and playing. It was the horrific tragedy of losing their families and then their teacher, of having to run from a fearsome force who wanted to exterminate them.

Kate was both sad and angry on their behalf.

Hoping to distract them, and with Halise translating for her, she made an attempt at conducting a simple geography lesson. She described places she had visited in her work, challenging them to name the countries. Their responses, nearly always correct, made her realize what an excellent teacher Enver Kastrioti must have been.

Her own instruction was rudimentary at best, but at least the children were interested enough not to be totally subdued.

As the tedious hours crawled by, Kate became increasingly conscious of Efrem's failure to reappear. He had indicated his absence could be a lengthy one, but when her wristwatch told her it was well past mid morning, she began to worry in earnest.

He could have encountered trouble in almost any form. What if the paramilitary had captured him or, far worse, shot him? What if he didn't return and she was left alone again with the children?

Stop it. You're not doing them or yourself any good.

In the end, it was one of the older, sharp-eyed girls, springing to her feet and calling out an excited *"tungjatjeta!"* who first sighted Efrem coming toward them through the pines.

Along with the other children, an immensely relieved Kate scrambled to her feet. As Efrem approached them, she saw that, like Santa Claus, he was lugging a heavy sack over one shoulder. But in this case the sack contained something much better than toys.

The children, already anticipating its contents, crowded around him with the first genuine enthusiasm they had expressed since leaving Reva.

"Breakfast," he announced, swinging the sack to the ground. "Or maybe by this time lunch would be more accurate."

"The village was there?" Kate asked as she helped him to pass around bread, cheese, sausages and apples.

"I found it all right. What's left of it."

"The paramilitary—"

"No, they haven't been there, but most of its ethnic Albanians have evacuated. Food isn't plentiful for the few families that are still hanging on, but when they heard about the kids they were ready to donate what they could spare."

Kate silently blessed the villagers for their generosity. She and Efrem waited until the children were eating before, seated apart from them, they talked in low tones.

"A phone?" she asked him anxiously after relieving the worst of her hunger with a thick chunk of the welcome bread. "Were you able to find a working phone?"

Efrem shook his head. "The lines are down everywhere. Leke thinks they must have been cut by the Serbs."

"Leke?"

"Yeah, Leke Berisha. A tough old guy who speaks English. Of a sort. Enough, anyway, that he was able to help me be understood in the village."

"But, Efrem, that means there's no way for us to communicate with the outside. What do we do now?"

"It's already been done."

She waited for him to explain while he helped himself to a sausage and she finished her bread, this time with a slab of cheese on it.

Efrem wasn't to be hurried. She remembered this characteristic from the past, how he'd liked keeping her in suspense. It had been an aggravation, but since then she had acquired enough patience to accept people's quirks.

"Leke is going to get us out of here," he said after eating the sausage.

"How?"

"In peacetime, he drives a public bus. Apparently in this part of the world, if you operate a bus you also own it."

"And sometimes the bus isn't a bus at all. It's a van if you're lucky, and if you're not, it's a truck with passengers seated in the open on the back holding on for dear life. I know, because it was that kind of excuse for a bus that brought me from the airport to Reva."

"No," Efrem maintained, "this is a regular bus all right. I've seen it. It's pretty old, but it's big enough to carry all of us."

"To where?"

"The border."

Kate shook her head. "I don't see how that's possible. Both the paramilitary and the regular Serbian troops must be constantly checking all the routes. They'd stop us, take the children."

"Maybe here in the north where they're more active, but there's less danger of that if we can reach the south. They're more likely to let us through when we explain we're evacuating the kids into Macedonia. That's what they want, isn't it, to clear the ethnic Albanians out of Kosovo?"

"But that clearing out," she reminded him quietly, "can be something like the horror of Reva. At least here in the north. And to try getting south on one of the major roads—"

"We're not going to use a main road. Leke knows a back road that winds through the highlands clear down to the border. It's seldom traveled because it isn't much of a road, which is why it will take us longer."

"How much longer?"

"Leke thinks we can make it in about two days. That is, if we don't run into trouble and providing we can find gas along the way when we need it. That could be a problem. He tells me gas is getting scarce."

Risks, thought Kate. The whole plan presented nothing but risks and potential dangers. But it seemed to be the only choice they had because to remain here was unthinkable.

"What is this going to cost us?" she asked Efrem.

"Leke doesn't want anything for himself. All he's asking in payment is that we tell America what's happening here in Kosovo."

"He doesn't have to ask that. I'll be shouting it when I get home." Make that, *if* I get home, she added to herself.

"The thing is . . ."

"You're going to tell me there's a catch."

"We can't expect Leke to cover the gas and what food we might be able to buy. He's a poor man. You got any money in that purse?" he wanted to know, eyeing her shoulder bag.

"Not a whole lot," she said, reaching for a sausage. "I have a fair amount of both marks and dinars and some American bills."

"Let's hope that, with what I've got in my wallet, will be enough. And, Kate?"

"Yes?"

"You might want to reconsider eating that sausage. They're pretty spicy. Unless," he added softly, his gaze riveted on her mouth, "you like them hot. I seem to remember you did like some things hot."

Was this a bold reminder of all his possessive, passionate kisses back in Iraq and Saudi Arabia? She was afraid it was and that, suddenly aware of his sensual mouth, she was susceptible to his suggestion.

"People change in their tastes," she informed him sharply. "I have."

Kate hastily placed the sausage back with the others in the butcher paper they'd come wrapped in.

Two days, she thought unhappily. Their plight wasn't something that could be quickly solved as she'd hoped, enabling her to get away from Efrem and be on her way home. She would have to be with him for at least two more days. Somehow have to endure the lure of their togetherness.

The bus was waiting for them, as Efrem had arranged, where the road they were to travel crossed the path that went down the mountain.

Kate thought it was a sorry affair, all battered and painted an ugly green. It was so ancient she wondered how it could possibly survive the journey.

Leke Berisha was there, leaning against the side of his bus

and idly smoking what smelled like a strong, Turkish cigarette. When Kate and Efrem arrived with the children, he pushed himself away from the bus, carefully extinguished the end of the cigarette, stuck the stub that remained behind one whiskery ear and ambled forward with a rocking gait to meet them.

"*Si jeni,*" he greeted Kate in what she had learned back in Reva was Albanian for "How are you?"

He shook her hand, then turned to the children with a friendly wink. They stared back at him silently.

Surveying Leke Berisha, Kate found him looking as old and rough as the terrain they were about to challenge, his face brown and seamed under a *geleshe,* one of those white skullcaps that was a common headgear among the older Muslim men. But there was an encouraging glint in his dark eyes that spoke of energy and capability.

She couldn't say the same about his bus. He caught her considering it again with misgiving and chuckled good-naturedly.

"She do for us all right," he assured her in his slightly mangled English. Then, turning his head to spit in the gravel, he rubbed his hands together and announced briskly, "Okay, we go now."

They boarded the bus, settling the children on lumpy seats, which in places had the stuffing coming out. Halise chose a seat in the rear, wanting Kate to sit next to her and insisting she have the window. To Kate's relief, Efrem selected a spot just behind Leke at the wheel.

The engine choked to life with fumes that smelled as bad as Leke's cigarettes. Then, with a grinding of gears, the vehicle lurched forward, laboring up the side of the mountain.

Kate immediately decided that to call the route a road was an exaggeration. It was nothing more than a neglected track, so rutted they were bounced and bumped and so narrow that boughs slapped against the windows.

"It's pretty, isn't it, miss?"

Halise was right. Now that the road had leveled off somewhat, Kate found that she could actually enjoy the scenery for the first time since they had left Reva.

The pines were still dominant, but they were no longer the only trees. Mixed among them were beeches and oaks. It was gratifying to find all these trees when so much of the land had been stripped of its timber during the Communist era.

Through gaps in the forest, she was able to see the plain far below where there were compact stone farmhouses with tiled roofs, vineyards against the slopes, fields whose dried stalks indicated sunflowers had been grown in them and pastures where sheep and goats grazed.

From this height it all looked serene and peaceful. Kate knew it wasn't, that it was a land locked in the jaws of war.

"Oh, look, miss! Chamois!"

Face pressed to the window, Kate was striving to catch a glimpse of the small, goat-like deer that the girl had discovered on a rocky spur above the road when she was startled by another voice. A deep and commanding one.

"Halise, would you do me a favor and switch seats with me for a little while? Leke could use those sharp eyes of yours to help him watch for any fallen rocks in the road."

Kate turned her head to discover Efrem towering over them in the aisle. She should have realized he wouldn't remain in his seat, that sooner or later he would ask to join her. And now with this interval that didn't demand some action on behalf of the children, he had his opportunity to talk to her about things she didn't want to discuss. The serious expression in his dark eyes, silently appealing to her not to refuse him, told her that.

Before Kate could object, Halise was out of her seat and moving toward the front of the bus. Efrem slid into the seat the girl had so willingly vacated.

The seats were not wide. Kate was instantly aware of his solid, male body squeezed beside her, of his enticing warmth in the unheated bus.

"About what I tried to say to you last night," he began.

"Efrem," she cut him off, "is this necessary? Because if it's about us, I think we should just let it go."

"I don't want to hurt you again, Kate. Don't you think I know how much—" He stopped to search her face she had turned reluctantly toward his. "Okay, I can see I don't deserve it, but I would like the chance to do some explaining. Please."

She hated that he had come into her life again, dragging up all the old emotions she had so resolutely put behind her. Still, she supposed she owed him this much.

"You didn't come on that plane just to make personally certain the children and I were safely evacuated, did you? You had another reason, and this is it."

"Look, I know I promised you I wouldn't bother you again, but I had to see you. I had to tell you what there was no chance to say back in Washington. That not a day has gone by since we parted at Dulles that I was free of the hell of having left you."

"Eight years is a long time to live in hell, Efrem."

And don't you think I knew that same hell? But it's in the past where I mean for it to stay. So what good are guilt and apologies now? They don't change anything.

She could have added all this, but she didn't. Maybe just because of the sorrow on his face. Of being unable to bear the idea of contributing to that sorrow.

"Kate, I don't expect you to forgive me. What I did was rotten, even if it was necessary. But it might be easier for both of us if I could make you understand about Jackie."

"What can you say now that you didn't already make clear that morning at Dulles?"

She hadn't meant to sound bitter. It was just there, maybe because the ache of the memory was still there, no matter how rigorously she had worked to free herself of it. To free herself of him. Except circumstances had brought them together again, and she didn't know if she could bear it.

There was something else that concerned her. "Efrem, you didn't go and tell Jackie about us?"

"Of course I didn't, but I guess she suspected something. I mean, we were all over the news after we were rescued."

Kate hoped his wife hadn't been more than just suspicious, hadn't suffered over their affair. It was enough she and Efrem had bled with the pangs of their separation.

"The sad thing is that your marriage didn't work out in the end, did it?"

"How did you—Oh, right." He glanced down at his hand. "The wedding band that's no longer there. No, it didn't work out. We shouldn't have stayed together as long as we did, even for the sake of Nell. Not when Jackie hated being an army wife. The divorce became final last month."

"I'm sorry. That couldn't have been easy on any of you."

He didn't react to that. Just as she had feared, he took their conversation in another direction, leaning toward her so closely she was aware of his breath mingling with her own.

"I was planning to contact you when I got home, Kate," he said, his voice raw with hope. "I was going to tell you about the divorce."

His nearness was making her woozy. And angry.

Damn him for cornering her like this. And damn her treacherous senses for threatening to betray the weakness his very presence still had the power to inflict on her. She knew now she'd been lying to herself out of desperation, making a massive effort to convince herself she'd gotten over Efrem. But, God help her, she hadn't. Not entirely.

Before she could frame an answer, he went on with a swift "Okay, I know I wasn't entitled to try to reach you, that the best thing I could do after you told me you'd moved on was to leave you alone. But now that this situation has thrown us together again—"

"Don't take this any further, please."

She didn't want to hear he still had feelings for her. She refused to risk her heart all over again, or her commitment to Gordon. But Efrem ignored her plea.

"You don't trust me. I haven't forgotten that was always an issue with you, Kate. I went and taught you to trust me back in Iraq, and then I went and deserted you."

"You're wrong. I grew up, Efrem. I no longer have a problem with mistrust. As for hurting me, yes, of course you did, but I put that behind me." She was being truthful about that.

What was the point of angry recriminations after the passage of so many years? Why make it any harder on both of them by telling him that her recovery hadn't been that easy or simple? That the despair of Dulles hadn't softened in the bleak months that followed it.

Not until Gordon entered her life, being there for her in the worst times, helping her through them, had the darkness finally lifted. She valued their relationship too much to put it in jeopardy now, which is why she firmly told Efrem, "You see, you don't have to worry any longer about your conscience. I forgave you long ago. I understood and forgave you. That's what you wanted to hear, isn't it?"

"Is that all you think this is about, my damn conscience? Because if it were, I wouldn't—"

"Efrem, don't say another word. We're finished here. Go back to your seat."

She was relieved when, after silently measuring her for a

long, uncomfortable moment, he got to his feet and went forward up the aisle. Or was she relieved?

Efrem reclaimed his place behind the driver with a smile of thanks for Halise and an encouraging "I think Kate is waiting for you to sit with her again."

The girl hurried off, happy to rejoin Kate in the rear of the bus.

Efrem settled into his seat, outwardly calm but inside seething with frustration. He could feel in his gut that Kate still cared about him, but something was holding her back from admitting that what they had once had was not as dead and cold as yesterday's ashes. That underneath those ashes were smoldering embers waiting to be coaxed into a fresh blaze.

Maybe it was the old mistrust she had so stoutly claimed to have cured. It was possible that mistrust was still there, making her too vulnerable to ever rely on him again.

Or maybe it was just his ego that had him convinced he still meant something to her. Could be she *had* moved on, found someone else. Why not? A woman like her would be the target of any number of men.

And Kate was more alluring than ever. He remembered thinking that back in Washington. How she had changed in her maturity. Her hair was longer and no longer streaked with blonde highlights. The warmth of its natural, light brown together with its simple styling suited her.

It was her inner self, though, that made all the difference. Kate had always been her own woman, but she had never been as self-possessed as she was now. That quality alone had to be an irresistible challenge for any intelligent male with functioning hormones. And although she hadn't mentioned anyone, it didn't mean she wasn't in a committed relationship. And if she were . . .

Efrem found himself seized by a sudden jealousy he had no right to feel.

In case you don't know it already, you're pathetic. Look at how you went on cheating on Jackie, sneaking down to the rec room whenever you got the chance just so you could catch a glimpse of Kate on the old TV. Anything to see her face again.

She had been like a drug to him, a fix he had to have. He'd even gone through a kind of withdrawal when CNA no longer carried her reports. But it hadn't worked. She was still in his blood. Hadn't he boarded that plane yesterday when there'd been no real need for him to accompany the capable rescue crew?

Oh, yes, there was a need, Chaudoir. An urgent one. You had to be with her again. Had to use the chance luck was tossing your way to test whether you did want her as fiercely as you'd wanted her during the Gulf War. Whether the passion you shared was real or only a tantalizing memory.

Want? Hell, wasn't the way he was squirming in his seat now, his body raging with a painful arousal, evidence enough of just how much he wanted her? Not that he deserved her.

Anyhow, he thought glumly, what did it matter when it looked like Kate wasn't going to let him get near her.

CHAPTER TEN

It was mid afternoon when the bus broke down.

Even at the back of the vehicle, Kate could tell something was wrong when the engine began to act up, in one minute surging and in the next dying back and threatening to stall. In the end, with a coughing sound, the motor quit altogether.

Leke coasted them to a safe stop at the side of the road. She heard him muttering something, probably an Albanian curse, as he slid from beneath the wheel, flung the door open and disappeared outside. Climbing to his feet, Efrem joined the old man.

Kate could hear what sounded like the hood being raised, and then there was silence. She tried not to worry as she and the children waited, but she couldn't help being anxious. What if they were stranded out here in the middle of nowhere with a bus that wouldn't run again? What then?

The long minutes passed. When Kate could no longer stand not knowing what was happening outside, she got to her feet and squeezed past Halise. The children started to follow her as she headed up the aisle, but she waved them back, signaling them to remain in their seats.

Efrem was at the door when she got there, offering his hand to help her down. She hesitated to accept it, not wanting to chance even a casual physical contact with him. Then she decided she was being silly. Even so, once she was on the ground, she quickly withdrew her hand from his. As brief as his touch had been, it had stirred an old longing. What's more, she was afraid he was aware of that.

She was grateful when Leke covered the awkward moment, lifting his head from under the hood to grin at her. "She be like my old woman," he informed Kate. "Stubborn until I give her what she want."

"What is he talking about?" she asked Efrem.

"His engine. The fuel pump is shot. He has to replace it."

"A new pump?"

"Well, another one anyway."

"This doesn't sound good. Where on earth is he going to find another pump?"

"No worries," Leke assured her. "I got her."

Kate looked to Efrem again for a translation.

"I'm learning just how resourceful these people are. Leke told me," he said, indicating the door of a luggage compartment in the lower body of the bus, "he carries not only his toolbox under there but all the spare parts he might need. Apparently, this isn't the first time the bus has broken down without a service garage on the next corner."

Kate wasn't surprised. "Yes, they have to be resourceful." She squinted up at the sun. "How long is this repair going to take?"

"I'm not sure. Could be an hour and a half or maybe two."

She looked around her. They were on a kind of small plateau with a level meadow stretching off from the side of the road. There was the sound of running water in a grove of chestnuts nearby, possibly a creek.

"We can't expect the children to wait in the bus all that time," she said. "They're probably thirsty, and if that water over there looks safe enough, I guess we can try it."

"Maybe they're hungry again, too," Efrem agreed. "We still have a few leftovers from this morning. Enough to hand around some snacks."

Leke took time to light a cigarette, his thickly callused hands shielding the flame of his match, before hunkering down in front of the luggage compartment. By the time Kate and Efrem had the children off the bus, the old man had his toolbox and the replacement fuel pump at his feet and was busy under the hood.

Kate led the children to the tiny creek where they lined up to fill their cups. The water was clear and cold from the recent melt on the mountaintop above them, so she could only hope it was all right to drink.

By the time they returned to the bus, Efrem had the leftovers ready for them. He handed around cheese and bread, which the children devoured in short order. Turned loose for the first time since leaving their village behind, they wandered around the meadow. Kate and Efrem seated themselves on a heavy log at the edge of the chestnut grove to keep an eye on them.

One of the boys produced a tennis ball from a deep pocket in his coat and began to toss it in the air. The others watched him with disinterest. Halise wandered over to the log.

"Everyone wishes that Almed could have brought a different ball with him," she confided. "One big enough so we could play soccer."

Kate knew that, like most everywhere else in Europe, soccer was the national sport here. Children and adults alike had a passion for it.

"I wish we had a soccer ball with us, too," she remarked to Efrem. "Look at them. They're bored. It's a good sign, I suppose. It means they no longer want to be anything but idle."

Efrem had no reaction to that, but a few minutes later he got to his feet and crossed the meadow to the bus. She watched him as he spoke to Leke, thinking he was checking on the progress of the repair. The old man leaned over to root around in his toolbox. Coming erect, he handed something to Efrem.

It wasn't until Efrem returned to the log that a puzzled Kate was able to see that Leke had given him a large folding knife and a roll of black tape. He sat both of them on the log.

"What are you going to do with those?" she asked him.

"You'll see," he said, keeping the secret to himself. "Be back in a minute."

He went off into the grove behind them. When he reappeared, he was carrying a three-foot length of a stout limb that tapered from a thick end to a narrow one. Settling himself on the log, he unfolded the sharp knife and began to whittle away at the wood.

"Uh, I'm assuming this has an explanation. Are you going to keep it to yourself, or would you like to spread it around?"

"Just a hobby, Kate. One day, when I'm retired, I plan to sit on my front porch and carve little animals that all the local shops are going to be wild to carry. When I'm not playing golf, that is."

Was he being funny? If so, it was the first evidence of it since he had arrived on that plane. Back in Iraq, even when the situation had been at its worst for them, Efrem had always been able to lighten it with an easy humor. It was one of the things she had loved about him. And missed. But if he hadn't lost it, if he was still capable of—

Don't go there, Kate.

Obeying herself, she emptied her mind of anything personal. She concentrated instead on his hands, watching him skillfully work the wood, turning it as he shaped it.

He certainly wasn't carving an animal. That was obvious almost at once. What on earth—

It was when he flattened both ends of the length, then chipped away at the thicker end until it was slightly rounded that Kate realized what was emerging from the limb.

"A baseball bat!"

"Hey, it can't be too bad if you can recognize it." After a few more strokes with the knife, he held up his creation. "A bit rough, but it should do."

She understood his intention then. "You're going to teach the kids how to play baseball."

"It's what I know. Or used to." He took up the roll of tape and began to wrap it around the narrow end of the bat, forming a grip.

"But they don't. I doubt they've ever had any contact with it. And what are you going to use for a ball? Oh, of course, Almed's tennis ball. This ought to be good."

Efrem got to his feet with a dry, "I bet you would've told Babe Ruth he'd never be a slugger."

Kate found herself smiling as he strode across the meadow, swinging the makeshift bat at his side as he signaled for the children to gather around him. Using Halise to communicate his instructions, he sent them flying in all directions across the meadow. Kate was puzzled until she saw them returning with sticks, which Efrem used for the bases as he paced out a diamond.

At least he's won their enthusiasm, she thought, watching him demonstrate the game before dividing them into two teams. That was an achievement in itself.

A tree limb for a bat, a tennis ball for a baseball, sticks for bases. But they worked. Sort of.

The children were clumsy and confused at first, but with Efrem yelling encouragement from behind home plate, where he was playing umpire, they began to improve.

They're enjoying themselves, Kate realized. Efrem even settled a quarrel with gestures and an English they somehow managed to understand. For this hour anyway they were able to be children again. Thanks to Efrem. Wise or not, she was moved by both his patience with them and the sight of his tall, virile figure.

Leaving the game in progress, with Halise standing in for him as umpire, he crossed the meadow to the log where Kate waited.

"Huh?" he said, one eyebrow lifted in a request for her approval.

"Okay, Major, you win points as a baseball coach."

"Damn straight I do."

She rose from the log, her tone serious now. "You're good with them, Efrem."

"You forget I've had practice."

"No, I haven't forgotten you're a father."

There was no strain about it. It was all very easy and natural this time when Kate found herself strolling beside him along the creek, managing to keep within sight and sound of the children as Efrem told her about his daughter.

"The worst of the divorce is not regularly being with Nell. It's hard, especially when you're in the service and not knowing where you'll be stationed next."

"What's she like now, your Nell?"

"Bright and bouncy. She's crazy about animals. Some stray is forever following her home. I just know that someday she's going to be begging for a horse. She already talks about having one."

Kate could hear the pride in his voice as he described his daughter. She was glad he felt he could share his Nell with her like this, but his exuberant description awakened an old yearning in her.

She stopped on the bank of the creek to gaze down wistfully at the rushing waters.

"Sorry to go on like that," he apologized, coming to a halt beside her. "I forget that people who aren't parents themselves find it hard to understand a father wanting to talk about his kid all the time."

Kate didn't answer him. She could feel him watching her.

"What is it?" he probed. "Is it because I stayed with Jackie for the sake of—"

She cut him off with a sharp "I told you I understood and forgave that, and I meant it."

"Then what's wrong because I can see that something is troubling you?"

She'd forgotten just how perceptive Efrem had always been about her. It seemed this hadn't changed, that he could still read her moods.

Kate hesitated. Well, why not? she decided. She'd told him this morning trust was no longer an issue with her. Maybe she needed to prove that to him.

Tearing her gaze away from the creek, she faced him. "I do understand about being a parent because I'm one myself."

He stared at her. "Let me get this straight. You're telling me that since I last saw you, you had a—"

"No, it was long before I ever met you. I was a teenager, and—" She paused to clear her throat. This was going to be more difficult than she'd expected.

"Look, Kate, you don't have to tell me."

"It's all right. I meant for you to know when we were together in the Gulf War, but . . . well, I guess on one level I was still battling with mistrust. I no longer work to keep it a secret now. Anyway, it was when I was sixteen and—there's no other way to put it but bluntly—I was date-raped."

Efrem blasted the air with a curse.

"Yes, exactly," she said. "I trusted these boys. I *knew* how to trust back then. And my parents trusted them."

"There were *two* of them?"

"We were on a double date. The other girl got dropped off

first on the way home from a party. I didn't get home. I got assaulted in the back seat of the car by a couple of guys who were drinking when they shouldn't have been drinking. They took turns holding me down while they . . . well, you can appreciate why I won't go into the details."

"Appreciate? Hell, I hope they both burned."

"They didn't. My parents didn't report it."

Efrem looked thunderous. "What kind of parents wouldn't go straight to the police?"

"The ambitious kind. Both of those boys were the sons of prominent Baltimore families. Families whose members were served by both my mother and my father. They would have risked their law practices if they'd brought charges."

"And you went along with it?"

"I was sixteen, Efrem. I was ashamed. I didn't want anyone knowing either."

"I hope you'll pardon me for saying it, but I sure as hell don't think much of these parents of yours."

"Oh, they cared. Enough to make sure I wasn't pregnant. I told them that part was all right, that both of the boys had had just enough sense left in them to use condoms."

"But your folks did take you to a doctor?"

Kate shook her head. "That would have been another risk, and I didn't want it myself." She laughed, but there was no mirth in her laughter. "Want to know the irony of it all? I was the one who got punished. Because that's what it felt like when my parents shipped me off to a boarding school in another state. Had to make sure it all stayed hushed up, you see."

"Damn it, Kate, your own parents betrayed you."

"Yes, that's exactly how I ended up feeling about it. Which is why I deliberately didn't tell anyone when I discovered I *was* pregnant until it was too late for an abortion. If they could punish me, I could punish them. Seriously dumb, huh?"

"Meaning one of those condoms failed to do the job."

"It happens, I hear. Anyway, it happened to me. I had the baby. Also out of state, of course. It was a boy. I didn't get to keep him. My parents argued I had a promising future ahead of me, but it would be jeopardized if I kept a baby I was far too young to try to raise."

"And you agreed."

"I agreed."

"Did you want your baby, Kate?"

She had no direct answer for Efrem, only a little shrug. "I thought I was doing the right thing when I gave him up for adoption. I never saw him again or knew where he was, not even his name. But . . ."

Her voice threatened to break. She hadn't planned on all this emotion getting dragged up from the past, threatening to overwhelm her with its intensity.

Efrem's insight was still at work, guessing her feelings. "But a part of you never stopped missing him. That's it, isn't it?"

She gave herself a moment to recover her self-control. "I suppose," she said slowly, "there aren't many women who don't go on aching all their lives in some measure or another for the child they lost. We're built that way, aren't we? But we learn to handle it."

"How? How did you handle it, Kate?"

"You know the answer to that. I did what my parents had done themselves. I went on and earned a degree, the best college, the highest grade average, all so I could wrap a career around myself. It worked. Most of the time."

"But there was a penalty in that," he said, knowing without having to ask this time. "Your problem with trust. It started with those bastards raping you, then your own mother and father letting you down. You couldn't rely on anyone. Until I came along. And what do I end up doing but walking out on

143

you just when—"

Before she could stop him, he had seized her by the wrist and drawn her behind a tree, trapping her against its thick trunk. His hands reached up to frame her face on both sides, his eyes stormy with self-anger and a deep regret as he gazed down at her.

"Oh, Kate, what have I done to you? What have I *done* to us?"

"What you had to do, so don't go all emotional on me. One of us is bad enough. Look at me. I'm a mess."

"You're entitled."

He went on searching her face. She was afraid he was going to kiss her. That couldn't happen.

But you're not as tough as you thought you were, are you?

That was true. In this moment, battered by a longing for the son she'd surrendered, she wanted to fill that void with the man who had once meant everything to her. Even though she knew it wasn't possible to substitute the one need for the other, she was willing to accept whatever comfort Efrem was prepared to offer her.

But a kiss? It was only with a strong effort Kate resisted that danger by trading it for something more acceptable. When his mouth angled toward hers, she escaped from the hands that steadied her face and leaned forward, resting her forehead against the solid security of his chest.

"I shouldn't have told you," she muttered, hearing the hollowness in her voice as she flattened her palms against the soft leather of his jacket. "It was wrong of me."

"It was right," he insisted, his arms wrapping around her.

It was a mistake to let him hold her close like this, to permit his soothing hands to stroke her back. Even worse than surrendering to his embrace was to relish it as she did. He would read in it something she hadn't intended.

It was the children who saved her. Before the situation could morph into something from which it would be impossible to retreat, there was a loud and angry commotion from the direction of the baseball diamond.

Kate lifted her head from Efrem's chest. "From the sounds of it, Major, I think you've got another quarrel that needs mediation."

She'd let down her guard with him. She'd have to be more careful after this. It was enough to be tormented by his nearness without submitting to any hazardous, physical contact from him.

Leke slammed down the hood of the bus with a satisfied "Okay, she is good again for rolling."

Kate was thankful for that but concerned over something else. The sun was beginning to sink toward the plain below. "We're not going to have a lot of light left to us for rolling," she pointed out. "Unless you mean for us to travel on in the dark." With the road being what it was, this wasn't a prospect that pleased her.

The old man shook his head. "*Jo.* Not good."

"So where do we spend the night?" Efrem asked.

Kate had a vision of trying to sleep in the bus parked at the side of the road. Well, as long as it was safe, she supposed it didn't matter. Better that than in the open or in a cave. But Leke had another plan.

"There is Monastery of Saint Nicodemus. Not so very far. You gonna like that place."

Kate was alarmed by his intention. In this part of the world monasteries were Eastern Orthodox, and that meant the Serbians. It was their chief religion.

"Leke, we can't take refuge there. You're Muslim, the children are Muslim. They would never take us in, and if we show up at their gate they might even report us to the military."

"*Jo, jo.* The father is a good man. He don't turn us away."

"Leke," Efrem asked him earnestly, "are you certain of this?"

"Sure, I know the father and how he helps all the peoples. You see that."

Kate and Efrem exchanged glances.

"I say we chance it," he said. "Kate?"

"It's your call."

"Then let's get the kids on board."

By the time Leke had stowed his toolbox and the old fuel pump in the luggage compartment, Kate and Efrem had the children settled in their seats. She didn't want any renewal of their conversation at the creek and was glad when he reclaimed his seat behind Leke.

Twilight was overtaking them by the time Leke turned off the road on a side lane that wound down the mountain. Through the trees Kate could see the scattered lights of a town below them. This wasn't good. If they had to enter the town to reach the monastery, the bus would be a subject of curiosity.

But Leke knew what he was doing. Their destination was located in a sheltered hollow at the foot of the mountain, with hills that divided it from the town on the plain. Kate sighted it in the last light of the day around a bend in the lane.

The Monastery of Saint Nicodemus was just beneath them in its little valley, a compact community behind high walls. She could see the whitewashed dome of the church and several buildings clustered around it.

Leke pulled up to an archway in the wall. They waited on the bus while he went and rang a bell beside a sturdy wooden gate under the arch. A few minutes later he was admitted through a door in the gate by a robed figure with a lantern. The door was shut behind them. More minutes passed as Kate gazed anxiously out the window.

When Leke finally reappeared, she went forward to hear what he'd learned.

"I explain to the father," he reported cheerfully to Kate and Efrem as he climbed aboard the bus. "He is waiting for you now. You take the children to him. The brother will show you."

"What about you, Leke?" Efrem asked him.

"I hide the bus in the trees back of the monastery. Then I come. Okay?"

They left the bus with the children, Kate leading the way and Efrem bringing up the rear. The young, silent monk was waiting for them just inside the open door. He conducted them through the thickening gloom across a cobbled yard and into a cloister. They trooped along an arcade and entered another door into a softly lit passage.

Kate could see icons on the walls, some of them looking very old. A bearded, robed figure came forward out of the shadows to meet them. He smiled at the children before turning to Kate and Efrem, shaking their hands.

"I am Father Basil, the abbot of Saint Nicodemus," he greeted them in a precise English. "You are very welcome."

After learning their names, he nodded toward the young monk. "We have food for everyone. Brother Johan will show you the way."

Kate and Efrem lingered behind after the children went off with the monk.

"Father, it's very good of you to take us in like this," Kate said, "but I hope it won't mean trouble for you."

"They never bother us here," he assured them. "And what would we be if we did not help the children? This ethnic cleansing ordered by our President Milosevic is very wrong."

Kate knew that, although the Muslims in the Serbian province were connected by culture, language and sometimes family to Albania, for most of them, whose ancestors had settled long ago in Kosovo, this was the only home they'd ever known. But now the Serbs, the militant ones anyway, wanted them gone.

Efrem had his own concerns. "Father, I'd like to contact my base back in Macedonia. Do you have a working telephone here?"

"I am sorry to tell you we do not. I understand the telephones everywhere are—I believe you call it down."

"What about gasoline? Is that available anywhere? The bus is pretty low on gas."

"There is a station in the town, but they tell me it has been closed for several days. The only supply of petrol in the area is kept for military use alone."

"Where is that, Father?"

"A few kilometers down the road from us. But the storage tanks are locked behind a high wire fence, and there is a guard. Would you like to join the children now?" he asked, leading the way along the passage.

Kate came suddenly awake sometime in the middle of the night. For a disoriented moment, propped up on one elbow, she failed to understand what had startled her into consciousness. One of the children calling to her?

She turned her head from side to side, her gaze searching through the dimness. The light from a single lantern left burning on one of the refectory tables, pushed against the walls to accommodate them, was very weak. But it was sufficient enough to tell her that none of the figures wrapped in their blankets on the floor around her was stirring. What then?

Kate listened. Seconds later, she heard it. The rumble of an engine somewhere outside the walls of the monastery. This must be what had awakened her. Just a vehicle passing by. The noise faded and was gone. There was silence again except for the low sounds of breathing from the sleeping children.

She lay her head back down on the pillow, grateful for both it and the warm blanket in which she was rolled. The monks had provided blankets for all of them, along with a supper of stew and the local, cheese pie known as *flia*. It had been wonderful to eat a hot meal again, not to mention the showers that had been available to them.

Kate hadn't felt clean since leaving Reva. That had been solved, even if she did have to wear the same clothes. Now all she needed was a few more hours of peaceful, uninterrupted sleep.

Closing her eyes, she was prepared to drift off when something brought her sharply alert again. Not a sound this time but a memory. She recalled Efrem telling Father Basil the bus was low on gas and the abbot informing him that the only supply of petrol in the area was restricted to military use.

Was it possible? Could the noise of the engine she'd heard have been the bus sneaking off in the night? She had to know.

Untangling herself from the blanket, Kate slipped on her shoes. She got to her feet and, as quietly and carefully as possible, she wove a path through the six, sleeping girls on the floor.

Leaving the refectory, she went down the passage. There was a chapel here to which the two men and the eight boys had been assigned. The door was open. A votive light burning on the altar made it unnecessary for her to enter the chapel. Its glow was enough that, just by hanging in the doorway, she was able to count the figures sleeping on the floor of the aisle between the rows of benches.

Eight of them. All boys, no adults. The two men were missing. Kate was convinced of it. Efrem and Leke had gone off to those locked and guarded storage tanks. The idiots! How did they think they could get the bus inside that fence without being shot, or at least apprehended?

There was no possibility of going back to sleep now. No way she could do anything but stay up and wait for them. And if they didn't come back, she would somehow have to rouse Father Basil. But what could the abbot do?

Feeling helpless and frustrated, she knew she had to go outside where she would be able to hear the first sound of the returning bus. *If* it returned.

Kate went back to the refectory, got her coat and checked on the girls. None of them was awake. She could leave them for a while.

She must have lost her way trying to locate the door into the cobbled yard where they had arrived earlier. When she finally emerged from the building, she found herself in what looked like an orchard on the back side of the monastery. A gibbous moon overhead shed enough light to illuminate the naked branches of the fruit trees. She could also glimpse the white-washed wall that framed the compound at the far end of the orchard. The dark mass of higher trees behind the wall indicated that must be where Leke had hidden the bus and where he would park it again when they returned.

If. Still that terrible *if.*

Kate began to pace through the orchard. It was a mild night. Or maybe she was just too worried to feel the cold.

Efrem. Damn him. What was she going to do if something happened to him? How was she going to get the children to safety without him? And Leke, of course, because this sick feeling roiling inside her had as much to do with Leke as it did Efrem. Didn't it?

Chapter Eleven

Kate wasn't sure how long she wandered aimlessly in the orchard through the rows of fruit trees. Her nerves were so taut with waiting it seemed like forever. In reality, it was probably no more than twenty minutes later when she heard the sound of a vehicle laboring up the hill from the direction of the town.

But was it the right vehicle?

She stopped beneath the boughs of a cherry tree to listen closely. A moment later the approaching vehicle slowed for a turn. It must have swung in at the side of the monastery. She could hear it crawling along the outside of the wall, feeling its way to the back side of the compound. She could detect no glow from the beams of its headlamps, which must mean it was traveling furtively without lights.

It had to be the bus. Thank God.

Needing to be certain it was not only the bus but that both men were on it, she went on standing there. Seconds passed. The vehicle came to a halt behind the wall where the engine was turned off. Then there was a moment of silence.

Something squeaked off to her left. Kate's head swiveled in that direction. A door in the wall she hadn't noticed until now opened to admit two shadows. The door was shut again. The shadows started toward the building. When the figures passed into a pool of moonlight, she was able to recognize them. Leke and Efrem.

"Over here," she called softly.

Startled, they looked her way. There was the low mutter of an exchange between the men. Then Leke went on his way. Efrem came swiftly across the grass to the cherry tree.

"What are you doing out here at this hour?" he challenged her.

"I might ask you the same thing. Except I don't have to." Her relief for their safe return became anger instead. "The two of you went down to those storage tanks to get gas, didn't you?"

"And we got it. Leke's old girl is full again."

"At what risk? By knocking out the guard, breaking through the fence to get in there?"

"Didn't have to. A generous bribe was all it took. Afraid we're gonna have to rely on your funds from here on."

"And what if the guard hadn't accepted your bribe? What if—"

"Worried about me, Kate?" His teeth flashed in the moonlight with a big grin that reminded her of the younger, cockier Efrem. But, damn it, why did the sight of it have to tear at her insides?

"What I was worried about were the children. If the two of you had been captured or killed and the bus taken, how would I have gotten them across the border?"

"A tough woman like you? You would have managed. No, I think you *were* worried about me."

"That ego of yours, Major, is nothing short of colossal."

He ignored that, his voice deepening. "And that means you still care about me."

He edged close to her. She would have backed away from him except she was pinned against the cherry tree, just like she had been trapped against the chestnut tree at the creek this afternoon.

"All right, I was worried. I was worried about both you *and* Leke."

"Do you remember what I swore to you that last morning

back in Riyadh? That we'd always manage to find each other? And we have, Kate, even if it has taken all this time."

"We didn't find each other. This meeting up again wasn't supposed to happen."

"And how much I loved you? The kind of love that never lets go. I shouldn't have waited until I got home again to contact you. I should have called you the day my divorce was final, even if you did tell me you'd moved on, even though I promised I wouldn't bother you again."

Why wasn't he listening to her? Why did he have to be so maddeningly persistent?

"Because I haven't let go of that love, Kate," he said, his voice like a caress, hypnotic, disarming.

She made a serious mistake then by admitting, "I do still care."

She meant to qualify that admission to prevent him from reading it as an invitation. But before she could utter a single *but,* his arms were around her and hauling her against his length.

It would have been foolish to tell herself she was caught against the tree without any defense. She could have easily escaped from his embrace. All she had to do was demand that he release her, and Efrem would let her go. He'd never been the kind of man who forced himself on a woman.

She had no argument to vindicate herself, either with being in his arms or accepting his mouth when in the next moment his mouth was on her own. She was not only willing to have him kiss her, she needed his kiss. Responded to it blindly, recklessly. It was compelling, his lips cherishing hers, their tongues tugging and teasing with their mutual longing for each other.

It was also an insanity, which Kate realized even before his mouth finally lifted from hers.

His voice was thick now when he confessed to her, "There wasn't a day that went by in all those years that I didn't think of you. And sometimes I wanted you so badly I couldn't stand it. Tell me you love me, Kate. I have to hear it."

It would be useless to pretend that, on one level anyway, she didn't want him. But there was a distinct difference between love and sex.

"Efrem, listen to me," she attempted to reason with him. "You have to understand—Would you let me go, please? I can't talk to you like this."

With a reluctance she could sense in his slowness to comply, his arms slid away from her. Even then she wasn't able to continue until he moved back far enough to put several safe inches between them.

"Efrem, we're no longer that man and woman who fell in love. We're different people now."

"If you're going to say you don't love me, I don't believe it. That kiss wasn't just moonlight in an orchard. It was real. Kate, I'm a free man now. There's no reason we can't build a life together."

She shook her head emphatically. "It wasn't love. It was just lust. They're not the same thing. Or haven't you heard? And even if I did love you, it wouldn't matter."

It was time. She had to tell him about Gordon, should have told him long before this.

"You might be free," she said, "but I'm not."

Even in the pale glow of the moon, she could see the scowl on his face. "Are you saying there's someone else?"

"That's exactly what I'm saying."

"Are you married? You can't be married because the first thing I looked for when I got the chance was a ring on your finger, and there isn't one, either wedding or engagement."

"No, but we're committed to each other."

"What the hell does that mean?" he growled. "Who is this guy, anyway?"

"Not that it matters, but his name is Gordon May. Look, there's something you have to understand, something I should have made clear to you before this and didn't."

"Like what?" he demanded.

This wasn't going to be easy, she thought. Efrem had called her tough, but she wasn't tough. Not when it came to him. Giving herself a moment to shape her words, she reached up and caught a thin bough on the cherry tree, dragging it down and rolling one of its twigs between her thumb and forefinger.

"I told you I got out of broadcasting because I could no longer stand covering all the global violence. That was true, but only partly true. The other truth was . . ."

When she faltered, he insisted harshly, "Say it."

"My career was everything I'd ever wanted, Efrem, but it wasn't enough. I tried to give it all I had after you left me, months, even years of it, but in the end it just wasn't enough."

"God, did I hurt you that much?"

"You weren't easy to get over." What was the point of describing for him just how difficult it had been, the awful loneliness and how she couldn't stop aching for him, how she'd barely kept herself from falling apart altogether? He'd had enough guilt heaped on him.

"Until this Gordon May came along. That's it, isn't it?"

"Until Gordon, yes." She went on worrying the twig as she made an effort for Efrem to understand. "We met at a fundraiser. He's in public relations and was there to promote it. You don't have to know all the rest. All you have to know is that Gordon helped me to heal myself. And he's been there ever since."

"Do you love this guy, Kate?"

"Not like I loved you. But he's a decent, caring man and deserves something better than my walking out on him. You ought to understand that, Efrem."

"Because of my not being able to walk away from my wife. But that was different. Jackie needed me."

And Gordon needs me now just as much as Jackie once needed you. But the reason for that need was Gordon's secret, and she had no right to share it. All she could give Efrem was a decisive, "We probably hurt your ex-wife, and we certainly hurt ourselves. I don't want anyone else getting hurt."

"Damn it, Kate, this doesn't make sense. You're going to sacrifice—"

"Don't!" She abruptly released the twig, letting the branch to which it was attached snap back up into the tree. "Because it isn't going to change anything. It ends here."

He was silent for a long moment. Knowing how vulnerable she was and that she might not be able to resist him if he pursued it, she prayed for him to let her go without a struggle.

"All right, Kate," he finally said, his voice resigned but carrying an underlying vein of bitterness, "if that's what you want, we'll do it your way. I'll keep away from you from now on."

Efrem's promise to Kate was one of the hardest things he'd ever had to make himself do, certainly not as tough as that scene in Dulles eight years ago but bad enough. Even worse than his pledge to her was the necessity of executing it. He learned that early the next morning before they even left the monastery.

Father Basil saw his overnight guests to the front gate of the monastery. They were waiting for Leke to arrive with the bus when two of the monks turned up.

"You will need food and water on the road," the abbot explained, indicating a pair of large plastic jugs and an old, bulky satchel the brothers carried.

"No, Father," Kate objected, "you've been more than generous already."

"This is little enough," he insisted.

"For the children's sake then," she agreed, accepting the satchel while Efrem and one of the older boys assumed responsibility for the jugs. "But I want to make a donation. It can't be as large as I'd like because we'll need money for gas, but maybe it can help someone who needs it."

Kate started to swing her shoulder bag around to get at her wallet while hanging onto the satchel with her other hand. It was an awkward maneuver that threatened to spill the contents of the bag onto the cobbles.

When the bag started to slip off her shoulder, Efrem sprang forward to save it. He hadn't meant his hand to connect with hers, but both of them reached out at the same time to prevent her loss. It was a little thing, yet it made him instantly aware of the electricity between them.

Kate's only reaction was a murmured, "Thank you," as she quickly recovered the bag.

How was he supposed to make good on his promise when they had to be almost constantly together like this? Efrem asked himself, taking his seat on the bus several moments later, when there might be other unavoidable contacts like that one, when just her presence alone drove him crazy with wanting her. Would this damn journey never end?

One more day. If Leke is right, you have just this one more day before we reach the border. You can hang on that long, and then—

But Efrem didn't want to think about that. Didn't want to have to imagine parting with Kate and how rough that was going to be.

So, okay, he would somehow handle it when the time came. Right now he had to concentrate on getting through the day, pray there were no more delays. It was an unlucky hope because the day turned out to be even more eventful than yesterday.

It started not long after they'd climbed back into the mountains. Leke halted them at the edge of a stream. Efrem rose from his seat to look over the old man's shoulder.

"There's no bridge."

"Fording place. She is always very little water here and the current nothing. No problem."

"Well, it's a problem now. Look at it. It's a torrent."

"Sure, thaw in the mountains. Makes her the bitch, huh?"

"We'll have to go back, find another place to cross where there's a bridge."

Leke shook his head. "No bridge. We go back, and it's lots of kilometers to another road. You understand?"

Efrem understood all right. It would mean losing hours of time, something they didn't dare to waste.

Wanting to know what the trouble was, Kate joined them at the front of the bus where the three adults put their heads together. Leke was sure he could bring his bus safely across the swollen stream, if the waters in the ford were shallow enough and if something could be provided to prevent the bus from sliding sideways into deeper waters. It would be at the mercy of the current. If that happened . . .

"Uh-huh," Efrem said. "And just where do we get this something?"

"She's no problem," Leke assured them with his usual confidence. "I got us a big rope down below." He indicated with his thumb and forefinger that the rope was a thick one.

Efrem wasn't surprised. There was everything else in that luggage compartment of his.

All of which explained why Efrem found himself several minutes later with his boots and socks stuffed into the big pockets of his leather jacket, his pant legs rolled up above his knees and wading barefoot into the icy waters of the stream. One end of the rope was snugged around his waist, the other end tied to a stout tree on the bank behind him.

Piece of cake, he thought. If you didn't count having to keep your balance in a current powerful enough to qualify as a cataract. Well, almost. Not to mention his sour mood. But in all fairness that couldn't be blamed on the roaring waters.

He was to blame for his mood. Or, to be more specific about it, his mounting frustration since leaving the monastery. He was angry with himself, angry with Kate, too. Why had he ever made that damn fool promise to her last night? Why had she demanded it? She belonged to him, not this Gordon guy somewhere back in the States.

Of course, Kate didn't see it that way. Nor was she angry herself. What she was was anxious about him. He could see that when he glanced back at the bus waiting on the lip of the ford. She had her face pressed to the window as she tensely watched his slow progress across the stream.

Efrem should have been pleased she cared enough to be worried about him. But he wasn't. He wanted more than that. He wanted *her*. Only there was nothing he could do about that.

The waters weren't as deep as he'd feared. They never came above his knees. Otherwise, he would have abandoned the whole effort as too much of a risk for the bus.

Making it to the other side, he replaced his socks and boots on his feet, stretched the line taut and looped it tightly around another tree before signaling the bus to come ahead. He stood on the bank, watching the bus lumber its way down into the wild waters, ready for action if it got into trouble.

His help wasn't necessary. The gravel bed of the ford was solid, its waters still shallow enough not to pose a threat to the engine. The bus crossed without ever having to depend on the chest-high rope waiting to stop it from being dragged into deep waters.

Recovering the rope, Efrem took his seat on the bus, and

they were underway again. His mood should have improved. It didn't.

Efrem didn't feel any better about himself when the next crisis occurred around noon. They had stopped at the side of the road, where boulders scattered in an open area offered them seats to eat a quick lunch from the satchel Father Basil had sent with them.

He was about to help himself to corn bread with kajmak cheese and ham, which Halise told him was called *proja,* when he caught the sound of a low flying plane approaching from the east.

Instantly alert, he got to his feet to scan the sky in that direction. He couldn't see it yet, but he knew from the pitch of its engine that it was a fighter jet. This could be trouble.

It was time to round up the kids and get out of here. Too late. The jet was already rushing in on them over the mountains.

"Into the trees!" Efrem shouted. "Out of sight and lie down flat!"

The children couldn't have understood his order, but both the presence of a plane and the urgency in his voice told them of the potential danger. Scrambling to their feet, with Leke leading the way, they raced for the nearby woods to take cover. All but the youngest boy. Confused, he flew instead toward the refuge of the bus. Kate tore after him to head him off.

Holy mother, Efrem thought, they were out in the open, and the jet was swooping in for a closer look at the scene.

He didn't hesitate. His legs pumping faster than at any time in his brief baseball career, when making it to first base was all that was important, Efrem covered the ground with lightning speed. The kid had already arrived at the bus and by this time had the sense to dive under it and roll out of sight. Kate, however, was still yards away from the bus and the plane almost directly overhead. Without any other choice, she flung herself full length on the ground.

Vulnerable! She was still vulnerable!

Reaching her side, Efrem threw himself on top of her, protecting her with his body. The jet zoomed by with a roar. Lifting his head, Efrem saw it out over the plain banking sharply for another pass. He could identify it now as one of the older Soviet MIGs that countries like Serbia had been buying from the Russians.

Kate was squirming under him, wanting to get up. "Keep still," he commanded her. "He's coming back."

Efrem knew they were perfect targets. Depending on the mood of the pilot, he could either strafe them or shell both them and the bus out of existence. But he must have figured they weren't worth his ammunition because the fighter thundered by them again without incident and disappeared over the mountains.

Efrem lifted himself away from Kate and helped her get to her feet. Their gazes collided in the sudden silence.

"Sorry," he muttered, apologizing for his damn heroics.

She nodded. "It's all right. It's not as though you meant it as some act of intimacy."

Maybe not, Efrem thought, only he sure as hell wished it could have been. Okay, it was instinctive of him to want to protect her like that, to care about her safety. But for Kate it hadn't been a need. He reminded himself, when it came to that, she had someone else now. Her Gordon had been there for her when her need had really counted. Efrem hadn't been, and his miserable guilt continued to eat at him.

"I think we'd better get everyone on board and away from here," she said.

"Yeah."

★ ★ ★ ★ ★

It was a couple of hours later when they stopped again to let the kids relieve themselves behind the trees on the left side of the road. After they'd galloped away from the bus, happy to be loose again, Leke beckoned Kate and Efrem to follow him.

"I gonna show you something. You will like her."

He led them to the other side of the lane. They crossed a narrow, open area to a spot where the mountain dropped off from a sheer height of several hundred feet. The overlook commanded a clear view of the vast plain.

As scenery went, Efrem thought, it was pretty spectacular stuff, guaranteed to lift just about any unpleasant mood. Or would have been, if it hadn't been for something Leke couldn't have anticipated.

Almost directly below them was one of the main routes to the south. Efrem heard Kate gasp beside him. He understood her reaction. He, too, was shocked by the sight of it.

The road was choked with refugees fleeing toward the border. Although many of them were on foot, Efrem could count in that thick, crawling traffic every mode of transportation imaginable.

There were beat-up Yugos, relics from the days when a united Yugoslavia had produced its own automobiles. Strapped to the car roofs were the belongings of its occupants. There were horse drawn carts, also heavily loaded. There were trucks and bicycles, even farm tractors. Anything that could accommodate the evacuees, including, of all things, an old woman being trundled in a wheelbarrow by a young man who might be her grandson.

It was a sad picture of the current, desperate state of Kosovo. There had been reports back at Efrem's base in Macedonia about the refugees, but actually seeing this stream of humanity was something else entirely. They had also heard the Serbian military had mounted checkpoints along all the main roads and were shaking down the refugees before they allowed them to pass. What a rotten comment on humanity.

"Better we are up here for the travel and not down there, huh?" Leke said.

Amen to that, Efrem thought.

He glanced at a silent Kate, figuring that she, too, was moved by the scene below them. Yeah, well, it was a humbling experience all right. It made you forget your own problems, or at least to rethink them. That's just what Efrem did.

He hadn't been fair about Kate, he decided. Why should he have supposed she wouldn't get on with her life when he'd turned his back on her eight years ago? Hadn't she said as much in Washington? She'd found someone else. That was what she'd meant. And she deserved that.

He had no right to feel sorry for himself. Regrets, yes, but not anger or self-pity. He was resolved to put those behind him.

There was something else, though. He knew he had to let her go when the time came. But how in hell was he supposed to manage that, lose her all over again, and live with the misery afterwards?

CHAPTER TWELVE

It was nearly mid afternoon when the bus rolled down off the highlands. The loftier, more rugged Sar Mountains loomed directly ahead of them. The Macedonian border lay within that range.

They were almost there, Kate thought, already feeling her tension beginning to ease. She'd been uncomfortably conscious all day of Efrem's longing glances in her direction. Glances that plainly said: *You belong to me, not this other guy waiting for you back home.*

She hadn't successfully convinced Efrem she was no longer in love with him. There was nothing else she could do but escape from those glances, escape from *him* when they'd safely delivered the children. Kate looked forward to that moment. They would go their separate ways. She would be free of him.

Then why, Kate wondered, was her heart so troubled about it? But it was better not to try to sort that one out. Too many pitfalls there. She distracted herself instead with the scene outside her window.

They hadn't met a single vehicle in their two days on the narrow, at times almost impassable, mountain lane. But now, as they approached a small town, there was light traffic on the road. Even though none of the several cars that passed them seemed at all interested in the bus, their presence made her nervous. What if they were stopped, challenged?

It didn't happen, but Leke himself must have been aware of

the threat. He stopped the bus near the outskirts of the town, signaling for Kate to come forward where he could confer with both her and Efrem.

"She wants the gasoline again," he told them, referring to his bus. "This place, she is called Gordana. I have cousin in Gordana. Maybe he is still here, maybe not. If I find him, he will help me to get the gasoline. But you and the childrens . . ."

"You saying it would be safer for the kids and us if we didn't show our faces in town?" Efrem asked him.

Leke shrugged. "Could be soldiers there. Maybe Serbs, maybe KLA."

Kate knew the guerillas of the Kosovo Liberation Army could be just as dangerous and unpredictable as the paramilitary. Even if Efrem's and her intention was to take the children out of the province, there was the potential for trouble if they met either force before reaching an authorized border crossing. It was best not to risk it.

"You want to leave us here and take the bus into town on your own. Is that it?" she asked.

Leke nodded.

Kate glanced through the window. A thin rain was beginning to fall. She didn't like the prospect of the children getting soaked out in the open while they waited for Leke's return.

Efrem didn't care for the idea either. "We'll need someplace where we can take cover, not just because of the rain but to keep out of sight."

"Sure. That's why I stop us here. I know this place. We go there, huh?"

Several minutes later, after turning off the road onto a grassy track, Leke delivered them to a hulking, isolated building with sagging doors and most of its windows broken. The old man explained it was an abandoned factory that had seen no activity since the Communist regime. He assured them they would be safe here.

Kate surrendered the last of her precious money to Leke to pay for the gas. If for some reason he was unable to return for them, they would not only be without funds but also without a bus to transport them to the border. Well, they had traveled on foot before this. They could do so again if necessary.

The interior of the factory was a vast cavern. What had once been manufactured here Kate had no way of guessing since the place had been stripped of its machinery, leaving it hollow and dismal in the gray light.

The roof also leaked, offering only one dry corner where they huddled on empty, overturned packing crates. The waiting was monotonous. In an effort to entertain the children, Efrem found a hunk of wood from one of the crates. Producing the folding knife that Leke had loaned him yesterday, he parked himself back on his crate and began to whittle.

The children, fascinated, crowded around him to watch. They buzzed with questions that Halise translated. "They want to know what you are making."

Efrem looked around at them with a mysterious smile. "Tell them it's a secret."

"We can't know?"

"Only when it's far enough along you can guess. Whoever gets it right wins what I'm carving."

They were silent after that, eagerly watching the work as Efrem formed it, each of them wanting to be the first to guess what emerged from the thick piece of wood.

Kate, perched on the crate directly opposite him, also watched, though it made her ache to see how wonderful he was with the children. Everything a father was supposed to be, strong and yet gentle at the same time.

There were other things that had her mesmerized. The look of his dark, tumbled hair as he bent his head over his task. The two day-old stubble on his jaw. Her glimpse of his strongly corded neck where the pulse beat in the hollow of his throat. The shape of his square, long-fingered hands as he applied the knife to the wood.

They were all of them evidence of a confident, magnetic masculinity that had Kate remembering the feel of his weight on her this morning when he had shielded her from the enemy plane. The recollection had the breath sticking in her throat, forcing her to acknowledge just why she wasn't entirely relieved by the imminent end of their journey. And it was wrong.

Efrem glanced up from his work and caught her gazing at him.

He knows. Not only that you're aware of him but that he can still arouse you just by being there.

It wasn't real or solid, not love. It was just sexual attraction, she reminded herself. And it made no difference. She wouldn't violate her loyalty to Gordon. Her parting from Efrem when the time came was still essential. But until then . . .

Impatient with her moment of weakness, determined not to repeat it, Kate got up from the crate and began to pace the length of the factory. She didn't care if she got wet from the leaks in the roof. All that mattered was putting distance between herself and temptation.

Where was Leke with the bus? Shouldn't he have been here by now? She hated to think something might have happened to the old man.

There was a sudden, excited clamor over in the far corner. One of the small boys sped across the expanse of concrete, triumphantly holding up the wooden figure of a bear for her approval. Kate smiled at him, admiring the prize he had won.

Moments later, to her immense relief, she heard the rumble

of the bus outside. Efrem joined her, and they went together to the open door to greet Leke.

"Any trouble?" Efrem wanted to know.

Cigarette in hand, Leke met them with one of his stoical shrugs. "Some good things I got for you, some bad."

"I guess we'd better hear the bad first."

"My cousin has news you don't like. All borders is closed. He knows this for sure."

This was not just bad news, Kate thought, it was devastating. "But why," she asked, "when Milosevic and his followers want the Albanians out of Kosovo?"

The old man went on to explain the rumor that the Serbian president had ordered the closing of the borders and Leke's people turned back in the hope the NATO bombers, who were destroying bridges and main roads to hinder Serbian military operations, would kill refugees along the highways. It would not only rid him of a great many ethnic Albanians, it would turn Western public opinion against America and its allies.

"Knowing Milosevic and his gang," Efrem growled, "it's probably more than just rumor."

"But we've come too far to end it here," Kate said. "There must be some way across."

"Let's hear Leke's good news."

Can there be any after the bad? she wondered. Mercifully, there was.

"Cousin Marko has guide for you. A Serb woman. She lives not far from border and knows way to walk through the mountains into Macedonia."

Kate found it hard to believe. "A Serb willing to help Moslem children?"

"Marko say she is good woman. She will help. He sends message to her to meet you. I take you there in bus. Okay?"

Without any other choice, Kate and Efrem agreed.

The bus bumped along a rough track that ran parallel to the mountains. With his cousin's help, Leke had been able to obtain gas. But an anxious Kate wondered how reliable Cousin Marko was when it came to the guide. With not much left of the afternoon, what would they do if she wasn't there to meet them at the specified rendezvous?

The track ended in a small clearing among the trees. This was as far as the bus could travel. To Kate's relief, a tall, bony figure waited at the edge of the clearing. With everything being a *she* to Leke, it wouldn't have surprised Kate if their guide turned out to be a man. But it was a woman with a head scarf tied under her chin, and she spoke a competent English.

With no expression on her long face, she came forward to greet them as they left the bus. "My name is Anna."

"We're very grateful that you're willing to help us," Kate told her.

"I do this for myself as well as the children. I want people on the outside to know all Serbs are not like Milosevic and his butchers, that most of us are decent."

"They'll hear it from us," Efrem assured her.

It was time to say goodbye to Leke. Efrem returned his knife to him and shook his hand. Kate would have hugged him, but she wasn't sure whether the tough old man would appreciate that. She settled for a handshake of her own and her warmest appreciation for all that he had done for them.

"What will you do after we leave you?" she asked him.

"I get a bed at my cousin's, and then when it is morning again I take her"—he jerked his thumb in the direction of his bus—"back to my village and my woman."

She was worried about that. "Will you be all right?"

"Sure." He laughed. "If they stop me, I tell them I have been carrying soldiers in my bus for Serbia."

Yes, she decided, the resourceful Leke would manage somehow. He was a survivor. When they last saw him, he was already back behind the wheel and leaning toward an open window to wish them a cheerful, *"Gjithe te mirat."* Kate remembered from her time in Reva that it either meant, "Stay healthy," or, "All the best." Whichever was correct, it was a satisfying way to part from friends.

The rain had stopped on their way to the clearing, which helped as Anna led them single file up through the thick woods on a path that was no more than a thread. But the climb was difficult.

Efrem brought up the rear. Kate, just behind their guide, was amazed at the woman's endurance. She had to be well past middle age, but she was so hardy that her breathing was never labored. Kate herself was puffing to keep up with her, hoping for a rest and thinking the children would appreciate a break as well.

Anna, however, permitted no pauses. Kate didn't ask, but she figured it was essential they keep moving while they still had the light. Thankfully, even in the gloom of the forest, the woman was so familiar with the terrain that she never faltered in her direction.

Kate hadn't checked her watch before leaving the clearing, so she had no idea how long they had been climbing up the mountainside. It seemed forever before Anna finally stopped, waiting for the children and Efrem to catch up with her, before she issued a firm instruction.

"We are not far now from the border. There are soldiers patrolling up here. No one must speak from this place on. It would be bad if any of the patrols caught us. Make sure the children understand they cannot make a sound."

The always reliable Halise interpreted the order for the other children.

Serb patrols. This was something Kate had never considered, and she couldn't help being concerned about the danger.

They must have been hiking silently for five minutes or so when Anna brought them to another abrupt halt, holding up her hand for their attention. "Listen!" she hissed.

Kate could hear it now, too. The sound of male voices somewhere up ahead of them and off to their right. A patrol!

There seemed to be two of them conversing in normal tones. They don't know we're here, Kate thought, but that will change if they sight us. And it could happen because from the sound of it the soldiers were coming their way.

Anna quickly motioned all of them off the path. There was a hollow among the trees a few yards away filled with leaves. She demonstrated how they must hide by dropping herself flat on the ground and burrowing among the leaves.

The leaves were damp from the rain, making it possible to cover themselves without any crackling noise that would betray them. They would have been safe in the hollow if one of the children hadn't yelped sharply when he flopped down on the ground.

Maybe a rock under the leaves, Kate thought. Not that it mattered what the boy had struck. The soldiers had heard his yip of pain. Their voices rising in excitement, boots pounding on the path, they sped in the direction of the hollow.

Her body hugging the earth, her arm around one of the children, Kate could feel her heart thumping as she waited for what was almost certain to be the discovery of them. Unable to stand the suspense, she lifted her head just far enough to determine how close the soldiers were. And that's when she saw Efrem.

Dear God, he was no longer buried in the leaves! He was on

his feet and charging toward the path! Making himself a perfect target!

Within seconds, he was on the path and racing down the mountainside. The soldiers couldn't fail to be aware of him, not when he crashed like cannon fire through the underbrush below in what must be an effort to dodge their bullets.

And there *were* bullets from their rifles, along with their shouts as the two soldiers flashed by the hollow without sparing it a glance, tearing down the path in pursuit of Efrem.

That's when Kate understood what he was doing. He was acting as a decoy to lure the soldiers away from the hollow, risking his own life for the sake of the children and her.

Oh, you terrible fool! Why do you always have to be such a damn hero?

She was furious with him. But not nearly as angry as she was frightened. If he were killed, how could she go on living knowing he was no longer in the world?

It was in this emotionally charged second Kate realized it was no use denying it to herself any longer. It wasn't lust she'd been feeling. That had merely been her poor excuse to hide from both him and herself what was much deeper, far more powerful. Love. She was still in love with Efrem Chaudoir, had never stopped loving him.

There was a dilemma for her in this insistent truth. No mistaking that. But this wasn't the time to address it. The children had to be saved.

When there was no longer the sound of gunfire, when the shouts had faded in the distance and there was nothing but silence again, Kate picked herself up from the leaves. The others also got to their feet.

The boy called Hajri rolled up his pant leg to expose his knee. Kate crouched down to examine it. It was only a scrape, nothing that needed immediate attention. He wore a sheepish expression when she glanced up at his face, as if apologizing for crying out when he'd hit the ground. She put a hand on his thin shoulder when she came erect, communicating her understanding with a gentle squeeze.

An impatient Anna whispered urgently, "We need to go before the patrol returns!"

She was right, but Kate was sick over the necessity of leaving Efrem behind.

Anna hurried them back to the path and up the mountainside, Kate following reluctantly. She kept an eye on Hajri during their swift progress to make sure he wasn't limping. The boy seemed fine. She wasn't. She was stricken with worry for Efrem. Had he been able to outrun the two soldiers, or had they shot him?

She ordered herself not to stop and look back, not to delay their flight. But she couldn't prevent the image burned into her brain of his body lying somewhere in the woods below them, either wounded or dead.

Survive, Efrem. You have to survive.

The path forked. Without hesitation, their guide selected the left branch. The going was easier now, the ground leveling off. As the ranks of the trees thinned, it was possible to glimpse the sky again. Kate could see the overcast had lifted, that the sun was dipping toward the horizon.

They reached a clear area where Anna halted, pointing to a gap in a broken ridge. "The border is just there. When you cross it, you'll be in Macedonia. You won't have any trouble. The path is very direct. It will take you down into a valley where there's a village. They'll help you there."

"You're leaving us then?"

"I have a home and a husband to go back to."

"It'll be night soon."

"I can find my way in the dark, and on my own I know how

to avoid the patrols. I'm sorry about your friend, but perhaps he was lucky and got away. God go with you."

Before Kate could thank her, she was gone.

Kate shepherded the children across the clearing and through the opening in the broken ridge. There was no marker to indicate the border between Kosovo and Macedonia, but she trusted Anna's direction. On the back side of the ridge, a clear path sloped down the mountain to the valley below.

She could see the village nestled beneath them. It was twilight now. Unlike the communities they'd left behind them, where electricity was either a luxury or not available at all, the houses down there were already blooming with lights. It was a gladdening sight.

They were in Macedonia now and safe. It was an achievement that deserved some expression of vast relief, but Kate wasn't capable of it. She could think only of Efrem.

The children, anyway, were happy. Sensing their liberation and that they no longer needed to be silent, they chattered with excitement as Kate led them down the winding path. Her own voice was also active with a fierce promise to Efrem. Internally, that is.

I'm not going to leave you out there. I can't *leave you. As soon as I deliver the children to that village, I'm coming back for you.*

It was a foolhardy intention. It involved the risk of another encounter with the Serb patrol and an impossible search in the dark. He might be anywhere in those woods. And even if he was still alive, how could she hope to find him when he could be wounded and unconscious, unable to call out to her?

She didn't care. She couldn't bear to abandon him over there on the other side. Whatever it took, no matter how long it took, she would look for him.

Kate was still seething with that reckless promise when there was a shout behind them. Danger? Alarmed, she swung around on the path to see a tall figure silhouetted above them against the last light of day.

"Hey," he called down to them in that robust, familiar voice that had her wanting to laugh with joy, "if you're trying to get away from me, it isn't going to work. Like it or not, guys, you're stuck with me."

Kate didn't laugh. She was too moved by Efrem's sudden arrival to do anything but stand there on the path trembling. The children were laughing, though, when his long legs swiftly carried him to where they waited. They swarmed around him, their hands reaching out to touch him.

Kate wanted more than just to touch him. She wanted to go to him, put her arms around him, hold him tightly. But all she dared permit herself to do was to meet his gaze over the heads of the children and to croak a hoarse, "Thank whatever god was looking out for you."

"Well, an angel anyway."

"How did you—"

"There's one thing Forrest Gump and I share. We can both run like crazy. I managed to shake them, bullets and all. Then when I cut around through the woods and picked up the trail again, I ran into Anna on her way back. Very good with directions, the lady is. So, what are we standing around here for? Let's get down to that village and see if they've got anything to feed us with. You hungry, kids? I know I am."

CHAPTER THIRTEEN

There was a stone-walled inn in the village, and the best thing about it was they accepted credit cards. Both Kate and Efrem carried them, and without any money this was a godsend.

There were also working telephones in the inn, and while its staff prepared a meal for them, Efrem was able to reach his base and relate their situation.

"You go on ahead with the kids to the dining room," he urged Kate after ending his call at the reception desk. "I'm going to wait here by the phone. My c.o. said he'd try to contact one of the UN refugee camps to take the children. He's going to call me back with the results."

"All right."

His gaze lingered on her, probing, worried. "You okay, Kate?"

"I'm fine." He didn't know about her revelation on the mountain. How it was tearing her up inside. Nor could she tell him because then he would never let her go. "See you in the dining room."

A wedding celebration was taking place in the village. Kate found the dining room crowded with out of town guests, but the innkeeper was able to provide a long table that would seat all of them.

While they waited to be served, she tried to take comfort in their surroundings. The warmth of a log fire on the wide hearth, the savory smells in the air, the vivid sight of red peppers strung against a whitewashed wall under a beamed ceiling. Not that these were anywhere near as important as being able to feel secure for both herself and the children for the first time in days. No threat here, only the pleasant sounds of clinking glasses and the hum of conversation from the other tables around them.

Safety. It was something you took for granted when you had it, and in places like Kosovo it was considered a luxury.

But how could she relax knowing she would have to surrender the man she loved just when in her heart she had found him again? No other choice, not when Gordon was waiting for her. She'd already decided the necessity of that, unbearable though it was.

Efrem joined them as their first dishes arrived at the table. "It's all set," he reported to Kate. "The camp is going to take the kids. The UN is working with the International Red Cross, and together they'll see them resettled in Albania. They're sending a bus to collect them first thing in the morning."

It wouldn't be easy parting with the children either, Kate thought. Not after all they'd been through together, not after she'd become so attached to them. Yet she knew her responsibility for them had to end here. Her one wish was for them to be placed with good people where they would have the opportunities to build new lives.

Kate couldn't help in that moment thinking with a pang of the son she had given up all those years ago. She hoped his life was everything he deserved, everything she wanted it to be for him.

Their server poured plum brandy for Kate and Efrem, a national drink known as *šljivovica*. Lifting his glass, Efrem smiled at her in an invitation to raise her own glass.

They drank in celebration of their success, sharing the victory of having together brought the children to safety. His eyes across the table seemed to tell her: "Whatever we didn't have, we had this." It was a bittersweet moment.

The food that was brought to them was both plentiful and rich. Freshly baked bread, cold cucumber soup and *sataraš*, a pork and veal dish flavored with onions and red peppers. She hadn't eaten like this since leaving home.

Nor had she slept in a bed since Reva. She didn't sleep in one that night either, but at least it was on a thin foam mattress, which was a vast improvement over pine needles or a hard floor. The landlord regretted that, with his inn full for the wedding, there were no bedrooms available. But he could accommodate them with mattresses and blankets in two downstairs lounges, one for the girls and one for the boys.

The arrangement was the same as last night's at the monastery. Kate slept with the girls and Efrem the boys. That, anyway, was an advantage. She didn't think she could rest if Efrem had been lying anywhere near her. Not after her admission to herself earlier of how she still felt about him.

As it was, exhausted though she was from the long, difficult day, she found it hard to fall asleep. Her agitated emotions kept her awake for some time. But she couldn't let them interfere with her intention. This must be their last night together.

Reality demanded that in the morning she part from Efrem. She dared not risk another day with him, fearing her senses would be assaulted in his company, her resolve weakened.

Oh, Efrem, Efrem, help me to be strong enough to leave you.

The bus for the children arrived just after breakfast. Kate and Efrem went out front to see them off.

At least this bus looked dependable, Kate decided after prudently eyeing the vehicle. Not like Leke's poor, old wreck. It was a disloyal thought, she knew, since that old wreck had managed to get them to the border.

The UN representative on board, who would accompany the children to the camp and see them settled there, was a stout, efficient looking woman. She turned out to be British. Kate didn't hesitate to question her.

"About the children," she asked. "What will become of them after they leave the camp?"

"You needn't worry, Ms. Groen," she assured Kate in her bright, crisp voice. "We'll be very careful to see they're placed where their welfare will always matter. You'd be surprised at how many refugees have relatives in Albania willing to give them homes, especially children."

Kate was satisfied. It was time to say goodbye. She didn't want this separation to be a tearful one, but that wasn't so easy to achieve when the children crowded around her, waiting for her hugs. All but the older boys, who solemnly shook hands with her.

Halise was the last. Kate had a special embrace reserved for the girl. "I don't know how I would have managed without you, Halise. I depended on you, and you never disappointed me."

"Miss?"

"Yes?"

"It will be sad without you."

"For me, too, Halise."

While Efrem made his own goodbyes, Kate pressed a slip of paper into the girl's hand. "This is my address back in America, Halise. When you get settled in your new home, I'd like you to write me and tell me how you're doing. The other children, too. You can share the address with them. Maybe when they go back to school, they'll learn enough English to write to me themselves."

Kate and Efrem waited until the bus rolled away, with the children waving from the windows, before they turned and went back inside the inn.

Efrem sensed what she was feeling. "Don't worry about them, Kate. They're kids, and kids are resilient. Given a chance, they'll recover from what happened to them."

She had no experience with children, but Efrem did. She could only hope he was right.

The landlord came forward from his reception desk to speak to Efrem. He spoke no English, but Efrem had picked up enough Macedonian while stationed in the country to understand him.

"He says one of the couples has checked out this morning," Efrem translated for her. "He's putting the room at our disposal. It has a bathroom with a shower, if we'd like to clean up before the car they're sending from the base arrives to pick us up."

"I would like that. Why don't you go first? There's a phone call I need to make."

He didn't ask her about the call, and she didn't tell him. But from the way he looked at her, he probably was guessing she intended to phone Gordon back home. He was wrong.

The shower was wonderful. There was plenty of hot water, enough to permit Kate to indulge herself by washing her hair, too. However, the heat in the bathroom itself was inadequate. She felt the chill the second she stepped out of the stall. Shivering, she dried herself quickly with one of the fresh towels that had been put out for them.

The innkeeper's wife had kindly loaned her a spare terry cloth bathrobe. It was too large for Kate, but she was grateful for the warmth its thickness provided when she bundled into it. Reaching for another towel, she rubbed her hair dry.

No blow dryer or hot air brush, of course. She had only her comb and a small brush, both of them in her bag which she'd left on the chest of drawers in the bedroom. The mirror in here was too steamed up anyway to see her reflection. But she remembered there was a large mirror attached to the old-fashioned chest of drawers.

Kate was in the bedroom, digging her comb and brush out of her bag when there was a rap on the hall door. It opened without an invitation to reveal Efrem standing there.

"We're all set," he announced. "I settled our bill, and while I was at the desk, the base called. The car is already on its way, but we should have time for another cup of coffee downstairs when you're finished here."

Kate felt an instant guilt. She should have informed him of her plans long before this. Instead, she had put off what was going to be very difficult to tell him but which had to be said.

She was still delaying the unavoidable when she turned back to the mirror and began to drag the comb through her hair. She could see his reflection as he went on standing in the open doorway behind her. Lounging against the frame, hands shoved into his pants pockets, he watched her with a slow smile that had her insides quivering.

"You're one of those women," he said.

Perplexed, she lowered the comb from her head. "What women?"

"The kind where the years only become them. You're even more beautiful now than when we were together in the Middle East."

Kate laughed self-consciously. "Beautiful? Looking like this, with my hair all limp and damp?"

"Yeah, even like that."

"Efrem, don't," she pleaded. He wasn't going to make it easy. He wasn't going to help her resist him as she had prayed he would last night.

Pushing himself away from the doorframe, he came on into the room, shutting the door behind him. "Kate, I've tried to keep my distance," he said. "Tried to stay away from you, just like I said I would in the orchard back at the monastery. Well, damn it, I can't."

She put the comb and brush down on the chest of drawers and swung around to face him. "Which is exactly why I went and did what I had to do."

He scowled. "I'm guessing this has an explanation."

Framing the necessary words was even tougher than she had anticipated, but he had to hear them. "Efrem, I'm not coming with you in the car that's on its way. I've made my own arrangements. The phone call I made at the desk was to the airport in Skopje. I was able to reserve a seat on a plane for Athens this afternoon. There's a truck from the village going into Skopje. The innkeeper's wife and I were able to understand each other enough for her to let me know the driver would be happy to give me a lift."

"Let me get this straight. You're going to Skopje, then Athens."

"That's right." It was the only call she had made. She'd had no time or state of mind for any further calls. She would wait until she reached the airport to phone Gordon and her editor. With Kosovo in the news, they would be worried about her. She had to let them know she was all right and on her way home. "I can connect in Athens with a direct flight to Washington."

"You're running away," Efrem accused her.

Yes, from you and from myself as well. The self I can't trust as long as I'm anywhere near you.

"Kate, you can't do this."

She had hoped he would stay on the other side of the room while they talked. He didn't. He crossed the room with his swift stride to stand in front of her, his closeness making her even more susceptible than she already was. She tried not to meet his gaze, focusing instead on a garish rug hanging on the pine-paneled wall behind him.

"Look at me," he demanded.

Whether it was because she didn't want him to think it mattered, which he would if she refused, or because in the end she couldn't withstand the temptation, she complied. Her gaze slewed back to his face.

"I saw it in your eyes the other morning at the factory when you were watching me carve the bear," he said, his voice gruff with his conviction. "And I saw it again when I caught up with you over the border. Just like I can see it now. Your love for me, Kate. The same love you can see in my eyes every time I look at you."

She didn't have to search his eyes to see it. She knew that love, deep and constant in his every action, in the timbre of his voice whenever he spoke to her, even in anger. She knew it because it was the love she had for him, equally strong, equally vital.

"It never went away, Kate, and it never will. That's why we can't leave each other. Not this time."

His gaze went on holding her own. Then somehow it was his arms that were holding her. His arms and his mouth. And in her weakness, her own mouth opened to welcome him. The realization flashed through whatever awareness she still possessed that this is where they belonged, what they were meant for, to ignite each other with their kiss.

Her senses overcame the last shred of her restraint with the raw passion that flared between them as she inhaled him, tasted him. As though they had a mind of their own, Kate's hands burrowed under his shirt and T-shirt to feel the firm, warm flesh of his chest, the vee of hair that trailed down to his taut belly. His own hands had parted her robe to cup her breasts, his fingers caressing the nubs into a rigid yearning.

Kate was only dimly conscious of a pop tune playing on a radio somewhere down the hall. A song that seemed to accompany her descent onto the bed behind her. Efrem came onto the bed with her, his hard body covering her own; their mouths locked in another kiss that consumed her with desire.

It was when his knee nudged her legs apart, when his hand began to stroke the heat that was the core of her womanhood that Kate was jolted by a spasm of pure conscience. Only then was she able to recognize the mistake she was about to make. To realize that in another moment Efrem would be inside her, and then any sanity would be too late.

She must have stiffened beneath him, telling him that something was wrong. He went still, his head drawing back with a questioning expression on his face.

Her breathing ragged, she managed a quick "Let me up."

He hesitated briefly before obeying her, levering himself off of her. Kate sat up on the edge of the bed, drawing the folds of the robe across her exposed breasts and thighs, avoiding the wounded look in his eyes.

For a moment there was only the sound of the radio. Then, easing himself off the bed to stand in front of her, Efrem's voice rumbled a low, "It's the guy waiting for you back in D.C., isn't it?"

"Yes."

She didn't look up, but she could feel him gazing down at her, challenging her.

"Kate, don't ruin both our lives out of loyalty for someone you don't love. If this Gordon is the man you say he is, he wouldn't want that."

"No, he'd let me go with his blessing if I asked him to. But I'm not going to ask him."

"You're still afraid I'll let you down again if you trust me."

"That's not it. It's Gordon I won't let down." It was time to put it into words for him. "He needs me like your ex-wife once needed you." Getting to her feet, she slid past Efrem, belting the robe snugly at her waist before she faced him again, finding the will to meet his gaze. "He's sick."

"Sick how?"

"He has leukemia. It's in remission now, but there's no guarantee he won't have a relapse. I told you I quit broadcasting because I could no longer stand covering the wars I was assigned to, as well as the trouble I was still having getting over you. Both true, but there was another reason I went home. It was because Gordon got ill and I wanted to be there for him. I wanted him to be able to rely on me like I'd relied on him when those first months without you were so awful."

"But you came to Kosovo."

"Only because I needed the money. Gordon's business has been doing okay, but his treatments are very expensive. His health insurance hasn't been enough to cover them. He did have some savings, but that went into his firm when things got tough."

"Why didn't you tell me all of this before?"

"I felt I didn't have the right to tell you. And I wouldn't have now, if this"—she waved her hand toward the bed—"hadn't made it necessary."

"But why keep it a secret?"

"Because of his work."

"Public relations. Isn't that what you told me?"

"I did, yes."

"And?"

"Gordon has some pretty valuable clients, and if it ever gets around he's battling a serious illness, he'll start to lose those clients. In a place like Washington, where PR is so important, people would be afraid they couldn't depend on his services. So far we've been able to keep it quiet, mostly because Gordon has a staff of two loyal people who've been able to cover for him when he couldn't be there himself."

"You're asking me to keep this to myself."

"More than that. I'm asking you to let me go."

He didn't say anything. She watched him, feeling his frustration in the way he plowed a hand through his hair.

"Efrem, it was very wrong of me to ever let things get this far with us. I should have been stronger about it, not ending up hurting both of us like this. So now . . ."

He looked at her, waiting for her to go on.

"Now," she appealed to him, "I need you to understand why I have to go back to Gordon, stay with him. To accept this just like I had to accept and forgive your decision to stay with your wife."

She could see him struggling with himself, his frustration mounting until, needing a release, he slammed his fist against one of the bedposts. "How am I supposed to fight something like this?"

The way I had to fight it eight years ago, Efrem. The way I'm fighting it now because, heaven help me, I do love you, and it's tearing me apart.

"I can't," he admitted.

There was the sound of a vehicle drawing up to the front of the inn just below the bedroom window. It was followed by the brief toot of a horn.

"That's probably your car. You shouldn't keep it waiting." She couldn't stand this. She wanted him gone.

"Yeah," he said, tucking his shirt back into his waistband.

"Efrem . . ."

"I know. Goodbyes stink, so let's not do them."

He looked at her like he wanted to add something, but what more was there to be said? It was finished. They were already out of each other's lives. And in the next moment he was out of the room as well, the door shut behind him.

Kate had sworn to herself eight years ago she would never repeat the despair of losing the man she loved. The self-promise had been worthless, because the ache was beginning all over again. But what she had achieved before, recovering from the loss of Efrem Chaudoir, she would, please God, manage again.

The radio was still playing down the hall when the car pulled away from the inn.

CHAPTER FOURTEEN

IN THE YEARS BETWEEN KOSOVO AND AFGHANISTAN

Washington, D.C.

Kate was in Hank Bushati's office at the *View* when the call came in. The editor was outlining a story he wanted her to write for the Sunday edition.

"See what I'm after, Kate? The weirdest and wildest of the unusual stuff the Smithsonian has acquired over the years. Keep it humorous. Yes, Valerie?"

Hank's assistant had appeared in the doorway. "There's this guy on the phone."

The editor's bushy eyebrows elevated. "So?"

"He's asking me for Kate's number."

"And?"

"I told him Ms. Groen isn't on our regular staff. He said he knew that but could I give him her home phone because she isn't listed, and he's been trying to reach her."

"Me? You didn't—"

"No, of course not. I said we didn't give out that kind of information. I didn't tell him you're here either. Only he's kind of persuasive, and since you happened to be in, Kate, I thought I ought to ask—"

"What does he want with me, Valerie? Who is he?"

"A Major Efrem Chaudoir, and he didn't say. I left him on the line. What do you want me to tell him?"

Kate had no immediate answer for the assistant. Efrem. It had been more than two years since they had parted in Kosovo. In all this time they had neither seen nor spoken to each other. He had been faithful about making no contact with her. What could he want from her now?

Hank was eyeing her. "You don't have to take this call, Kate."

No, she didn't. And probably shouldn't, not when her breath had quickened at the mention of his name. But if it was something important . . .

"Would you mind, Hank?"

"Go," he growled. "We'll finish up later."

Kate followed Valerie out to her desk.

"You can take it on Phil's line," the assistant said, indicating a neighboring desk. "He's out on assignment."

Kate seated herself in the privacy of the reporter's cubby, hesitating before reaching for the phone. Calming herself, she picked up the receiver.

"I'm here, Efrem."

"Kate? I can't believe I lucked out."

His mellow voice could still warm her at the mere sound of it. She didn't explain to him why his call had found her at the *View*. It wasn't important. "What is it, Efrem? Is something wrong?"

"No, I'm good. It's just . . ."

"What?"

There was a brief silence before he continued, his voice almost gravelly now. "Look, I know I don't have any business calling you like this. And maybe you'll think I'm crazy. But, hell, Kate, I couldn't help myself. I just had to hear the sound of your voice again. That's all. You know?"

"It's all right." It wasn't all right, but he sounded so lonely she couldn't bear to tell him that. "Where are you calling from, Efrem?"

"Georgia. I'm stationed back at Fort Benning again."

She was relieved about that. She'd been afraid he was here in town and would ask to see her. There would have been too much risk in that. Too much ache. As it was, just to talk to him again, even though they were hundreds of miles apart, had her heart in jeopardy.

"How have you been, Kate?"

It was a banal thing for him to ask, totally unlike the inspired dialogue that had once flowed from him so energetically. But then her response was just as innocuous. "Keeping busy."

The rest of their conversation was equally stilted. She asked about his daughter, and he told her he didn't get to see Nell nearly often enough. He questioned her about her work, and she told him she was still freelancing, mostly for the *View,* and had no plans to return to broadcasting.

Yes, stilted, but also safe. And that was a good thing because she could detect an underlying yearning in Efrem to express things that weren't safe. Things that would be intimate and fiercely emotional. She couldn't have handled that any better than the sight of him if he had walked right now into the newsroom.

Running out of polite things to say to each other, they ended the call. Kate went on sitting there in the cubby, thankful that, after so alarmingly confessing his need to hear her voice, Efrem had managed to restrain himself. But she was also puzzled. He'd never once mentioned Gordon, never asked her about the current state of Gordon's health.

It took her a moment to understand. Efrem was a good man. No matter how diplomatically he might have worded such an inquiry, it would have seemed insensitive. As if his interest were purely personal.

Efrem would never do that, never selfishly hope for the convenient death of a man who was standing in his way just so he could have the woman he longed for so earnestly. And that Efrem did still long for her Kate had no uncertainty.

Oh, God, why did life have to hurt everyone so much?

Washington, D.C.

Gordon's leukemia was still in remission, but he had the occasional bad day. This was one of them.

Kate left him napping in their bedroom while she caught the late afternoon news on TV. They had given up the apartment in Georgetown and moved into a more affordable condo near Rock Creek Park. It was an attractive place, but it was small. Sound had a way of traveling through its four rooms, so she kept the volume low on the living room set, not wanting to disturb Gordon.

The newscaster on the CNA channel was an experienced reporter who handled herself well on camera. She was about the same age as Kate. That could be me seated at the anchor desk, Kate thought. *Would* have been her by now, had she pursued her ambition. She didn't regret it, though, didn't miss that scene. The writing suited her.

She listened to the update of another unit of American troops being deployed to Iraq. Was Efrem over there in the midst of this latest war? She had no way of knowing. She hadn't heard from him since his phone call to the *View* almost three years ago, and even before then she'd made Dara Weinstein, her friend at the Pentagon, stop telling her where Efrem was stationed.

It was better to sever all ties, less tempting, less painful. But sometimes, in unexpected moments, she would catch herself thinking about him. Wondering where he was, what he was doing in that very second and whether he was safe. She couldn't help those moments, couldn't prevent the wistful feelings that accompanied them.

Switching off the TV, she went into the bedroom to check on Gordon. His eyes were closed, but he had to be awake and sensing her presence because he stretched out his hand to her, inviting her to join him.

Kate sat on the edge of the bed, folding her hand around his. His clasp was steady and strong, but he'd lost weight. He's much too thin, she thought.

His pale gray eyes were open now. "I want you to promise me something," he said. He was smiling at her, but his voice was serious.

"If it's chicken for dinner, you're too late. I've already got a meat loaf ready to go into the oven."

"I like your meat loaf, and that's not it. I want you to promise me, after I'm no longer around to nag you about it, you'll write that book you've been planning for as long as I can remember."

Stiffening, Kate tried to withdraw her hand from his. "What brought this on? I thought we agreed we were never going to talk about things like this."

His fingers tightened around her hand, refusing to let her go. "Kate, listen to me. We need to stop kidding ourselves. We both know the reality, that in the end I can't beat this thing. Not without a bone marrow transplant."

And a bone marrow transplant wasn't possible. Gordon had no brothers or sisters. His only surviving relative was a first cousin. The cousin had been willing to be a donor, but a test had shown he wasn't compatible.

Yes, Kate knew the dismal reality. She lived with it daily and just as constantly denied it, even as she stubbornly opposed it. "There hasn't been a sign of a relapse in a long time."

"Yes, I've been lucky to have had all these years. But it isn't a cure, and all the drugs and blood transfusions aren't going to change that. Sooner or later . . ."

"Gordon, please."

"All right, we won't talk about it. But I still want that promise."

"You have it. I'll write the damn book. Now, are we through here because I've got a meat loaf waiting for me."

"Just one more thing." He brought her hand to his mouth, placing a kiss on it. "My thanks to you."

"For what?"

"For being in my life. You'll never know what that's meant to me, Kate."

She found his words so moving, so endearing that it was only with a considerable effort she was able to prevent herself from crying. She knew he wouldn't want that.

Washington, D.C.

Kate remembered Gordon's heartfelt declaration fifteen months later at the memorial service for him in the chapel of the Grace Methodist Church. In those last, sad days, his body, no longer able to tolerate repeated treatments that had been his only hope, surrendered to viral pneumonia. Unable to fight it, he'd slipped away. He had wanted to be cremated without a funeral. She had honored his wish, but all of his friends and business associates, and they were many, expected some form of tribute to him.

The chapel was crowded with people waiting to express their condolences to Kate following the simple service a week after his death. As she received them one by one, enduring all the inane murmurs of people who never knew what to say on these occasions, she kept thinking of Gordon's words of thanks to her that afternoon in their condo.

For being in my life. You'll never know what that's meant to me, Kate.

She was glad she had been in his life, that they had been there for each other. She felt, though, she hadn't been entitled to his gratitude, not when he'd deserved the kind of love she'd been incapable of giving him. He had understood that and never seemed to mind it, but still . . .

Kate went on receiving people, many of them strangers to her. But they had known and appreciated Gordon and told her how much they would miss him.

Then, suddenly, there was someone who was anything but a stranger. She had swung around to say goodbye to one of Gordon's assistants. When she turned back, he was there in front of her, tall and imposing and completely unexpected.

It seemed impossible she wouldn't have noticed him before this, not in that immaculate uniform with all the ribbons across his chest. She'd sat in the front, though, during the service, and afterwards there had been all those people around her.

"You don't mind my being here, do you, Kate?"

He didn't try to take her hand and press it, as so many others had. He just stood there, army beret in hand, dark eyes meeting her own.

"No, certainly I don't mind, but how did you—"

"I'm stationed in Virginia these days. Fort Belvoir. We regularly get the *View* there." He smiled wryly. "I seem to be at that age when a man starts reading the obituaries."

He was approaching his mid forties, anything but old, and the years had been kind to him. She had noticed that right away.

"I never met Gordon, of course," he went on, "but from the way you talked about him, he must have been one hell of a guy."

"He was."

Fort Belvoir, she thought. It was only a short distance from Washington, and she had never known he was there. But after what she had learned a few weeks ago, she should have realized he was close by.

"Anyway," he said, "I just wanted to pay my respects."

"I appreciate that, Efrem." She paused, summoning the fortitude to acknowledge the change in his own life. "Actually, your being here gives me the opportunity to congratulate you on your engagement."

One of his eyebrows arched in surprise. "The *View*?"

"Well, it does print social announcements, as well as obituaries. Especially when it's the betrothal of a senator's daughter to an honored army officer."

Kate hadn't read that announcement herself. It was Dara who had told her of Efrem's engagement. She'd been stunned by the news, unable to believe it, at least until she gave herself time to think about it. That was when she remembered the loneliness in his voice the last time he'd spoken to her. So why shouldn't he have found someone to share his life with? He deserved that. She had no right to mind.

Ironic, though, wasn't it? Now that she was free, Efrem wasn't. Well, the timing had never been right for them. Kate had to accept that, had to understand that a man couldn't wait forever. And if he had fallen out of love with her and in love with Senator Reade's daughter, then that, too, she had to bear.

"I wish you every happiness, Efrem," she told him, her tone as genuine as she could make it.

"Kate," he said, his voice low and thick now, "I wanted to . . ." He hesitated.

"What?"

"Nothing. I'd better move on. There are others here waiting to speak to you."

He left as abruptly as he'd appeared, his broad-shouldered figure weaving through the crowd. She never learned what he'd started to tell her before he changed his mind.

Washington, D.C.

"Merlot for me," Kate told their server after Dara had placed her own order for a margarita.

When they were alone again, Dara leaned toward her across the table. "Look, I know you probably didn't want to handle any more calls and that's why you weren't answering the messages I left, but it's been two weeks since the memorial service. Don't you think it's time you got out and about again?"

"What do you call this?"

"Yeah, but if I hadn't threatened in my last message to come over there and break down your door, you probably wouldn't be here."

Kate had agreed to meet Dara for a drink in the little bar where the redhead sometimes hung out after a day at the Pentagon. She owed her friend this interlude.

"You wouldn't have found me there because I haven't been hiding in the condo grieving. I miss Gordon, and a part of me will always miss him, but I haven't been idle. I've been on the go ever since that service, which is why I haven't had a chance to get back to you."

"Doing what?"

"Taking care of a million little things, like signing papers and arranging to have my furniture put in storage."

"You're letting the condo go? Why?"

The server arrived with their order. When he had departed, they sat back in the booth with their drinks while Kate explained her intention.

"You know about the book I always meant to write."

"Yeah, I remember. Your experiences as a reporter in all the hot zones around the globe."

"I promised Gordon I would write that book. The thing is, I've realized that before I have the right to tell America about the rest of the world, I need to see my own country and meet its people. Right now I know more about Angola than I do about Iowa."

"So?"

"So now I have the time and the funds to go to Iowa and Nebraska and wherever else my mobile home takes me."

"You bought a mobile home?"

"A small one, along with an SUV to pull it. Turns out Gordon left me his business, and his two assistants are buying it from me."

"How long will you be gone?"

"As long as it takes me and my laptop to get the job done. Who knows? Maybe the book will end up being about America instead."

Kate needed this journey across the country, not just for the sake of the book but for herself as well. Being on the move would give her the opportunity to recover from Gordon. And maybe the hard reality of Efrem's forthcoming marriage, if she were lucky.

"What am I going to do without you?" Dara lamented.

Before Kate could answer her, her friend's attention was riveted on the door that opened from the street.

"Whoa, check out what just walked in. Now *he's* what I call hot."

Kate laughed. "I don't think we have to worry about what you're going to do without me."

Washington, D.C.

Things had changed in Kate's absence. One of them was the feature editor at the *View*. Hank Bushati had retired. He had been replaced by Lew Dekker, a longtime staff reporter who had surprised everyone when he'd been elevated to Hank's position.

The lanky, bearded Lew could be just as exacting as his predecessor, but he was familiar with Kate's work and had always admired it. She hoped this was still true as she waited for his reaction to the story idea she had just pitched to him in his office.

Lew gazed at her suspiciously for a long moment. "You wouldn't be looking for a last chapter to that book of yours, would you?"

"That isn't my motive at all."

She was being honest about that. He didn't have to know that, although she would give him the best writing she was capable of if he agreed to her proposal, she did have another, far more urgent motive for wanting to be sent to Afghanistan.

In the months Kate had been on the road, she had met and talked to families everywhere across the country. It was the children in those families, so cherished by parents and grandparents, who had awakened in her a need she had long dreamed of realizing. It was that need that ultimately sent her to Chicago and would, if she was successful in winning this assignment, take her on to Afghanistan where she was determined to fulfill a promise.

"Come on, Lew. Everything has been focused for years on the Iraqis. Isn't it time Afghans had some of that same kind of coverage?"

He shook his head. "I don't know."

"You said how much you liked my feature on Kosovo. I remember at the time, you calling me over to your desk in the newsroom out there just to tell me that. Well, this would have the same appeal, how the people of Afghanistan are faring after the Taliban, even though the war is still on in the south."

Kate won the editor's approval, giving her a legitimate reason for going into a region which ordinary travelers were generally not permitted to visit. There were problems in her intention, one in particular. Efrem Chaudoir.

It was Dara who had warned her. "I know you made me stop

telling you where he is, but if you're going over there you have to know. Kate, he's stationed in Kabul. You'll have to be careful not to run into him."

Problem or not, she *would* run into him because she meant to contact him when she arrived. Whatever they no longer were, or could be, to each other now, she hoped Efrem was still her friend. At least friend enough to help her. She didn't want to have to rely on him, but he could make things so much easier. If he was willing.

It was a big *if*.

Chapter Fifteen

Part Three:
Afghanistan—2007

Kate told herself she had every reason to be nervous as she waited in the lobby of the Hotel Babur. Efrem's support was important to her mission. He could either help her or turn her down, even refuse to listen to her appeal.

But with him or without him, she had promised herself she would succeed. There had to be a way. Somehow. She was determined.

She checked her watch. He was late. Or possibly he wasn't coming at all. She couldn't blame him if he failed to turn up. Not when there had been no contact between them since Gordon's death. Not when their parting at the memorial service had carried such a note of finality to it.

It was all of this that had Kate anxious. And there was something else.

Be honest with yourself. You're worried he might still have strong feelings for you, and how are you going to deal with that? Or are you afraid he won't feel anything at all, and that would be even worse?

She was a fool. After all this time, why should anything like that still linger for either one of them? He had someone else now, and Kate herself—Well, she had a direction of her own and no business focusing on anything but that.

Trying not to squirm with impatience, she made an effort to

distract herself by gazing around the lobby. Kabul, like everywhere else in Afghanistan, had suffered in all the wars that had bled the country. The Hotel Babur was no exception.

In the years since the occupation of Afghanistan by the coalition forces, the hotel had made an effort to recover itself. There was fresh paint on its walls, new draperies at its windows, but evidences of shabbiness still remained.

The fabric of the chair in which Kate was seated, selected by her because it afforded her a view of the front entrance and the street outside, was faded and threadbare. There were crystals missing from the chandeliers overhead, and the carpeting was worn, needing replacement. This was considered a luxury hotel. By Western standards, however, it was poor, sharpening her sorrow for the devastated land and its people.

Through one of the tall front windows that faced the street, Kate sighted an army jeep pulling up to the front of the hotel. She sat forward on the chair, watching it intently.

There were other jeeps in Kabul, other soldiers. This might not be the man she was waiting for. But it was, although she caught only a glimpse of Efrem as he slid out of the passenger seat and headed for the entrance. She couldn't mistake that energetic gait. It was still familiar to her across the span of the years.

She came to her feet, aggravated by the flutters of anticipation in her stomach. He was in the lobby now, casting his gaze around in search of her. Kate took the opportunity to measure him.

Efrem was still a dashing figure in his army green uniform. Still very fit, though maybe just a bit thicker around the waist. Well, changes were to be expected, weren't they? If memory served her, he had to be somewhere in his mid forties.

She started to lift her hand to signal her presence, but he had already spotted her. Removing his beret, he came striding across the lobby toward her. There was an authority in his bearing that hadn't been evident in their last meeting. And why not? Efrem was a colonel now.

He was suddenly there in front of her, tall and solid. She'd had no opportunity to examine him at the memorial service. Their time together had been too brief. She could see now that his face was a little fuller and with more lines in it. She could also detect the first slight signs of gray in his dark hair. But the sight of him still had the power to stir her senses.

Nothing wrong with that, Kate told herself firmly. As long as it didn't go beyond that, and she intended to see it didn't. Their meeting this time was strictly a business one.

They didn't speak for a few seconds. They just gazed at each other. She was almost forty herself, so she knew he must in turn be seeing the differences in her. She had her own faint lines around the mouth and the corners of her eyes.

Kate was the first to break their silence, holding out her hand with an uncertain "Colonel Chaudoir."

In the past, he would have grinned at her formal greeting or maybe growled an embarrassed, "Cut that out."

But his mouth didn't widen in a grin. It was tight, and all he had to say finally was a low-voiced, "Kate."

He did take her hand, though, holding it warmly in his own big hand for several seconds. She had forgotten how long his fingers were, the strength in them.

"I appreciate you meeting me like this," she said.

He nodded and released her hand. "Sorry I was out when you phoned. But they made sure I got your message."

"Did you know I was coming to Afghanistan?"

"I heard. Your name appeared on the roster of journalists."

This wasn't going well, she thought. They were too stiff with one another. She made an effort to ease the awkwardness of their reunion, resurrecting his pledge to her all those years ago in Saudi Arabia. The same one he had repeated back in Kosovo. "We'll always find each other. Do you remember, Efrem?"

"I haven't forgotten." His dark eyes looked both wary and wise. "Except those words have another meaning for you now, don't they?"

"You always did have an irritating talent for reading me. You're right. I did find you because there's something I want that has . . . well, nothing to do with the past. *Our* past, that is."

"I appreciate your honesty," he said dryly. "But you were always that, weren't you? All right, Kate, what is it you need? The army's approval to do a story? I'm assuming that's why you came to Afghanistan. That you've gone back to your job of covering trouble spots around the globe."

"No, I haven't returned to that kind of thing and don't plan to. All I've been doing are some pieces for the magazines and working on a book I'm afraid isn't very good. That is, I was until—" She broke off, not wanting to get ahead of herself. "Actually, I have agreed to do a feature for the *View* while I'm here."

"Yes?"

"How Afghanistan's people are living now under another government, the kind of stuff that brought me to Kosovo."

"But that isn't your essential reason for being here," he guessed, as insightful as always.

"No, it isn't," she admitted. She looked around the lobby, which suddenly seemed to be too crowded. "Could we go for a walk? After being on a plane for so many hours, I could use the exercise while we talk."

She did feel the need to stretch her legs. More than that, however, she was hoping the action would ease their stilted exchange, make them less uncomfortable with each other. It was going to be difficult enough telling him why she was here without that obstacle.

"I have the time," he agreed.

They started toward the Hotel Babur's main entrance, where Efrem paused.

"Uh, you wouldn't happen to have something to cover your head, would you? The Islam they practice here isn't the same as it was in Kosovo."

He was right. Appearing on the street with her head uncovered would be offensive. "I came prepared," she assured him, opening her purse and removing a scarf, which she settled over her hair, fastening the ends under her chin.

Leaving the hotel, they traded the gloom of the lobby for an April sun in a hard blue sky. There was a silence between them as they headed down the street. Kate tried not to be worried about that, tried to see it as an opportunity to relax themselves with each other.

If nothing else, it permitted her to digest the sights and sounds of the city. She had done her homework before coming to Afghanistan, learned that Kabul was located on the Campanie Plain framed by barren mountains. That when the wind blew, it swept clouds of yellow dust into the city. That sections of Kabul had been reduced to rubble by the war.

But research, as Kate had so often discovered, couldn't compare with experiencing a place in person. Couldn't let her see, as she did now, the blocks of apartment buildings whose concrete walls were pockmarked by bullets. Or the traffic in the streets consisting of bicycles, ancient buses and taxis directed by policemen in peaked hats. Couldn't let her smell the exotic odors from the bazaars with their arched passages.

The walks were crowded with pedestrians, some of them in Western clothes, others in traditional dress with baggy trousers and turbans. Three women passed them clad in burqas, not the drab black of the *abbayas* in Saudi Arabia, but a blue that echoed the color of the sky overhead.

There was color, too, in the postcards and posters of Hindi actors offered by a stall where Kate and Efrem paused to eye the cheap wares arranged along sagging shelves. She decided they had been silent long enough, that she needed to say something, even a trivial something.

"About calling you Colonel back in the lobby. I didn't mean to be flip. I'm afraid it might have come out that way. Actually, I'm impressed you've risen to that rank."

His broad shoulders, with the silver eagles on them, lifted in a dismissive little shrug. "If you're commissioned and in the service long enough, it's what happens. You advance through the ranks. Providing you keep your nose clean."

"I don't believe that. I don't think you'd be a colonel if you hadn't earned it."

"Maybe."

They were quiet again as they moved on, stopping finally on a bridge that spanned the Kabul River. Efrem leaned against the railing, his face moody as he gazed down into the brown waters, swollen from the spring thaw in the mountains.

Kate, beside him, couldn't help noticing his hands resting on the rail. No ring. That might mean he and his fiancée preferred a long engagement and were yet to be married, or else they had decided he wouldn't wear a wedding band. Either way, she had no intention of asking him about it. It was none of her business.

There would have been no hesitation about discussing a subject with the old Efrem. Whatever it was, no matter how difficult, he would have listened to her sympathetically. But Kate wasn't sure she even liked this new Efrem. He seemed so brittle, and this subject was such a sensitive one.

She was still searching for a way to begin when he went and anticipated her again. Turning his head to look at her, he asked her bluntly, "You want to tell me now what this meeting is all about?"

Jean Barrett

He had relieved her of any more nervous delays. She could now be, and was, just as direct when she answered him. "I need you to help me find someone."

One of his thick, dark eyebrows lifted, expressing his puzzlement. "And who would that be?"

"My son."

He stared at her blankly for a full moment. "I know this has got to have an explanation," he finally said, "and maybe I'll be sorry asking for it, but you'd better let me hear it."

"I'll try to be brief, but it's a little involved."

"Some of my officers would probably tell you patience isn't one of my virtues, but let's find out if they're wrong."

The traffic behind them trundled over the bridge in a steady stream as Kate related her story. She told him about the book she had promised Gordon she would write and how and why she had traveled across America after his death.

"The families I met and talked to everywhere . . ." She spread the fingers of her hands, palms up, in a gesture meant to indicate her difficulty in describing their effect on her. "I'm a writer. I should know how to say it. All I can tell you is the experience had me realizing all over again how I'd never known that kind of family closeness growing up and that I suddenly missed it very much. Maybe just because I'd lost Gordon."

Efrem's rigid expression softened. "Yeah, that would have done it."

She appreciated his understanding. In that respect he hadn't changed. At least in this instance.

"Whatever it was, it left me with a need to try to connect with the son I gave up for adoption. Not," she went on hastily, "that I would either see or speak to him if he didn't want it. Not as his birth mother, anyway. I wouldn't inflict that on him."

"And you're asking me to help you locate your son? Kate, we're in Afghanistan. How does this make sense?"

206

"I've already located him. His adoptive parents, that is. It isn't hard to do these days. There are even online services that specialize in it, although I didn't use one. All I had to do was go to the agency that handled the adoption. They contacted the couple, who were willing to see me."

"Why would you have gone to his parents first? You couldn't have needed their permission to meet with him, not when your son has to be well beyond the age of consent."

"I didn't legally need their permission for that. But I felt it was only right to let them know what I wanted, both to get their approval and to learn whether he'd been told he was adopted."

"And?"

"I was informed by them through the agency he does know he was adopted, and they had no objection to my seeing him. They even thought he would like to meet his birth mother. And I would have met him, only—" She paused to select the right words, not wanting to risk Efrem's refusal by rushing her plea. "—he's not currently available."

"Uh-huh, and you need to find him." Efrem's dark eyes narrowed suspiciously. "That is what you said, isn't it? Just where is all this going, Kate?"

"I'm trying to explain it to you. How his parents had the agency tell me their name and address. How the Secrists agreed to have me come to their home outside Chicago. Efrem, it's a wonderful home in the suburbs, and they're fine people."

"Their son," he prompted her. "*Your* son. Where is he?"

"Here in Afghanistan."

Pushing himself away from the railing, Efrem gazed at her for another silent moment before issuing a slow, almost grim, "It suddenly occurs to me that maybe I don't want to know where all this is going."

Even if he didn't, she intended for him to hear her out. "The army," she said. "He's with the army here. Listed as missing in action when his chopper was shot down. Marion Secrist refuses to believe he isn't still alive."

"Kate—"

"All right, I know what you're going to say. That I'm not being rational, that with all the wars I've covered I should know better. But a parent isn't rational when it comes to the survival of a son or daughter. You should understand that, Efrem."

"You went and promised the woman, didn't you?" he guessed. "That, being an authorized journalist, you could arrange to come over here and recover this—"

"Sean. Corporal Sean Secrist. I had to promise her, Efrem. I *wanted* to promise her. She's ill, just recently diagnosed with cancer. It's treatable, but—"

"Gordon. This is all because you lost your Gordon to cancer," he said, his tone sympathetic.

"No, this is all about Sean. Because this is the one thing I can do for my son. I can find him for the only parents he's ever known."

She watched Efrem press one hand over his eyes, blowing out his breath at the same time, as if with both actions he was searching for the patience that was still in question. He looked around before telling her, "Let's go find some place to sit, and we'll talk about it."

The metal tables and chairs on the sidewalk outside the tea shop could have benefitted from fresh coats of paint. Chipped and in places spotted with rust, they were meant for summer use. But the morning was mild enough for Kate and Efrem to occupy them.

He ordered tea for them, explaining it was the preferred beverage in Afghanistan and that coffee was not common. When the hot tea came, it was served in glasses accompanied by a samovar.

"I should warn you before you taste it," Efrem explained from his side of the little table, "that it comes sweetened over here."

"I don't mind," Kate assured him. "I've been to so many places I've learned to be grateful for whatever they serve me."

She didn't remind him of the tea they had been given when they were imprisoned in Iraq had also been very sweet. Reaching for the glass, she sipped the steaming tea, finding it bracing.

"You've seen it all, haven't you, Kate? That ought to make you a realist. Most veteran war correspondents are, even after they've left it behind them."

She set her glass back on the table. "Only you think I'm being a sentimental idealist, don't you?"

"As you pointed out, I'm a father. I know how strong paternal instincts can be. But sometimes you just have to accept the facts."

"Do you know what those facts are?"

"I think so. We've lost only one chopper in the last six months, which means the one you're talking about has to be it. I wasn't in charge of the operation, but I am familiar with it."

"I read the report, but I'd like to hear the particulars."

She watched him lift his glass, saw how his Adam's apple bobbed in that old, disturbing way as he swallowed the tea.

"Are you sure?" he asked her when he'd lowered his glass. "They're not pleasant."

He had to realize there wasn't anything she hadn't heard in her years as a war correspondent for CNA, but it was different when it involved her own son . . .

"I'm sure."

"Okay," he said decisively, "it was a reconnaissance mission."

"For?"

"The illegal opium traffic. With our aid, the new government has been trying to stop the flow of the stuff out of the country.

But the Afghans are so poor and growing poppies so profitable, it's been impossible to control."

Kate already knew this, but she didn't interrupt him.

"Corporal Sean Secrist was evidently a member of the team sent to check out a reported source of opium processing that allegedly is supporting terrorist activities."

"And the folks who operate it wouldn't have liked that. Are they responsible for shooting down the helicopter?"

"It seems likely, but there are so many unfriendly forces out there we can't be sure. What made it so difficult is the terrain. A remote region west of here."

"But the army did send out a search and rescue, didn't they?"

"They did. Only the crash site is a narrow mountain ledge. It wasn't possible to land a Pave Hawk there. Before they could drop a recovery team, a spring storm slammed into the area. The winds in Afghanistan can be brutal, and this wind dumped several feet of snow. By the time it cleared and they were able to get in there, there was nothing left to recover. Do you want me to be specific about it?"

"Yes."

"No survivors." His voice hardened. "Not even the remains of bodies. There were enough signs to determine they'd been dragged away by animals. There are wolves in Afghanistan, Kate. A lot of them, and at this time of the year they're hungry."

He was right. The details weren't pleasant. Had he wanted to discourage her? Is that why he had related those details with such tough cynicism? Or was this just the evidence of the new Efrem Chaudoir, something that maybe came with the territory of being a colonel?

When she started to reach for her glass again, her wrist suffered a spasm of pain. In an effort to relieve it, she dropped her arm to the side of the chair, swinging it slowly like a pendulum.

"What are you doing?" he asked her.

"What I shouldn't be doing. I keep forgetting, even though it seems the natural thing to do to put my arm down and start turning it every which way. What I'm supposed to do is lift the hand up and back to ease pressure on the nerves."

"What's wrong? Are you okay?"

She smiled at his concern. "Carpal tunnel syndrome. Aggravated by too many years at keyboards, they tell me. I'm planning to have it corrected by my orthopedic surgeon when I get home."

"That surgery could have been done before you came over here. But I suppose you refused to schedule it because you had something else you wanted to do."

"*Needed* to do, Efrem."

"Kate, be reasonable. The army has made a conscientious effort to retrieve those men. They weren't there."

"Because your evidence says they'd been dragged away by animals. But that evidence isn't enough to prove that one or more of them didn't either crawl or walk away from the site right after the crash. Sean is listed as Missing in Action, remember, not dead."

"That's the procedure when there isn't a body. It's not the reality. And you're too intelligent and experienced about that reality to deny to yourself that MIAs seldom, if ever, survive in these kinds of circumstances."

"*Seldom.* That's a word with hope in it. It means something is still a possibility, not a certainty." She leaned toward him earnestly. "I want your army to try again."

"Even if I was convinced there's still time for it, which there isn't when it's been over four weeks, I don't have the authority to order another search."

"No, but your Brigadier General Carl Boynton does."

"What do you know about Boynton?"

"That it was his operation. That he isn't willing to conduct

211

another search. I learned that back in Washington, Efrem. I also learned he has great respect for Colonel Chaudoir, that he listens to him."

"You're exaggerating my influence there."

She ignored that in her urgency to win his help. "I know I'm using you, Efrem. Taking advantage of our past relationship to ask you to do this thing for me. I apologize for that. But if what we once had still means anything at all to you—"

He held up his hand, cutting her off. "You're as stubborn as Boynton, but you don't need to take this any further. I'll go to him, but don't expect any miracles, Kate. He isn't known for them."

"Thank you." She sat back in her chair, satisfied. For now she had done all she could do. Anything else would have to wait until Efrem got back to her.

Her wrist was still aching, but at least this time her arm wasn't numb.

Efrem paid no attention to the scene outside his window as the jeep, with his driver behind the wheel, bore him back to headquarters and a session with the general he knew wasn't going to be easy.

He wasn't interested in the blocks of concrete villas and the plane trees lining the avenues. He was still seeing Kate where he'd left her in the doorway of her hotel after removing her scarf.

Her hair was short again. About chin length, he thought, with a slight wave to it and bangs swept off to one side. But he didn't care about the style. All that interested him was the way the sun had gleamed on it, making golden highlights in its thickness and how the sides of her hair brushed her cheeks when she leaned forward.

He saw, too, the tweed pantsuit she wore with those same

flecks of gold in it. Or, more correctly, what he'd noticed was her figure in that pantsuit, still as slim and eye-catching as it had always been.

Damn it, why did she have to look so great? Why didn't she grow old? Look old?

Yeah, as though that would matter. If she had wrinkles and was sagging, it wouldn't make any difference. You'd still want her.

"Sir, I noticed buds on the willows beginning to open," his driver said pleasantly. "Looks like spring might finally be underway, huh?"

Private Rosinski. That was the young man's name. A good soldier who deserved better than a grunt, which was Efrem's only response. Well, he was in no mood for small talk. He was too angry for that. Angry with Kate, angry with himself.

He didn't want her back in his life, a temptation all over again. Not when he couldn't have her, when she was here only for the sake of the Secrists and their son. *Her* son.

It isn't me she wants, Efrem thought. I'm only a means to an end.

Okay, he was a father, and if it were his Nell who was missing . . . Yeah, he'd agreed to help Kate, for that reason if no other.

You're being an ass. Let it go. You have no right to resent her because she needs you for something other than yourself.

But he couldn't help it. He did resent her. He wanted her to care about him, about them. But that no longer seemed to matter to her.

Chapter Sixteen

The dining room of the Hotel Babur adjoined the lobby. The lunch crowd was in there. From the babble that drifted through the room's open doors, Kate could tell without looking that its occupants were from the West. She caught snatches of dialogue in English, German, Dutch and other European languages she couldn't identify.

A lot of them were journalists, some of whom she'd recognized when they had passed through the lobby. Others, she assumed, were officials of one kind or another, maybe UN related.

Not that it mattered who they were or what they were talking about. She made herself deaf to their conversations. Her only interest was in hearing what Efrem had to say to her. He was seated just across from her, directly outside the dining room in the now deserted lobby.

Kate leaned forward to hear him, wanting him to tell her positive news but fearing from the sober expression on his face it would be negative. She was right.

"Kate, I did try, but Boynton flat out refuses to order another search. Insists the army has already done everything possible to recover those MIAs."

She sat back in her chair with a disappointed "That's it then."

"I'm sorry, Kate. I know you were counting on the general. I know how hard this is for you to accept. Look, maybe it doesn't help for me to say it, but at least you can get your story for the *View* before you go home."

"Oh, I'm not going home," she informed him matter-of-factly. "Not without my son. It may be over where your general is concerned, but it isn't finished for me. I'm not leaving Afghanistan until I find Sean."

"This is crazy. What do you think you can do on your own? Hike over every mountain in the country looking for him?"

"Yes, if I have to. But that won't be necessary. I'll hire a car and a guide. Sean's out there somewhere, Efrem, and unless I get positive proof he isn't alive, I'm going to go on believing he survived."

"My God, listen to yourself. You don't know what you're saying. Kate, we're still fighting a war over here."

"So they tell me," she said dryly.

"Did they also happen to tell you just what that means? Like there are still Taliban and al-Qaeda strongholds?"

"Concentrated along the Pakistan border, not in the west."

"No, in the west you've just got your routine Taliban sympathizers, drug trafficking, primitive villages and hostile warlords with their own private armies. All in a rugged, isolated land where even the weather is freaking unfriendly."

He wasn't telling her anything she hadn't already made it her business to learn before leaving Washington.

"Haven't you heard?" she said confidently. "Kate Groen knows how to get in and out of troubled areas from her days as a war correspondent. No one will consider her a threat just for traveling around the villages in the region of the crash, showing them her son's photograph and asking if anyone has seen him."

"You can't do this, Kate. I won't let you do it."

"There's no way you can stop me. I have my visa and the credentials as a *View* reporter to travel through Afghanistan, even permission from the Pentagon and the Afghan government. Turns out it's useful having a few influential friends in the right places."

"I bet." Efrem exhaled loudly in exasperation. "What am I going to do with you?"

"Let me go without any more arguments."

"Like you say, I can't stop you."

She gazed at him suspiciously. "This is too easy. What's the hitch?"

"I go with you."

"I don't think so."

His face as hard as steel, he hunched forward on the chair, hands planted on his knees. "You don't have a choice. Because if you don't agree, I'll make it my business to see to it there isn't a car or guide in Kabul available to you."

She knew he meant it. "Efrem, why are you insisting on this?"

"Let's just say it doesn't look good when a journalist gets herself killed in a war zone. America expects its citizens to be safeguarded by the military, even the reckless ones."

"Your Brigadier General Boynton will never let you go."

"Oh, I think he will, and not just because I'm due for a leave anyway. Of course, he won't be happy about it, but he'll be less unhappy when I point out to him that Ms. Groen will have protection from one of his officers. Makes for good public relations with the press, and Boynton cares about that. Up to a point, anyway."

Efrem got to his feet with a crisp "I'll get back to you later this afternoon with all the arrangements."

Before she could offer any further objection, Efrem left her, his tall figure swinging across the lobby and through the front door into the street.

Kate went on sitting there after he was gone. Then she opened her shoulder bag and took out the photograph the Secrists had given her back in Chicago. She stared at the grinning, good looking face of the young man who was her son, searching for a resemblance to herself. Except for his blue eyes and light brown hair, there was none she could see. And yet she had given birth to him. He shared her genes, maybe even something of her temperament.

Careful. If you don't watch yourself, you're going to get all emotional over this, lose the clear head you're going to need.

To prevent that risk, she put the photograph back in her bag. She thought instead about Efrem, even though that was a risk of another kind.

He didn't believe in her mission, was convinced it was a hopeless effort. Only he was determined to go with her. She could have examined his motives, but it was probably safer not to do that, to instead accept just what he'd claimed was his reason for accompanying her.

There should be no danger in that plan. Efrem was engaged to be married, she reminded herself. Or possibly was already married. No reason for her to feel uneasy. But she did.

When Kate exited the hotel early the next morning, she was wearing a sand-colored, belted tunic over a pair of dark brown slacks with a matching scarf covering her hair. The outfit was in no way meant as an effort to pass herself off as a native but simply a garb that would make her acceptable to the Afghans. It was also practical for the journey, as were the leather boots on her feet and the warm jacket over her arm.

In her other hand, she carried a canvas tote crammed with a few changes of clothing and several other necessary articles, including a digital camera. She had learned in her days as a war correspondent the wisdom of traveling light.

Efrem had yet to arrive. While Kate waited for him on the broken, brick sidewalk, the tote at her feet, she checked her shoulder bag. Conscious that she was, after all, on assignment for the *View*, she wanted to make sure she had included a spare notebook. Although she'd brought her laptop from home, she had decided to leave it behind in the hotel with her other luggage. It would just be something else to haul, and she preferred making her story notes on paper anyway.

She was restoring the bag to her shoulder when the same jeep that had delivered Efrem yesterday pulled up to the curb. He was carrying his own bag of essentials when he swung himself out of the jeep.

"Morning," he greeted her briefly, eyeing her clothing with a nod of approval.

His own outfit was just as nondescript. Jeans, a sweatshirt and a baseball cap. She certainly hadn't expected anything like dress greens but maybe a camouflage-patterned army combat uniform.

"No field gear?"

"Like I told you on the phone last night, going out there looking like some military convoy would only invite trouble."

"Right," she said. "We're just an ordinary couple on a peaceful errand. I'd make that a trio, except I don't see the guide and the car you promised." The jeep that had deposited Efrem at the hotel was already gone, and at the moment the street was empty. "Where are they?"

"Coming."

Efrem was checking his watch when another jeep roared around the corner, sped recklessly down the street and rocked to a halt in front of them. Kate stared at the vehicle with dismay. It looked like something left over from the Second World War.

"Uh, is this it?"

"Don't let the body fool you. This isn't Leke's rattletrap," he said, referring to the old bus that had been their only means of transport in Kosovo. "She's sound and dependable, with new tires and a new engine."

"But like us, I suppose. Meant to blend in with the scenery."

"That's right."

Well, why not? she thought. There were enough dents and rust on what remained of the faded, khaki paint to make it convincing. She wondered if the Afghan driver had put them there.

Even if she'd had the nerve to ask the man, he gave her no opportunity. Bounding from the jeep, his feet barely hit the pavement when chatter spilled out of him like one of his country's magpies.

"*Salaam aleikum,*" he greeted her cheerfully, hand to his heart.

There were two Dari phrases Kate had made the effort to learn. *Salaam aleikum,* which meant, "Peace be with you," and its customary reply of *waleikum salaam,* meaning, "And also with you." She managed to murmur the latter, which he welcomed with a delighted grin.

"Oh, very good," he said in a flawless English. "But is that the extent of your Dari? Don't worry if it is, because I am fluent in both Dari and Pashto, as well as many of the dialects of our country. Language is my business. That makes me the perfect guide for you, don't you agree?"

She was saved from answering him by Efrem's intervention. "Kate, meet Nadir Fawad."

"You will call me Nadir," the guide instructed her, "and I will call you Kate and Efrem. We'll be friendly, like Americans always are."

"Okay," she agreed, amused by this man who seemed to be all buoyant energy. He was also something of a contradiction. Unlike most Afghan men, he was clean shaven but wore a *pakul* cap, which was almost as common as turbans. A pair of bright, intelligent eyes looked out at her from round, dark framed glasses perched on a large nose.

"If you're ready, Nadir," Efrem said, "let's get the bags in the jeep and us on the road."

"Immediately. But first—" Nadir held up a camera. "—we

will make a photograph to mark the start of your adventure."

Kate certainly wasn't thinking of it as any adventure but only as a journey that, like it or not, she had to undertake.

"Is this necessary?" Efrem complained.

"Please," Nadir urged.

Seconds later, Kate found herself facing the camera in front of the hotel with Efrem beside her. The closeness of his tall, hard body was familiar. And also unsettling, although it could have been worse. He could have slid his arm around her in one of those traditional, just-between-friends poses.

She was also relieved when, after the bags were stowed, Efrem turned to Nadir, insisting, "You guide, I drive."

From what she'd observed, Nadir was a menace behind the wheel. He climbed into the back seat without an objection, however, which left Kate occupying the front next to Efrem. She refused to let herself consider that the cramped arrangement might be a problem.

It was Nadir who ended up being the problem. He hung over the back of Kate's seat, talking nonstop. When he wasn't giving Efrem directions on the best route out of the city, he maintained a steady flow of one-sided dialogue on an endless variety of subjects.

". . . taught languages at the university. That was before the Taliban came to power, you understand. Now the university is open again, but there are no teaching jobs for me. There are too many of us and not enough funds. So I wait, hoping for a position as an interpreter for my country at the United Nations. I would be a very good interpreter. In the meantime, I must make a living as a guide. You turn left here, Efrem. If you turn right, it will . . ."

Kate managed to listen to him with a minimum of attention while focusing on her real interest outside her window. Now that they had left Kabul behind, the terrain was both bleak and awesome.

There was very little vegetation, mostly grass that was beginning to turn green with the season. Otherwise, the somber hills, ranging in shades of brown from pale taupe to coffee, were bare. From time to time, they passed through roadside hamlets where the houses were mud brick with flat roofs.

". . . no education for my people, not here in the villages. They are illiterate, which is why they believe in evil jinns and think to protect themselves by wearing amulets and hanging colored pieces of cloth on poles near the shrines. Watch the man on the donkey, Efrem. They both look so old that, as you say in America, they are an accident waiting to . . ."

Kate stole a glance at the silent Efrem, amused by his expression of mounting aggravation.

By the time the road took them through a river gorge, where cowslips and anemones were beginning to bloom along the banks, Nadir's running monologue had shifted direction again.

". . . my cousin, Ahmad. I told him he must stop thinking like the Taliban. They are gone. Forever, I hope. Now Afghans must be forward thinking. But does Ahmad listen to me? No, he does not listen . . ."

Kate wasn't sure just when she became aware of the silence in the jeep. Probably sometime after her fascination with the sight of a feudal castle, whose octagonal towers were beginning to crumble. She was still thinking of the castle on its ridge long after it had passed from view. It was her curiosity about it that had her wondering if Nadir could identify it for her.

And why hadn't Nadir pointed it out? For that matter, why was he suddenly—

Kate twisted around in her seat for an explanation. Nadir was sprawled across the back seat, eyes shut, hands folded across his stomach.

"He's asleep," she reported to Efrem.

"Yeah, I know. I could hear him snoring back there. I was just giving thanks to his Allah for the blessed quiet. I swear, if he hadn't finally worn himself out, I would have stopped the jeep and taped his mouth shut."

"I like him."

"I do, too. But if he's going to yammer like that for the whole trip—"

"The road forks up ahead," she interrupted Efrem. "Which way do we go?"

"I don't know."

"Oh, for a road sign. I guess I'd better wake up Nadir and ask him."

"You do, and I'm going to toss both of you out of this jeep."

"Efrem, we can't just guess."

"We won't have to."

He braked the jeep where the road divided. Producing a map from the pocket on his door, he unfolded it, spreading it across the wheel in front of him. She watched him as he bent over the map, trying to consult it. Then, grunting, he reached into the door pocket again, this time coming up with a pair of reading glasses he tucked over his ears.

Kate didn't comment on the glasses, though she had never known him to wear them before. But why not? They were both getting to the ages where such things were necessary.

"Okay, think I've got it," he said after studying the map for a few minutes. "We take the right branch."

She eyed him skeptically. "You don't sound very certain about it. Why don't we just ask Nadir?"

"Forget it. I'm sure."

She had known other men like him. Stubbornly driving around in circles instead of just stopping somewhere and asking the way. The male ego, she supposed.

Replacing the map and his glasses in the pocket, Efrem proceeded into the juncture, bearing to the right. The road began to climb after a half mile or so, winding around the side of a mountain. Its condition also deteriorated.

Almost none of the rural roads in Afghanistan were paved, and the wars had left them in a deplorable state of disrepair, marked with potholes and sometimes missing bridges. The route they had been traveling before the fork had been bad enough, but this branch was as rough and rutted as a farm track. It had also dwindled to a lane so narrow that, if they met an oncoming vehicle, there would be no room to pass.

Kate held her silence as long as she could. But when it became obvious they were headed nowhere but into a lonely wilderness, and all because Efrem had insisted on relief from poor Nadir's busy tongue, she found her own tongue.

"Uh, I hate to point it out, but—"

"Don't say it. I chose the wrong branch. I'd have turned back before this," he pointed out, "except there is no place to turn without the risk of going over the side of the mountain. Maybe up ahead."

Another mile of twisting road brought them around the shoulder of the mountain and into a small, high valley that would permit Efrem to swing the jeep around with ease. But Kate's cry brought them to a halt on the level floor of the valley.

"Efrem, look!"

The little valley was not empty. The ruins of ancient buildings were on all sides, most of them no more than jagged foundations. Except for one structure on the far side that was almost intact.

The minaret was impressive, soaring to an incredible height and, even from several hundred yards away, an obvious work of art. It was a temptation not to be resisted.

"We can't pass this up," Kate said. "It will only take a few minutes, just enough to have a look and for me to get a picture."

Efrem hesitated, clearly not happy with the idea. He must have been thinking about a possible danger, but the area was silent and deserted.

"All right," he agreed, "but let's make it fast."

Nadir had yet to stir when Efrem extracted their jackets and Kate's camera from the back of the jeep.

"Should we wake him?" she wondered.

"Let him sleep."

They left the jeep parked where it was and set off in the direction of the minaret. It was cold at this elevation, with a sharp wind from the snow peaks, which made Kate grateful for the warmth of her jacket.

"Judging from the ruins," she observed, "it must have been a sizable community before it was abandoned. Why do you suppose it was built in such an isolated spot?"

"Probably a holy place that would have included a mosque."

A large one, if the minaret was any indication, she thought. The mosque was long gone, but somehow the minaret had survived. When they reached its octagonal base and looked up, Kate realized what a magnificent tower it was.

Constructed of beige brick, its entire length was sheathed in intricately carved terra cotta, turquoise tiles and elaborate mosaics. High on its crown were the remains of balconies. What was left of the open fretwork that once formed their railings was as delicate as lace.

She was fascinated by the minaret, but Efrem didn't seem nearly as interested as she was. He was quiet. When she looked at him, she caught him eyeing her intently.

"There's something I've got to know," he finally said.

She was startled, not just by the sharpness of his tone but by his timing as well. Whatever he wanted to ask her, it seemed to come out of nowhere and at an odd moment.

"What is it?"

"Didn't you get any of my messages? You must have gotten at least one of them. I left them everywhere back in Washington."

"What messages? What are you talking about?"

"Kate, I tried to phone you. Your line had been disconnected, and no one I called—the *View*, the new owners of Gordon's public relations service, your former associates at Cable News America—knew where you were or how to reach you. You'd just disappeared."

Dara, with whom she'd left her cell phone number, could have told him how to reach her. Except he didn't know about Dara Weinstein. She'd never had any reason to tell him.

"Efrem, you know where I was. I told you about that yesterday. And, no, I didn't get any of your messages. When did you leave them?"

"A few months after the memorial service."

"And I was working my way across the country by then, and gone so long that by the time I got back those messages must have been forgotten by the people you left them with. Efrem, why didn't you tell me this back in Kabul? Why did you wait until now?"

"Maybe because all you could think about was recovering your son. Or maybe . . ."

"What?"

"Hell, Kate, it was like you were keeping me at a distance. Like you should have gotten my messages and just hadn't wanted to contact me. That we were history, and you wanted it to stay that way."

She gazed at him, not knowing what to think. He looked and sounded so resentful. "These messages . . . what did they say?"

"That I needed to hear from you. That I had something important to tell you. Important to me anyway."

"Tell me now."

"Kate, I'm not engaged. Susan and I called it off. I started to say something to you at the memorial service, how it wasn't working out. Only with you just having lost Gordon, that would have sounded like—Well, you know how it would have sounded."

This was the explanation for why he wasn't wearing a ring. He had never married his fiancée. She could still remember how she'd felt when Dara had told her of Efrem's engagement. Dismay followed by a mixture of loss and relief. Loss because he could never belong to her, and relief because she no longer had to live with the guilt of having sent him away. But now . . .

"I figured I had to wait a few months to tell you, and by then—"

"I'd left Washington. Why, Efrem? Why was it called off?"

"You know why."

Kate was afraid she did. She didn't want his broken engagement to be because of her, didn't want to suffer the guilt all over again. But Efrem went on to make it clear she *was* the reason.

"I couldn't forget you, Kate. I did my damndest to get over you, only I was never able to manage it."

She didn't know what to say, but Efrem did.

"I was lonely, Kate. Lonely for you, and when Susan came along I hoped—Well, it doesn't matter. No one got hurt. We both realized we couldn't go through with it, that it was a mistake."

She wasn't prepared for this, was still unable to find the words to express herself. Maybe because, beyond confusion, she wasn't certain what she was feeling.

"I need to know, Kate. I need to know whether you kept that promise to always love me."

He must have been edging toward her without her being aware of it. But she was conscious of him now standing so close to her that she could see how suddenly stormy his black eyes were. There was nothing gentle about his voice either. It was harsh when he demanded, "Tell me we still matter."

Was he so desperate he was willing to force an acknowledgment out of her? Was that why his arms wrapped around her so insistently, hauling her against his body? Why, before she could pull back, he crushed his mouth over hers in a savage kiss that was an explosion of urgency.

Kate longed to respond to him, ached for the tender Efrem of earlier years. But he wasn't there. All she could experience was shock at the intensity of his kiss. At the anger in him that was somehow made more pronounced by the hard bulge pressed against her. Not his arousal. A handgun in his pocket. She could feel the shape of it through the material of his jacket.

In that moment, she was actually afraid of him. When she tugged against his embrace, he let her go. Stepping away from him, she looked up into his now anxious face with a soft "I don't think I know you anymore."

Efrem didn't try to stop her as she turned and started back toward the jeep. She was still shaken when she met Nadir hurrying toward her.

"What are we doing here?" he wanted to know, looking around nervously. "This is a very bad place."

"It seems innocent to me. Nadir, you aren't afraid of those evil jinns you told us about, are you?"

"I am not a superstitious man. It is the living I fear."

Efrem had caught up with them by then. "What is it that's got you worried, Nadir?"

"This is an ancient place," the guide explained. "There are many old things buried in the ruins. Things that collectors in the outside world pay money for. My people are very poor. Some of them dig for these things to sell, even though the practice of sending them out of the country is illegal."

Kate was beginning to understand. "Looters," she said.

Nadir bobbed his head. "Yes, and they can be dangerous if they find us here. Please, *let* us go."

"I think," Efrem said slowly, "it's a little late for that."

Both Kate and Nadir cast their gazes in the direction Efrem was looking. Off to their right, less than a hundred yards away, was a broken ridge that formed one side of the valley. At its base was a scree down which four men with turbans and beards, and carrying rifles, were swiftly scrambling.

"Kalashnikovs," Efrem muttered.

"The men?" Kate asked.

"Their rifles. Russian designed, Iranian made and very lethal."

Nadir was instantly alarmed. "Oh, cripes!" He whirled around with the intention of fleeing to the jeep.

"Both of you stay right where you are," Efrem instructed them. "They could cut you down before you ever got anywhere near the jeep."

If their dogs don't tear us apart first, Kate thought. The four figures were accompanied by as many mastiffs. Great, mean-looking brutes who had outdistanced their masters and were already racing toward them across the floor of the valley.

Before Kate could object, Efrem had snagged her by the arm and thrust her protectively behind him. His other hand rested over the deep pocket of his jacket, ready to whip out the weapon inside. She prayed that wouldn't be necessary, although the existence of the gun seemed justified to her now by the potential menace of the Afghans and their animals.

The snarling dogs reached them. Whether they would have attacked, Kate never learned. One of their owners, who had cleared the scree and was running toward them, shouted a command. The four mastiffs obeyed his order, sinking down on their haunches. They were still a threat, however, guarding the three interlopers with warning growls low in their throats.

"*Allah-u-Akbar,*" the same man hailed them.

"I know that one," Efrem said. "God is great. It's a peaceful greeting. Nadir, go talk to them."

The guide was plainly unwilling to do anything of the kind and only went reluctantly to speak to the four arrivals. Kate and Efrem tensely watched the exchange among the men. To her relief, Nadir was smiling when he returned.

"It's good," he reported. "They are not looters. They are hunting wolves. The wolves have been a great problem. Their dogs have been trained to also hunt the wolves."

Although the four men couldn't have understood what Nadir was telling them, they nodded their approval. The mastiffs were called off, and a minute later, with friendly waves of farewell, the hunting party retreated.

"I think," Nadir pleaded, "it would be a very fine thing if we now left this valley."

I don't think I know you anymore.

The words she had spoken to Efrem back at the minaret were still with Kate as they retraced their route to the fork below. She glanced at him close beside her. He was silent, concentrating on the road.

Nadir, too, was mercifully quiet behind them. He wasn't asleep this time. When she turned around to check on him, he had a pouting look on his round face, perhaps because they hadn't bothered to rouse him either at the fork or during the trip up the mountain to a place he would have warned them not to go. She would have to ask his forgiveness, but right now she was occupied with the words that kept repeating themselves in her mind.

I don't think I know you anymore.

They were true, those words, whatever her regret for having expressed them. She didn't know this Efrem. He was no longer the man she had fallen in love with back in Iraq. However compelling he still was, this was a darker, often cynical Efrem. She had glimpsed the first signs of the changes in Kosovo, but they hadn't been sufficient enough to prevent her from falling in love with him all over again. Those changes must have deepened since then, although their infrequent encounters in the years between Kosovo and Afghanistan had been too brief for her to notice. They were very evident this time.

He was hard-edged now, without his fun-loving spirit in Iraq, or even to some degree during their flight out of Kosovo. Whatever had toughened him, and she hadn't the courage just now to ask him about it, she missed that other Efrem. Mourned the loss of him with a sadness so deep she was deaf to whatever he was saying to her.

"Sorry," she apologized, shaking off her despondent mood. "You were saying?"

"You didn't get your picture of the minaret."

"That's right, I didn't. It doesn't matter. There'll be other opportunities for photos."

CHAPTER SEVENTEEN

The first of those photo opportunities occurred that evening after supper when Kate shot a portrait of the headman of a village located beside the Hari Rud River.

Efrem noticed that Nadir, who looked on while Kate posed the preening Hussein Ali Karzai, was very proud of himself. The guide had secured them accommodations for the night in the headman's extensive compound.

Nadir had made certain that Kate and Efrem understood how privileged they were to be honored guests in the compound, because Hussein Ali Karzai was a very rich man. By the standards of rural Afghanistan, Efrem knew Nadir was right.

There were such luxuries as a coal brazier to warm the common room where they were gathered, family photographs displayed on a low table along with an elegant Koran box and a richly figured carpet on the floor, even though that floor was nothing more than hard mud.

Their host had served them a meal of kebabs, *nan* bread and the familiar sweet tea followed by *basraq*, which were tiny, curled pastries. Nadir, wanting to make certain Efrem was impressed, had leaned over and whispered to him between courses, "This is a very fine banquet."

Efrem had agreed, though he was more grateful for the gas that Hussein Ali Karzai was willing to provide them for the jeep. Neither this kind of food or fuel would be easily available when they reached the more remote areas.

The stout headman, who was very pleased with Kate's camera work, was now showing her his prized lapis lazuli prayer beads. It didn't surprise Efrem that in this particular Muslim society she was the only woman present in the company, an exception because she was both a Westerner and a journalist.

Efrem watched her as she admired the beads. Even though, with her head covered, he couldn't see the silky hair he had once spilled with such pleasure through his fingers, she dazzled him in the soft glow of an oil lamp. The sight of her could still produce that tight longing deep in his gut. *And always would.*

Returning the beads to her host and thanking him for his generosity, Kate excused herself. "I'd like to organize my notes."

With Nadir's help, she had interviewed several of the villagers in preparation for the feature she had been assigned to write. She went on into an adjoining room, shutting the door behind her. Efrem wasn't interested in the game of chess that Nadir and Hussein Ali wanted to play before they turned in for the night on their pallets.

He was still dealing with the remorse that had gripped him after that episode with Kate at the minaret. He'd been an absolute fool manhandling her like that. He wanted her forgiveness, and this was his first chance since then to beg it. Getting to his feet, he followed her into the next room, closing the door again so they could be alone.

Kate's head wasn't bent over her notebook. It was the photograph of her son that Efrem found her examining. Though they had yet to reach the region of the crash, she had been showing his picture around the village here, asking if anyone had seen the young man. No one had.

She looked a bit embarrassed that he had caught her with the photograph. "I'm trying to learn his face," she excused herself. "You never know. I might just spot him somewhere, and I'd like to be sure without having to whip out the photo every time."

Efrem hated to see her like this, so certain she would find her son she was intense about it. He didn't want to remind her again how unlikely the possibility was. All he said was a sympathetic, "Sure."

She laughed self-consciously. "Okay, that isn't exactly true. What I was really doing was trying to connect with him on some level. Silly, isn't it? I know Sean will always belong to the Secrists. That's as it should be. But I thought if I could just share some little part of him . . ."

"I understand."

"Yes, I guess being a parent you would."

She smiled at him brightly, easing the burden of his remorse. He hoped her smile meant she was no longer angry with him.

"How is your Nell, anyway?" she asked him. "Did she ever get that horse she wanted?"

"I wish. These days she's far more interested in boys than horses."

"Ah, yes, that age."

"It worries the hell out of me."

"That's what fathers are supposed to do when it comes to their daughters. Or so I've been told."

There was a moment of silence between them. She gazed up at him expectantly from her stool, as if waiting for him to tell her why he was here.

"About what happened this afternoon at the minaret," he said awkwardly. "I had no right to treat you like that. I just want you to know how sorry I am."

"Let's just agree to forget about it, shall we?"

She didn't add it, but Efrem sensed she also meant: *As long as it doesn't happen again.*

There was another silence. He was conscious then of a transistor radio playing in one of the other rooms. The Taliban had forbidden music, but it was legal again, though not common. Surprisingly, this was an American song. He couldn't name it, but he remembered it had been popular when he was a kid.

Long ago, he realized. It made him think sadly of the other years. The years that had separated Kate and him. Too many years.

Hearing the old ballad seized him with a sudden, powerful need. "Dance with me, Kate," he urged her impulsively.

His proposal brought a startled expression to her face. "Here? Now?"

"Do you realize we've never danced with each other?"

"I don't think—"

"Please. Just for a minute."

She hesitated. He thought she would refuse him, tell him his intention was crazy. And was relieved when, instead, she got up from the stool, placed the photograph in her shoulder bag on the floor and went into his waiting arms.

She stiffened when his arm went around her waist, letting him know he was drawing her too tightly against his body. Resisting the mistake he'd made at the minaret, the desire to embrace her possessively, Efrem instantly loosened his hold. She relaxed after that, trusting him.

Their slow waltz was easy, fluid. It felt so natural to him, so right the way they moved together in perfect harmony to the music that he could have sworn this couldn't be the first time they had danced together. That they must have been dancing like this all their lives.

The ballad ended abruptly and all too soon. He couldn't bring himself to release her. He went on holding her, swaying with her.

Efrem had been careful not to fit himself too closely to her, but it didn't seem to make any difference. At his age, he ought to be able to control his urges. Yet, here he was with a raging hard-on, like some randy teenager. But then Kate had always had this effect on him whenever his body came into contact with hers.

Had she been able to feel the heat of his aching arousal? Was that why she freed herself, leaving his arms empty? Leaving all of him with an empty feeling.

Maybe not. Maybe she'd had another reason for stepping away from him. One that had her now lifting both of her hands. He watched her as she flapped them slowly back and forth at the wrists in a kind of ritual exercise.

"The carpal tunnel bothering you again?"

"A little. I'll take a couple of aspirin before I go to bed."

Efrem read it as an invitation to depart. "I need to find my satellite phone. I think I left it in my jacket in the other room. I promised to check in with headquarters every night."

He started for the door, then stopped and turned around. There was something else that had brought him here. A question for her. He knew he probably shouldn't raise it, that she might put up another barrier if he risked asking it. But he couldn't bring himself to leave without an answer of some kind.

"There's something I'd like to know."

She nodded warily. "All right."

"If you hadn't learned of my engagement, would you have tried to see me again after the memorial service?"

"But you *were* engaged."

He had his answer, and it didn't satisfy him. He wanted something more. But he could see he wasn't going to get it, that she would resent it if he tried to pressure her for it. And maybe . . . maybe he wouldn't like what he heard.

"Thanks for the dance," he told her, unable to prevent the sour mood that overcame him as he went in search of his satellite phone.

★ ★ ★ ★ ★

Kate went on standing there after the door closed behind Efrem, struggling to understand why she had panicked at his question. Why she hadn't been able to tell him what he wanted to know.

I wouldn't have hesitated to get in touch with you. I would have told you, now that I'm free there's nothing to stop us from being together.

That's what Efrem had wanted to hear from her. But *would* she have tried to see him? She honestly didn't know. Maybe not. Maybe fear would have stopped her.

But fear of what? That he wouldn't still love her, want her? That he had moved on without her? Or that her love for him was no longer the vital force it had once been? And without that . . .

It was the last fear that gnawed at her through a long night of fitful sleep. That continued to demand an answer she didn't have when they moved on again in the morning. Kate tried to put it out of her mind, making their search for Sean her top priority. It was the only way she could survive the frustration of being so close to Efrem every waking hour.

They traveled from village to village through the raw, barren landscape, showing Sean's photograph to everyone they met, asking through Nadir if anyone had seen a young American or knew anything about one. The responses were always the same. The seamed, ageless faces of the villagers would go blank, there would be a long pause and then would come the slow, but emphatic, shaking of heads.

She appreciated how patient Efrem was about it. Just as he refrained from making any further mention of his feelings for her, he kept equally silent about his conviction that hunting for her lost son was a hopeless effort. In the end, however, after scouring the vicinity of the downed helicopter and finding nothing, he was no longer able to hold his tongue.

"Kate, be reasonable," he appealed to her. "I know how tough it is, but you've got to accept it. He just didn't make it."

She didn't want to be reasonable. "He's out here somewhere," she insisted. "I won't believe anything else. I *can't.*"

"All right, let's suppose your Sean *was* able to walk away from the crash. Then where is he? Why haven't we heard something from him or about him?"

"Maybe because he was captured by an enemy. Or else he suffered injuries that make him unable to contact his base."

Although Efrem didn't oppose her argument, she knew he didn't think either one of her explanations was a solid one. Maybe if she allowed herself to think about it, she wouldn't either. Only she refused to do that, fearing she would be subjecting herself to doubts. Instead, she went on clinging to her certainty, resolved to exhaust every possibility.

Those possibilities carried them from village to hamlet. Even though none of these places offered anything that was encouraging in their quest, they were welcomed everywhere. Kate had learned from her research that Afghanistan was famous for its hospitality. She just hadn't realized its poverty was so extensive that sharing a meal with guests sometimes meant no more than a chunk of *nan* bread and a glass of tea.

Kate, Efrem and Nadir were always fed whatever was available, perhaps even a bit of chicken when their hosts were fortunate enough to provide it, and given beds for the night. Those same hosts only reluctantly accepted the afghanis, the currency of the country, when the money was pressed on them in the morning by Kate or Efrem.

Obtaining gas for the jeep was more of a problem. But Nadir seemed to have enough connections, along with his talent of persuasion, that they managed somehow to get what they needed.

"This is Majnun, the village of my cousin, Pekka," Nadir said, leaning forward from his seat in the rear of the jeep. "Pekka is the *khan* here. The headman, you understand. If anyone knows anything, Pekka will know it. He will be very happy to see us."

As Nadir chattered on, Kate gazed at the place in the late afternoon light. It was like most of the other villages they had stopped at with its dun-colored walls, flat roofs of reed matting covered with clay and the ever-present mosque, this one situated in a grove of silver poplars. Oxen, stirring the dust along the road, indicated Majnun was a farming community, like nearly all of the villages.

"What's the building up on the hill?" Efrem wanted to know, parking the jeep where Nadir had directed. "It looks like a fort."

"It is a fort, a very old one. But most of it is in ruins. The Russians shelled it when they occupied my country."

The subject of the fort was forgotten, but it came up again after Nadir's cousin had joyfully welcomed them into his small home and fed them on a feast of cabbage, rice and salted mutton.

At the end of the meal, Nadir came to Kate and Efrem where they were seated on one of the cotton mats placed along the edges of the room. His dark eyes behind his round glasses looked concerned.

"Pekka knows nothing about an American soldier?" Kate guessed.

"I am sad to tell you he does not, nor do any of the other men here with us. But this is not the trouble. It is the sleeping arrangements."

"Why has that got you looking so serious?" Efrem asked him.

"Pekka is worried he will offend you because he has no room for you to sleep here in his house. It is seldom I'm able to come to his village, and when I do it is an event of significance. He has sent for my kinsmen in the hills where they are with their flocks. You can see how many of them have joined us already, and all will remain for the night to celebrate."

Kate wondered how many other cousins the tiny house could possibly accommodate. The common room was so noisy and crowded now that she was squeezed up against one of the big jars that stored grain for the family.

"Tell Pekka not to worry about it," Efrem said. "Kate and I can sleep in the jeep tonight."

Nadir looked horrified at his proposal. "Pekka would never permit an honored *meman*—a guest, you understand—to suffer such an indignity. What he wishes instead is to place you in the fort. There is one room there still whole and with a good well just outside."

The guide waited anxiously for their decision while Kate and Efrem traded glances. She didn't know how wise it was to spend a night alone with Efrem, but there didn't seem to be any other choice.

"Let the *khan* of Majnun know we will be pleased to occupy the fort," she informed Nadir.

There was still light in the sky when the whole party insisted on escorting them up the terraced hillside. Bearing pallets, blankets, a pair of oil lamps and Kate and Efrem's bags, they laughed and shouted and sang all the way to the fort.

The brick-floored room into which they were conducted carried an odor that made Kate think its last tenants must have been livestock, but it had been swept clean for them.

The silence after the party retreated, taking Nadir with them back to the village, seemed altogether too pronounced. It made Kate conscious that she and Efrem were suddenly alone together. She could feel him gazing at her perceptively.

"Relax, Kate," he said, the tone of bitterness creeping into his voice again. "Nothing is going to happen here that you don't want to happen."

"I'm not as worried about that as I am about you."

Even though the gloom was thickening in the room, she could see his scowl. "Care to explain that?"

Kate hesitated only briefly before summoning the courage to be honest with him. "I told you back at the minaret I didn't know you anymore. And it's true. You're not the man I fell in love with. You've hardened in the years since Kosovo. What happened to change you, Efrem?"

"You should know the answer to that. You covered enough wars during your years as a TV correspondent. You saw all the suffering."

"Yes, but I didn't let it make me callous."

"Yeah, well, it's different when you're looking on. It isn't the same as being directly involved in those conflicts, watching both the men under your command as well as the enemy die, not to mention all of the innocent civilians caught up in those actions. And if you take it seriously, feel in some measure responsible for the carnage, and I did, then, yes, it changes you."

"But if your compassion is strong enough—"

"What? You can overcome all the rest? You can't. Not in the end. All you can do is teach yourself to become immune to it. Because if you don't build a tough shell around yourself, it'll drag you down, make it impossible for you to go on."

She stared at him unhappily. "My God, Efrem, if it's doing all this to you, then you've got to get out, leave it behind."

"And do what? The army is all I know."

"But if a man or a woman won't let themselves in some way be vulnerable, refuse to have any weakness—"

"I have a weakness, Kate. You're my weakness."

His voice was no longer brittle. It had softened, and she could hear the yearning in it. *And you're my weakness.* That's what she wanted to tell him, but she didn't trust herself to say it.

The room had darkened. It made an excuse for her to turn away, to cross through the shadows to one of the oil lamps that had been placed along with matches on a stool. She lifted the chimney, struck a match and applied it to the wick. Light bloomed in the room.

She was replacing the chimney when she became aware he was beside her. Coming erect, she faced him. The glow of the lamp bathed his angular features, revealed to her how his naked gaze seemed to caress her face.

His voice was thick and husky now when he spoke to her. "I wonder if you have any idea just how beautiful you are."

To be beautiful in a man's eyes, even when you knew you weren't, was irresistible to almost any woman, making her susceptible. And Kate, God help her, was just that when Efrem drew her slowly into his arms. When his mouth angled across hers in a deep, riveting kiss that fired her senses, she was lost.

Mistake or not, she didn't try to fight what followed. Not this time. She contributed to it willingly, even with a kind of blissful release that seemed nothing but right when she shed her clothes, sank with him on one of the pallets. When his body consumed hers in a dynamic joining that taught her what she and Efrem had once shared hadn't been diminished by the years. It was sweet torture to her.

It was afterwards she paid the penalty. Holding her securely in his arms, he whispered a fervent, "Do you know how scared I've been of losing you again? I never stopped loving you, and I'm never going to."

She knew he expected her to echo his feelings. She couldn't and didn't know exactly why.

"We're a part of each other, Kate. There's nothing now to keep us from being together."

He was right. She knew that. They were both free now. Just

as he'd said, there was nothing to keep them apart. Nothing except—

"Unless you no longer love me." Releasing her, he braced himself up on one elbow in order to look down at her. "Is that it, Kate?"

Was it? But how could it be when she had never stopped loving him? If she'd been uncertain about that since coming to Afghanistan, she no longer questioned it. Not after tonight. She did love him.

Or at least the man he had once been. But this new, abrasive Efrem . . . you're not so sure about him, are you?

"Kate, talk to me. I want to know what's holding you back. Is it the old issue of trust? Are you still dealing with that?"

"I told you back in Kosovo I overcame that problem. I meant it. This has nothing to do with mistrust."

"Then what?"

"Maybe it's because we're too different now. Maybe too many years have gone by to make it work, even if we do still love each other." She didn't add she feared she couldn't count on that love being enough to make a relationship last, which she supposed was a form of mistrust after all.

"We've missed too many of those years, Kate. I don't want to miss any more."

How could she explain how confused she was about them and make him understand? "I can't think about this. You're going to have to give me time, Efrem, because right now my mind is on finding my son."

"Kate," he pleaded, "don't give up on us now that we've found each other again."

She saw the misery on his face, in his eyes, and she couldn't bear it. Pulling one of the blankets around her, she got up from the pallet and went to the lamp, using the excuse of turning the wick down for the night to escape from him. He didn't try to follow her. She knew he understood they would be sleeping on separate pallets.

The sun was just clearing the horizon when Nadir arrived at the fort, breathless and excited.

"I have blessed news!" he announced, ignoring the fact they were still dressing as he burst in on them. "Word has come to me that Sean Secrist may still be alive!"

Kate, in the act of covering her hair, stared at him with the breath sticking in her throat. "How? Where?" she managed to croak.

Talking even more rapidly than usual, his words spilling over one another, Nadir explained it to them. "My cousin's son, who is Rashid . . . oh, yes, he arrived a few hours ago . . . a good boy, you understand, very reliable . . . we spoke of family at some length . . .

"Nadir, please get on with it," Kate urged him impatiently. "Tell us what you learned."

"Rashid . . . only just now did he ask what brought me to Majnun . . . when I told him . . . when he understood of our search . . ."

"For the sake of Allah, man, will you just spit it out?" Efrem demanded.

The guide gazed at him with an injured look. "I *am* telling you this. A few days ago Rashid bought a goat from a nomad. At a very good price, I think. Do you know about the nomads in my country?"

"Is this necessary, Nadir?"

Ignoring Kate's interruption, Nadir went on with his story. "The nomads follow the grasslands with their herds, sometimes spending the winter in one place and then moving on when the season turns. The nomad who sold Rashid his new goat spoke to him of a foreign soldier who stumbled into their winter camp several weeks ago. That he was injured and very ill."

"Sean," Kate whispered, hardly daring to breathe the word aloud for fear it wouldn't be true.

"The nomad did not tell Rashid the soldier's name. It was of no matter to him."

"Where is this soldier now?" Efrem asked. "What did the nomads do with him?"

"They took him with them when they moved on."

"To where?"

Nadir shook his head. "Rashid doesn't know. They could be anywhere now."

"Without reporting to someone in authority that the soldier came to them?"

"The nomads wouldn't do this. They are shy of outsiders, have as little to do with them as possible."

"Did your Rashid get a glimpse of this soldier?" Efrem wanted to know.

"He did not. Rashid was not in their camp. The man with the goat heard Rashid wanted to buy a good goat and came to his house."

"I suppose," Efrem conjectured, "Rashid also doesn't know whether the foreign soldier was American."

"Regretfully, no."

"But he must be Sean," Kate said. "He *has* to be. We've got to find those nomads."

To her relief, Efrem didn't try to point out to her what she refused to consider. That the injured soldier needn't be either the survivor of a helicopter crash or her son. Even that he could easily be some other member of the downed reconnaissance team.

"All right," he said decisively, "let's pack up here and get rolling. Nadir, your all-nighter with the family has got you looking like hell, but you can sleep in the jeep."

Chapter Eighteen

They traveled from village to village, asking everyone they met on the road or in the villages themselves whether they had seen the nomads. Or, rather, Nadir asked while Kate waited impatiently for the responses.

The answers were almost always disappointingly the same. No one knew anything about the nomads. On two occasions, however, they *were* directed to nomad camps. They went to those camps, only to learn that the nomads in them were not the band they sought. No soldier, foreign or otherwise, was traveling with them.

Kate wouldn't let herself be discouraged. The band they wanted was somewhere out there, and she wouldn't permit either herself or Efrem and Nadir to give up until they found it.

Only one thing troubled her as they moved from place to place. The guilt that gnawed at her for being unable to give Efrem what he waited for so earnestly. He never introduced the subject again, but whenever she caught him looking at her, she could see by the intensity of his gaze just how much he wanted to hear her tell him they had a future together.

Kate couldn't do that. Not yet, even though her uncertainty was eating at her soul. And probably Efrem's, too.

Her indecisiveness was on her mind, distracting her, when they stopped for water at a well in a deserted hamlet where the houses were nothing more than blackened shells. Kate had seen other hamlets like this, which Nadir told her had been burned when its inhabitants resisted either the Russians or the rule of the Taliban.

An old man with a wisp of a beard had also stopped at the well to water his camel. While Kate and Efrem waited in the shade of a cedar for the traveler to finish drawing water, Nadir went to speak to him. The pleased look on the guide's face when he returned a few minutes later had Kate alert again and hopeful.

"He is a trader," Nadir informed them. "Only yesterday he stopped to barter for sheepskins with a band of nomads. He knows nothing of a soldier, but he was able to tell me where their camp is located."

Kate sent up a silent prayer when they were underway again in the jeep on the trail of the nomads.

Let them be the right band this time. Let them still be there.

Less than an hour later, and to her immense relief, they sighted a collection of tents woven out of goat's hair. The nomads had not moved on. Their herds were grazing on the open grasslands of a broad plain, to which the old man had directed them.

The members of the band gazed at them with impassive, silent faces when they arrived in the camp. As in the other two camps they had visited, Kate knew that the nomads would greet them politely but with a wariness reserved for strangers. These people weren't like other Afghans. Their lifestyle permitted a freedom that had them even dress differently. The men wore vests and caps of karakul instead of the more traditional turbans. And the women, who were less restricted than women elsewhere in the country, weren't required to wear veils, needing only to cover their hair with shawls.

The burly headman, a swarthy figure with no beard but a full mustache, came forward to learn their business while the other nomads hung back, watching the scene. Hand to his heart, the headman greeted the visitors with the customary *"Salaam aleikum."*

Nadir returned the greeting before launching into an explanation, none of which Kate could understand except for the mention of Sean's name. She looked on anxiously, not liking the headman's solemn silence when Nadir had finished his explanation.

These aren't the nomads we want.

That was her first thought. But she decided otherwise when the headman began to reply at some length, tugging one end of his mustache as he spoke. The grave expression on Nadir's face as he listened was all she needed to tell her she was about to hear something she wouldn't like.

The guide turned to them at last, his voice sober with regret. "I am sorry to say the news is not good."

He hesitated before Efrem ordered him, "Just give it to us, man."

"There was such a soldier with them. As we already know from Rashid, he was in a bad way when he staggered into their camp and collapsed. They tried to help him, carried him with them when they left their winter camp. The headman's name is Yussuf. He tells me some of his people have knowledge of medicines and nursed him, but the soldier did not recover. He died only yesterday evening. They buried him this morning on the grasslands."

Nadir's account must have left Kate looking as stricken as she felt, because Efrem's hand closed over her arm, steadying her. She didn't want to believe her son was dead. *Couldn't* believe it.

She was only dimly conscious of the headman turning his head and barking a command to a young boy, who had been hovering just behind him. The child raced off, vanishing into one of the tents. When he reappeared only seconds later, he had something cupped in both of his hands. Whatever the article was, he carried it back to the headman as though it were very precious.

When the headman took it and passed it almost reverently to Efrem, Kate caught a glimpse of metal glinting in the sunlight.

"Dog tags," Efrem identified the article for her. "They saved his dog tags before they buried him."

The boy spoke up, addressing Kate with an enthusiastic, "English, English."

Was he telling her he knew her language or asking her if she were English? Before she could answer him, the headman, Yussuf, silenced the child with a frown that presumably told him he was being disrespectful.

Efrem, examining the tags, turned to her. "Ware," he said. "His name was Ware, not Secrist."

She was so numb by then she didn't know how to react. "Then it wasn't Sean," she said slowly. "But who—"

"One of the other members of the team. Sergeant Edward Ware. I knew him."

The boy plucked at Yussuf's sleeve. The headman was prepared to ignore him, but the child persisted. There was a whispered exchange between them. Then Yussuf turned to Nadir, speaking rapidly.

"There is more," Nadir informed Kate and Efrem after listening again to the headman. "Something the boy—whose name I now have been told is Hamid—said Yussuf must tell us. He knows a bit of English, this Hamid. How he learned it I didn't ask. It is of no more matter than how the Sergeant Ware came to learn a bit of Dari. Enough that, when he first came to the camp, he and Hamid between them were able to communicate a little. This was before the sergeant went into a state where he was not able to speak again, you understand."

"What is this *something?*" Kate asked, a tiny flame of hope beginning to burn inside her again. "Is it about Sean?"

"Yussuf doesn't know, but it is possible. What the sergeant told young Hamid had to do with one other survivor. A soldier who was also injured but unable to walk. The sergeant carried him on his back down the mountain as far as his strength would permit. In the end he had to leave him, promising he would get help."

Kate's hope was burning brighter now. "Where is this other man now? The nomads did try to rescue him, didn't they?"

"Oh, yes. Yussuf and two of his men went up the mountain to the place the sergeant described to Hamid. A stunted fir that grew beside a fork in the path to the valley. They found no soldier there or anywhere nearby. Nothing."

"But he could have crawled off seeking shelter. A cave maybe."

Nadir shook his head. "There was no cave. Yussuf thinks the other soldier never existed. That, because of his fever, the sergeant was not making sense. Either that or Hamid didn't correctly understand him. Whatever the explanation, no one could question the sergeant again. When the nomads returned to the valley, he was unconscious and remained so to the end."

With a sense of renewed urgency, Kate turned to Efrem. "If we leave now, there's enough of the day left to get back to the mountains. Nadir, please ask the headman for specific directions to their winter camp in the valley and exactly where the mouth of the path they searched is located."

To her frustration, Efrem had a different order for the guide. An almost casual one. "Nadir, ask the headman if someone will be good enough to take me to Sergeant Ware's grave."

Hamid, dancing now from foot to foot, understood his request before Nadir could relate it to the headman. "Come, come," he beckoned to Efrem.

The boy took off at an eager trot. Slipping the dog tags into a pocket of his jacket, Efrem strode after him. For a moment

Kate was too dismayed to act. Then, driven by a tight-lipped determination, she swiftly followed them through the tough, scant grasses waving in the wind that blew over the open plain.

By the time she caught up with them at the grave, which was mounded with rocks, probably to prevent wild animals from digging up the body, Efrem was jotting something in the small notebook he carried.

"What are you doing?" she cried.

"Describing the site of the grave for the recovery team," he said mildly without looking up from the notebook. "Ware's remains will need to be returned to Kabul for shipment home."

"But that can wait. We have to find the other survivor."

Closing the notebook, he returned it to his pocket. When he lifted his head to gaze at her across the grave, his face was grim. "Because you just know he was Sean Secrist. Right?"

"Of course, I don't know that for certain. But as long as there's any chance—"

"Of what? Finding him still alive? Providing another survivor ever existed and wasn't just some product of Ware's delirium. And even if he was a reality, it doesn't mean he was your son. There were other members of that team, Kate."

"Why do you keep using the past tense like that?" she challenged him, anger beginning to surge through her.

"Because it's been weeks since the crash. You heard what Ware was supposed to have told the kid here. That this other guy was in worse shape than he was and had to be carried out of there. It was still winter then with all that cold and snow on the mountain when Ware had to leave him behind. What are the odds of someone badly injured, unable to walk, staying alive in those conditions?"

"You don't have to tell me that. I know the odds. I also know people are capable of incredible things when they're facing death."

"A miracle, huh? Well, not this time. It just isn't in the cards. Kate, give it up. We've exhausted all the possibilities. You'll only be letting yourself in for some serious heartache if you try to go on."

Although she was aware of an alert Hamid listening to them from the foot of the grave, his gaze traveling from Efrem's face to hers and back again, his puzzled expression told her his English wasn't good enough to comprehend their conversation. She could say what had to be said, and she did.

"I let myself go and forget what was there from the start, didn't I? How you thought the whole thing was a madness. How you had no faith in my need to recover Sean, which was the same as saying you had no faith in me. And that hasn't changed. You still don't."

Kate was no longer undecided about them. However much it tore at her soul, this settled it. "You can think like that, and at the same time you want us to be together." She shook her head. "I don't know, Efrem. Maybe you do love me, but there's no way I can build a life with you."

She had deeply hurt him. She could see it in his eyes. Well, she was hurting, too. But there was one last thing she had to make him understand before she turned and left him here.

"This may be the end of the line for you where finding my son is concerned. But not me, Efrem. Not me."

What else could he do? Even if he'd refused to let her have Nadir and the jeep, she would have found a way to go up that blasted mountain. On her own, if she had to. He couldn't let her do that. Not and live with himself afterwards, even if nothing did happen to her.

She was in his blood, a part of him, and Efrem damned her obstinacy.

Of course, she objected. Didn't want him to accompany her,

not when he was so pessimistic about continuing the search. But he insisted, and in the end she accepted the wisdom of having both his experience and his protection. That hard-headed she wasn't.

They spent the night in sight of the mountains at a centuries-old caravansary that was still in use. Efrem didn't sleep much on his lonely pallet.

He kept hearing the tone of finality in Kate's voice there at the grave. Knew that, ass that he was, he had gone and thrown away his last chance with her. When this search was over and done with, she would leave Afghanistan and he would never see her again. And all because he wouldn't believe her son might still be alive, which by her definition was his failure to believe in her.

Well, why not, Colonel? If the situation were reversed, if it were your Nell out there, wouldn't you move heaven and earth to find her, even if all the evidence said she'd perished?

Absolutely. He'd gone and forgotten where the heart is involved, logic doesn't play a role. It was a lapse that had cost him the woman he loved. He would have to live with that unbearable loss for the rest of his life.

At first light they set off in the jeep, traveling to the valley where the nomads had spent the winter. Kate was nothing but polite to him, but Efrem could detect a faint chill in her voice whenever she found it necessary to address him. It didn't do much for his spirit. Nor did the sight of the valley when they reached it.

He could see why the nomads had camped here. It was spacious enough to feed their goats and sheep, and it was sheltered against the worst of the winter winds by high, sheer cliffs on three sides. But those cliffs also cut off the light, making it a somber place.

At the far end of the level valley, about a mile or so away, he could make out a number of gorges that sliced through the heart of the sandstone cliff. A maze of deep canyons that could ideally conceal an opium refinery, providing there was one somewhere in there and that its operators had been responsible for bringing the helicopter down. The nomads had certainly not mentioned the existence of one, which meant nothing since they were people who minded no one's business but their own.

At the moment, however, it was this end of the valley that claimed Efrem's attention. Obeying the headman's directions, he drove the jeep across the grassland to the mouth of the path that ascended the mountain looming over them.

The mouth was wide enough to accommodate the jeep, but after a few hundred feet it narrowed, becoming impassable when they were blocked by boulders that had tumbled from the mountain.

"We'll have to leave the jeep here," Efrem indicated.

Nadir was uncharacteristically quiet as they picked their way around the boulders and across a rocky hollow to the trail on the other side. Maybe he didn't like this place either, Efrem thought. Kate was also silent, probably saving her breath for the climb.

She would need it, Efrem decided. All three of them would. Because, as arduous as their earlier climb to the crash site had been on the opposite side of the mountain, that ascent had been gentle compared to this forbidding terrain. The path, only a thread in places, was steep and rugged, made worse by a powerful wind that punished them at every step, threatening to blow them off the side of the mountain.

How an injured man could possibly survive this brutal mountain was something Efrem was careful this time not to talk about. But his mind couldn't silence a question that troubled him. If there was another survivor, why hadn't the search and rescue team that had swept the area discovered either him or his body?

He had no answer for that. Nor did he have any observation for either Kate or Nadir when they finally reached the stunted fir. They could see the obvious for themselves as they stood there listening to the howl of the wind. There was nothing here.

Just as Yussuf had told them, the trail divided at this point. The branch to their right went off around the side of the mountain. Efrem presumed that somewhere along its length was the ledge where the chopper had crashed. The path offered the only possibility of finding something that might have been overlooked.

The other branch, which wound toward the top of the mountain, could be dismissed. That's how Efrem saw it, anyway. Kate did not. Without a word, she headed up the path.

"Kate, what are you doing?" he shouted after her. "It's useless to go that way. Any survivor would have gone down, not up."

Paying no attention to him, she rounded a shoulder of rock and vanished from sight. Damn the woman! Fuming, Efrem started after her, with Nadir trotting behind him.

When they rounded the shoulder themselves, Efrem halted so suddenly that Nadir bumped up against him, squealing a startled, "Oh, cripes!"

And with good reason, Efrem thought. Because what confronted them was not an encouraging sight. Just beyond an astonished Kate was a towering, skeletal figure in a baggy robe whipping in the wind. Efrem told himself it was probably the black turban and his piercing gaze that made the Afghan so sinister looking. On the other hand, it could be the Kalashnikov rifle cradled in his arms.

Efrem acted swiftly, putting himself between Kate and the Afghan. His hand rested on the pocket where he carried his Beretta, but he didn't attempt to withdraw the pistol. Unless it became necessary, he knew better than to make any threatening movement.

"*Salaam aleikum,*" he greeted the Afghan.

Efrem received a brief nod, which apparently was as friendly as the guy was prepared to get. He turned his head to call for their guide.

"Nadir, come up here and ask him who he is and what he's doing on the mountain."

A less than willing Nadir stepped forward and began to nervously question the stolid stranger, who listened with his head bowed. Efrem changed his mind about the man when he answered the guide. There was a solemn dignity in his deep voice.

Looking perplexed, Nadir turned to Kate and Efrem. "His name is Kushal. He is hunting for ibex. Sometimes he is lucky enough to shoot one that will put a bit of meat in the rice pots of his village. The village is not far from here along this path."

Efrem was astounded. "A village up here on the mountain?"

"Yes, it is strange. Not at all to be expected. But there is something more strange. When I told Kushal why we are here, he said they knew that someone would eventually come. They have been waiting for us."

Kate, who had been silent until now, uttered a little cry that seemed to Efrem to be a release of every taut emotion that had driven her since her arrival in Afghanistan.

"Ask him to explain," Efrem urged the guide.

There was another quick exchange that Nadir translated for them. "Kushal said he and his brother found an injured soldier in the snow by the fir. They carried him to their village where they have been caring for him all this time."

"His name," Kate asked. "Did Kushal tell you his name?"

Nadir shook his head. "He pretends not to know it, but I

think it is because he does not fully trust us yet. However, he is ready to take us to his village, and if the soldier is willing, we will be permitted to take him away with us."

Kushal set off along the path with Nadir beside him and Kate and Efrem bringing up the rear. As they climbed through the rocks, the guide and Kushal spoke again.

"He and his people have had a bad time of it," Nadir said, falling back to explain it to Kate and Efrem. "It has left them suspicious of outsiders. They were not always on the mountain. Their village was below, but when the Taliban destroyed it, they had to find new homes. They wanted them isolated enough they would not be bothered again."

Efrem was still puzzled by the choice of such a rigorous location. "A top of a mountain is isolated all right, but it just doesn't make sense."

"True," Nadir agreed, "and I said as much to Kushal. He assured me we would understand when we reached the village."

Efrem figured they must have climbed another quarter of a mile when the path suddenly dropped, taking them around another shoulder of rock to an overlook. He found himself gazing down into a deep, natural cleft in the mountain. The cleft was narrow, no more than a hundred feet or so in width and perhaps three or four times that in length.

It was amazing! He could see people down there, moving in and out of doorways hacked through the sandstone along the sheer faces of the cleft. The place was honeycombed with such doorways, as well as windows at different levels.

Kushal told Nadir about the village as they stood there on the overlook. Once again, Nadir passed the knowledge on to Kate and Efrem.

"His people did not have to create their new village. It was already here waiting for them. Many centuries ago, before the Islamic faith came to Afghanistan, this was a Buddhist community. The Buddhist monks carved cells for themselves in the rock, which are now the homes of the village."

The path seemed to sink into the mountain itself as Kushal led them down a series of slopes and steps to the floor of the cleft. They left the sharp wind behind them, moving into a stillness almost as mild as the valley below. Efrem realized this sheltered place would not be easily visible from any aircraft overhead. No wonder the search and rescue choppers had missed it.

Without pause or explanation to any of the villagers who regarded them curiously, Kushal led them directly through one of the doorways, not into any cave-like affair but an actual room hollowed out of the sandstone. It was occupied by a woman wearing a pillbox hat fastened with a bright scarf over her hair. Seated at an upright loom weaving a carpet that would be sold at one of the markets, she glanced at them silently when they entered, then returned to her work.

Efrem could sense Kate's anticipation as they approached a pallet in one of the shadowy corners and looked down at the figure lying there. Efrem had seen the photograph she carried so often that, even under several weeks' growth of beard and what remained of the soldier's soiled and tattered uniform, he could recognize him.

Kate had gotten her miracle.

Finding Sean was all that had mattered. Kate hadn't thought beyond that, hadn't planned what she would say to him when that moment arrived. Now all she could do was stand here, speechless and with tears threatening to sting her eyes, gazing at the young man who stared up at them with both hope and bewilderment in his blue eyes. *Her* eyes.

Whatever all his earlier objections, Efrem himself was at no loss for either action or words. Hunkering down at the side of the pallet, he briskly addressed her son.

"I don't suppose you know who I am, Corporal."

"I do, sir," Sean managed to answer him in a raspy voice. "Everyone at the base knows who you are. You're Colonel Chaudoir."

"That's right. Now, none of that," Efrem ordered, lowering Sean's hand when he tried to salute him. "How are you doing, soldier?"

"I've been better, sir. How did you—"

"We'll save any explanations for later. You're going home, son, but right now we're going to see what we can do about getting you out of here."

Efrem got to his feet, his satellite phone already in his hand. "I may have to go up on the rim to get a signal," he told Kate. Lowering his voice, he added a soft, "Talk to him."

He was right. Although this was certainly no time to tell Sean she was his birth mother, she needed to at least introduce herself. After Efrem and Nadir left the room, she knelt beside the pallet, keeping her emotions in check as she spoke to her son.

"I imagine Colonel Chaudoir has gone to phone your base, probably to arrange for a helicopter to carry you back to Kabul and a hospital."

Sean was plainly awed by Efrem's presence. "Ma'am, what's a colonel doing here?"

"He's a friend who's been helping me to search for you. And it's *Kate*. Kate Groen. I'm a reporter for the *Washington View*, Sean. I promised your parents before I came to Afghanistan I would do my best to find and recover you."

"You know my mom and dad?"

"I met with them, yes."

"They okay?"

If Sean didn't already know about his mother's cancer, it

wasn't her place to tell him. "They're worried about you. Me, too. You were pretty banged up in the crash, weren't you?"

"Yeah, but I was lucky enough to get out of it still alive. The other guys . . ."

He didn't go on. She could see by the anguished look in his eyes this was something he couldn't bring himself to talk about. She was afraid, though, he would ask her about Sergeant Ware, and she would have to tell him the sergeant had died. Kate was glad when he didn't mention him. This was also something for later.

Just now all she wanted to do was gaze at her son, reassure herself he was going to be all right. There were shallow lacerations on his face, probably from flying glass when the chopper went down, but they seemed to be healing.

There was also a fringe of unruly hair pasted to his forehead. It had nothing to do with his condition, but Kate found herself longing to gently smooth it back from his brow. A maternal urge, she supposed. She resisted the impulse. Sean wouldn't have understood it.

"I was told you have a broken leg. Would you mind if I . . ."

"Sure."

A rough blanket covered him to his waist. She carefully peeled it back to expose his injury. The leg of his trousers had been cut away, a rudimentary splint attached to the break. The flesh above and below the splint was swollen.

"They did their best for me," he said, "but I don't know."

He's worried he might never walk again, Kate thought. It was a legitimate concern. "What else?" she asked, eyeing the dressing on his upper arm where the sleeve, too, had been cut away at the shoulder.

"This," he said, indicating the dressing with a nod. "It's a pretty nasty gash. Hurts like hell. I saw it when they changed it. It's all raw and red. I think it's infected."

Kate wasn't surprised. The dressing looked none too clean. She couldn't blame the good people who were caring for him. Water had to be scarce up here, probably melted snow in the winter and in other seasons whatever rain they were able to collect.

"Are you running a fever?"

"Maybe a low one. I got pretty cold out there in the snow and cold before they discovered me."

Kate thought it was more likely his fever was a result of the infection. "Well, medical treatment at a hospital will have you feeling just fine again," she assured him, making a concentrated effort to believe it herself.

"Ma'am?"

"Kate," she corrected him. "What is it?"

"I just want to thank you for finding me," he said, his voice still raspy, as though speech were difficult for him. "Both you and the colonel."

"We wouldn't have had it any other way, Sean. You try to rest now."

Getting to her feet, she smiled at the woman at her loom, wondering if she was Kushal's wife. The woman smiled back at her shyly, pointing to the open doorway where Efrem, accompanied by Nadir and Kushal, was just returning along the path. Kate went outside to meet him.

"I've got a chopper coming to collect us," he reported. "There's no chance of Sean's being airlifted out of here, not with the overhang of these cliffs or the velocity of the wind on the mountain. They're going to meet us back at the jeep."

She was glad a helicopter wouldn't be violating the sanctity of this peaceful place. She was also concerned. "How are we going to carry him down to the valley?"

"We'll have to devise a stretcher."

There was no question of it, Kate thought, watching Efrem

in action. In a situation that required it, he became the take-charge, impressive figure of authority his high rank demanded.

Asking through Nadir for a strong blanket, rope and two stout poles, he somehow got all his requests without delay. Then, assisting Nadir and Kushal, he showed them how to lash the poles tightly to the blanket, producing a primitive but serviceable stretcher.

While Efrem and Nadir carefully transferred Sean from the pallet to the stretcher, making certain he was secure and warmly covered for the trip down the mountain, Kate drew Kushal aside. Taking the last of the afghanis from her bag, she placed them in Kushal's hand.

These people were very poor. It must have been a sacrifice for them to share their precious food with Sean, yet they hadn't hesitated to rescue and care for him. The money was a demonstration, a small one at that, of her gratitude.

Kate hoped she wasn't insulting Kushal's hospitality. He tried to give the afghanis back to her, but she squeezed his fingers over them, managing to make him understand she would be pleased if he would accept them. He did finally with a grave *"Zinde bashi."*

Both Kushal and his brother insisted on guiding them as far as the stunted fir where Sean, reaching up from his stretcher, clasped their hands, expressing his own thanks to his saviors. The brothers parted from them here, returning to their village.

The haul down the mountain, with Efrem and Nadir bearing the stretcher and Kate leading the way, was a strenuous business, especially on the steepest slopes where care had to be taken not to spill Sean from the stretcher.

One thing was in their favor. The wind was beginning to ease, and by the time they reached the rocky hollow at the foot of the mountain, there was a blessed stillness. The jeep was nearby, just on the other side of the massive boulders at the mouth of the trail, but Nadir pleaded for a brief rest.

"Please, may we not lower the stretcher for a moment before we cross those boulders?"

Before Efrem could answer him, there was a loud whoosh from somewhere on the other side of the boulders. Startled, Kate was at a loss to identify the fearful sound. Efrem wasn't.

"RPG!" he yelled. "Down! Everyone down!"

A nervous Nadir, literally obeying the command, dropped his end of the stretcher, his action pitching Sean onto the scattered rocks. Before he could be recovered, the hollow was rocked by a deafening blast that kicked up a cloud of dust. When it cleared, Kate found herself hugging the ground, unable to explain to herself whether she or the explosion itself had flung her there.

Nadir was also flattened on the ground beside her. "I am shaking," he whimpered. "Is it an earthquake?"

Efrem, on his stomach behind them, translated his shouted RPG with a grim "It was a rocket propelled grenade."

"Oh, cripes!"

Who? Kate wondered. Why?

"Anyone hurt?" Efrem asked.

She lifted her head and looked around. *Sean.* He was still lying there where he had landed, his head twisted to one side. And groaning softly in pain.

Kate went to him, wriggling her way across the gravel. Efrem reached him first.

"Were you hit, soldier?"

"Not by the grenade, sir. I struck one of the rocks when I went down. It's my neck now. I think something is wrong. It hurts like the devil."

"What are you doing?" Kate asked Efrem as he positioned himself behind Sean, his legs stretched out on either side of her son's body, his hands on both sides of his head.

"Something I saw performed in combat by a medic," he said, bracing himself as he gently drew Sean's head toward him and held it there. "If I don't provide traction until that chopper gets here with a collar . . ."

He didn't have to finish. Kate understood him. Without traction, Sean could end up being paralyzed by his neck injury.

"Sir, are we under attack?"

"Keep still, Corporal. Yeah, looks like somebody has ambushed us. Kate, Nadir," he called to them with the confident, efficient voice of a colonel under fire in the field, "I'm gonna need both of you, and you're going to have to act fast before whoever is out there starts swarming over those boulders. Kate, get the Beretta out of my pocket."

Crouching low, she rounded Sean's body and started to reach for the pocket in Efrem's leather jacket.

"No, not that one. The other side. And take the extra clip, too." Leaning over, she withdrew the pistol and the clip. "Give them to Nadir. Nadir, I don't want to hear any more cripes out of you. I know you know how to shoot a gun. Just get over there with the Beretta behind those boulders."

"Colonel, I am a miserable shot."

"You don't have to hit anyone, man. Just be prepared to return fire. If they know we have a weapon, they won't be eager to try and rush us. And, all of you, keep your heads down."

Clutching the Beretta and the clip, Kate took them to Nadir. The trembling guide accepted them, reluctantly crawling over to the boulders that screened them. Kate went back to Efrem and Sean.

"Who is it?" she wanted to know. "Who could it be that has us trapped here?"

Sean answered the question for her. "Maybe the same guys who shot my chopper down."

"Don't talk," Efrem cautioned him. "Yes, it could be the

same people. And if it is a nearby opium operation they're protecting, you can bet that as soon as I get back to the base, I'm going to order a thorough search of those gorges across the valley out there. If there is an operation, it needs to be cleaned out."

Kate was conscious of the strained, uneasy silence now. There had been no further sound or sight of aggression since the launch of the grenade. Perhaps the foe had retreated from the scene.

The hope had barely registered in her mind when there was a hail of bullets from the other side of the boulders, none of which were capable of striking them as long as they kept low in the hollow. Still, it was a terrifying assault. Nadir must have thought so. He yelped with surprise before answering with the Beretta, his aim a wild one since he plainly had no intention of peeking over the boulders. Kate didn't blame him.

Efrem addressed her with a new urgency. "Our rescue Chinook needs to be warned about what's happening down here. Get my satellite phone for me, will you? It's programmed for a fast contact with the base. It's in my upper pocket. I'll tell you what number to punch."

"Efrem, let me take over with Sean. You can make the call yourself."

"No, we can't risk that, not with your carpal tunnel. You might not be able to maintain a steady grip if your wrists start acting up."

He was right. She slid the phone out of his pocket, checked the signal, then dialed the number he gave her. "It's ringing."

"Hold the phone to my ear," he instructed her.

She listened to him as, seconds later, he identified himself, reporting their position and that they were pinned down by an unknown enemy. All the while she could hear Nadir muttering rapidly on the other side of the hollow in what sounded like

Dari. Although she couldn't understand him, she had an idea he might be praying.

Efrem ended the call, telling her, "That was the base. They're relaying my message to the Chinook."

"It will be armed even if it is a medical helicopter, won't it?"

"None of our choppers go out without fire power."

Kate had lowered the phone, but she went on clenching it in her hand. There was spasmodic gunfire from the other side of the boulders as the long minutes passed. She worried their attackers might close in on them before the rescue Chinook arrived. If that happened, there would be no way for Nadir to hold them off with the Beretta.

She also worried about Efrem. His hands and arms must be numb by now, but he never faltered in his sustained support of Sean's head. It was only when she suddenly became aware of something else that she had cause for genuine alarm.

Blood. There was blood oozing from a small tear in his trousers in the upper area of his thigh.

"Efrem, you've been hit!"

"Not by a bullet. Must have been a piece of shrapnel from the grenade."

"Why didn't you tell me?"

"Relax. It isn't serious. They'll dress it for me on the chopper."

Relax? How could she? Where was that helicopter? Why didn't it get here?

It seemed like a light year later when she finally heard the beat of the twin bladed Chinook overheard, watched it as it descended to the valley. She could see the figure of a gunner stationed in the open doorway at the side. That he wasn't returning any fire was an indication their attackers must have fled at the sight of the heavily armed craft.

The helicopter sank out of sight. There was silence then. A

few blessed moments later two uniformed medics, accompanied by a pair of armed escorts, appeared. They carried bags and a stretcher as they clambered over the boulders.

With the swift skill that was the result of rigorous training and experience, the medics assumed responsibility for Sean, fitting a traction collar on him, loading him on the stretcher. Kate followed the stretcher, Nadir joining her, as Sean was borne toward the waiting helicopter.

It was only when they reached the boulders she realized Efrem wasn't with them. She stopped and looked back. He was still there behind them, collapsed and unconscious on the rocks.

CHAPTER NINETEEN

She was a handsome woman, tall and stately. Kate couldn't help thinking the green hospital scrubs she wore made a curious contrast with the shawl that covered her hair. Although her dark, prominent features were strongly Afghan in looks, her accent was pure American.

"I'm Dr. Samira Karzai," she introduced herself as Kate rose from her chair in the waiting room to shake the slim hand extended toward her. "Colonel Chaudoir is in my care."

Dr. Karzai must have noticed the surprised expression on Kate's face. Her intelligent, black eyes wore a look of amused understanding.

"I know. Afghan female doctors treat only female patients. It's true I am Afghan by descent, but I'm American by birth and training, which is why the Muslims tolerate me. They also badly need surgeons, and that's why I'm here in Kabul."

"I'm sorry," Kate apologized. "You must be weary of explaining this to everyone. How is Colonel Chaudoir?"

"Yes, he said you would want to know. Let's sit down."

When they had settled themselves on side by side chairs in the waiting room that was empty except for the two of them, Kate leaned toward her, anxious for her report.

"Here's what we have," Dr. Karzai explained. "The X-rays show us the fragment of shrapnel is lodged up against the femoral artery leading to his left leg."

"That's not good, is it?"

"No, it's not. He hasn't lost much blood from the entry wound, but the shrapnel is sharp and if it should shift, which it's in danger of doing, then it will rupture the artery and cause massive bleeding. And if that happens . . ."

"He could die." There was no emotion in Kate's voice, but inside she was seething with fear.

"We're going to prevent that. I'm going to operate. The shrapnel has to be removed."

"How delicate a procedure is that?"

"There's some risk."

"Meaning he could hemorrhage on the table."

"I'm a very good surgeon, Ms. Groen."

Kate had already sensed that, but however confident Dr. Karzai was, the risk was still there. Efrem might not survive.

"Look, the stress he suffered before he got here didn't help, but this is a man who's in good condition. That's very much in his favor."

"Can I see him?"

"No." Dr. Karzai got to her feet. "He's being prepped for the OR, which is where I should be right now. Try not to worry."

Not worry? Kate thought when she was alone again. That wasn't possible. Not remotely.

Perhaps she shouldn't have sent Nadir home to his family. They could have worried together. But the poor man had been in such a nervous state Kate felt she couldn't have endured his company.

The notes for her *View* story were in her bag. She could be using this time to compose the story. No, bad idea. She'd never manage to concentrate on it. It would be useless to even try. Besides, there was something else she needed and wanted to do.

Sean. They should be finished with him by now. Leaving the waiting room, she went to the far end of the long corridor where her son had been taken. Having already spoken to the doctor who had been summoned to treat him, and been promised Sean wasn't in a life-threatening state, Kate was less worried about him than Efrem. Still, she would like to know his current condition as well as visit him, if they would let her.

The army doctor Efrem had insisted on before they had wheeled him away was just coming out of Sean's room when Kate arrived. They spoke together in the corridor.

A balding, genial man, he had nothing but cheerful assurances for her. "Considering everything Corporal Secrist's been through, he's in fine shape. The broken leg has been set, and he's on antibiotics for the infection in his arm. The fever is already on the way down. Being young and strong, he should make a full recovery. Of course, it could have been a different story where his neck is concerned if it hadn't been for the quick action of Colonel Chaudoir."

Efrem's fiercely sustained attention to Sean when he, himself, had been wounded was the stuff of heroes. Something Kate would never forget. Something for which she would always be grateful.

"Can I look in on the patient?"

"I think he would be glad to have a visitor."

Thanking the doctor, she went on into the room. She found Sean partially elevated on the hospital bed, wearing a traction collar, hooked up to an IV drip and his leg encased in a cast. A big grin spread across his face when he saw her, a boyish grin that triggered a maternal lump in her throat.

Swallowing the lump, she managed to greet him with a casual "You look in good spirits."

"Yeah, I'm cool. Or would be if I wasn't thinking about the colonel. How's he doing?"

"He's in surgery. They're removing the shrapnel." She didn't want to worry Sean by telling him how serious Efrem's situation was.

Parking herself in a chair beside the bed, she diverted him with a quick "They've given me permission to contact your parents with the good news you're alive and have been recovered. I haven't done that yet. I wanted to be sure you were going to be all right. Besides, I think they'd like to hear it from you. Would you like me to make the call?"

"Could you? That would be great."

Kate slid her satellite phone out of her bag. Sean eagerly gave her the number without waiting for her to find it in her notebook. While she dialed, then waited for the connection, she remembered it would be the middle of the night in Chicago. Receiving a call at that hour would probably alarm the Secrists, but they would forgive her when they heard their son's voice.

It was Sean's father who answered with a slurred "Hello," his voice hesitant and with the rasp of someone who has been awakened from a deep sleep.

"Mr. Secrist, this is Kate Groen in Afghanistan. Can your wife share the phone with you? There's someone here who is very eager to speak to you both."

She passed the phone to Sean.

"Mom, Dad, it's me."

The cries of shock and joy on the other end were so loud Kate could hear them. She got to her feet, knowing she wasn't the mother Sean wanted to talk to. This should be a private moment between him and the only parents he had ever known. Her time would have to wait.

Anyway, Kate tried to tell herself when she came away from Sean's room, how could she miss what she had never had? This was how it was supposed to work, but the truth was that leaving those three happy voices behind gave her a lonely feeling of being left out of something vital.

It was a pang that lasted only briefly. Efrem was too much in her thoughts to dwell on anything else.

She went back to the little waiting room to keep her vigil. It was a dreary place, with drab walls in need of painting and the lingering smell of tobacco in the air. Unlike American hospitals, this one apparently had no rule about smoking.

Sitting there on a lumpy chair, Kate realized she'd given herself almost no time to think or feel since leaving the nomad's camp. Her entire focus had been on finding Sean and bringing him back to Kabul. Now all she had was time. Time to examine her emotions about Efrem. They poured into her mind and heart, those seething emotions.

She remembered what Sean's doctor had said about Efrem's quick action preventing Sean's paralysis. It was true. That and so much more. Because whatever Efrem's resistance to their search, in the end, when it had counted, he had known what to do and had done it, including risking himself to save her son.

How could she have failed to realize that, although Efrem might have changed, the fundamental, decent core of him was still there under a skin of cynicism, making him as protective and caring as ever? Those were the values that really mattered.

As for the other, his bitterness . . . well, maybe she was as much to blame for that as he was. She had shut him out, both in Kosovo and here in Afghanistan.

He loves you. All he asks is to share his life with you, to cherish you. No woman can ask for more than that.

Except . . . yes, to know an equal love for him.

It struck her forcefully then. How much she still loved him in return, deeply and fervently. Always had and always would, whatever her earlier misgivings. Anything else could be worked out, if—

If he survives.

Dear God, why had it taken this, his life in the balance, to make her understand just how essential Efrem Chaudoir was to

271

her? If she lost him now, it would leave an unbearable emptiness from which she would never recover.

Hands clenched in her lap, she was so busy praying she wasn't aware of Dr. Karzai's arrival in the room. When the woman cleared her throat to gain her attention, Kate looked up, unable to voice the question that must have been apparent in her pleading gaze.

Dr. Karzai smiled and nodded. "He made it. He's going to be all right."

Kate sagged with a vast relief. "Can I see him?"

"You can, but you won't be able to speak to him yet. We did wake him briefly in the OR, but he's been medicated for pain and is sleeping now in recovery."

"I just want to be with him."

"Come on. I'll take you there."

Dr. Karzai led her down the hall to the recovery room. Before they parted, Kate took her hand and squeezed it with a simple but heartfelt "Thank you for saving him."

Kate slipped into the room and stood at the foot of the gurney where Efrem lay. Except that he was on an IV drip and in an unconscious state, he looked as fit as ever, his face neither ashen nor drawn. Whatever dressings had been required for the entry wound and the surgery were concealed under the sheet that covered him.

Pulling up a chair, she seated herself at the side of the gurney. It didn't matter that Efrem never stirred as the minutes passed. All she asked was to gaze at him, watch him breathe and know with a deep gratitude he was going to recover.

Even in sleep, he was a compelling figure. Always would be, right into old age. The feelings she had for this man, and which she had finally recognized as the kind of love that would never leave her, swelled inside, making her understand how lucky they were to have found each other. And how glad she was to have come to her senses.

The time that passed while she sat there with Efrem had no meaning for her. It could have been as much as an hour, maybe even more before she became aware they were no longer alone in the room.

He stood just inside the door, a compact figure probably somewhere in his mid fifties and with the kind of face decades of combat had seasoned. The silver star on the shoulders of his uniform identified him as a brigadier general. She didn't need to guess which brigadier general, but he told her anyway in a crisp voice that was anything but gentle.

"Carl Boynton. And you'd be Kate Groen, I suppose."

She got to her feet as he moved to the foot of the gurney to examine the inert officer under his command.

"How's our boy doing?"

"He's going to be all right," Kate told him.

The brigadier general grunted his satisfaction. "Damn fool, almost getting himself killed on us. He's too good a soldier to lose."

Before Kate could respond, Dr. Karzai joined them. "Time to check on my patient before I move him to a room with a bed."

She asked them to wait outside. Boynton and Kate left the recovery room to stroll side by side down the corridor. She could feel him looking at her critically.

"I haven't been very happy with you, Ms. Groen," he informed her gruffly. "Taking away my colonel like that."

"But you let him go."

"No choice. He would have gone AWOL."

Moved by his admission, Kate stopped and turned to gaze at him in wonder.

"No, I'm not exaggerating. He was prepared to risk everything, including his career, in order to be with you on the search. Well, I had to meet the woman who was that important to him."

"And?"

He nodded curtly. "I guess I can see why."

"Is that a compliment?"

He snorted. "It is, if you'll promise not to take Efrem Chaudoir on any more rescue missions."

"But it *was* a successful one."

"Yes, you and my colonel did find Corporal Secrist for us. On behalf of myself and the U.S. Army, I thank you for that."

Kate knew it was as much of an apology as she was going to get for his refusal to order another search. She was satisfied with it.

The brigadier general glanced at his watch. "Tell Efrem when he's awake I'll look in on him again." He started briskly along the corridor, then paused to look back over his shoulder. "Take good care of him, Kate Groen."

"I intend to do just that," she called after him.

When she turned to go back to recovery, an orderly accompanied by Dr. Karzai was wheeling the gurney to a room across the hall. Kate waited outside, giving them a chance to settle Efrem in a bed.

A few minutes later, the doctor joined her in the corridor. "He's awake now and impatient to have you with him. Less than two hours out of surgery, and he's already getting feisty on us. I've noticed that colonels are especially bad about that."

The doctor chuckled and went off on her rounds, the orderly following her. Kate entered the room to find Efrem with his head lifted from the pillow and watching the door. When she appeared, his gaze eagerly followed her to the chair at the side of the bed, where she seated herself.

"I've been told you aren't behaving yourself," she said, leaning toward him.

"When do I get out of here?" His voice was hoarse, probably a result of the anesthetic.

"See, the doctor was right. How are you feeling?"

"Like I don't want you to fuss. How is Sean?"

"In a better mood than you are. When I left him, he was on the phone with his parents."

Efrem relaxed, dropping his head back on the pillow. "That's good. He'll recover then?"

"He'll recover."

He was silent for a few seconds, his gaze never leaving her face. "Kate," he said earnestly, "I'm sorry about Sean. I mean about forever telling you there was no chance he could still be alive."

"You're forgiven. After all, you saved him from paralysis."

"I guess." He hastily changed the subject. "So, where's Nadir?"

"I sent him home to see his family. He'll be back to visit you. You did have another visitor already, though. Brigadier General Boynton."

"I suppose the old man is royally pissed off with me, huh?"

"Maybe a little, but only because he values you, Efrem. Is your throat sore from the anesthetic? It sounds like it is."

"I just need some water."

Water had been left on the table beside his bed, so she assumed it was all right for him to have it. She helped ease him up on the bed and drink from the glass.

"Maybe you shouldn't be trying to talk."

He handed the glass back to her. She could see by the way his eyes searched hers he had no intention of obeying her suggestion, that their exchange so far wasn't what he wanted to talk about. He had been waiting for something else, and he could bear to wait no more.

275

"I suppose you'll be going home now that you got what you came for."

He was trying to be casual about it, but she didn't buy it. His tone was too forced, too anxious beneath his nonchalant observation. Suddenly impatient with his performance, he rushed on before she could respond.

"Kate," he implored reaching for her hand, clasping it in his own big one, "don't leave me. Not this time. I couldn't take it. I know you don't like the man I've become, but with you beside me I can change. I can become the mellow guy you once loved." His other hand thumped the area of his heart. "He's still here somewhere inside me, and together we can find him again."

He gave her no opening for a reply, as if determined to prevent something he couldn't stand to hear. His words became even more rapid and intense, his fingers tightening around hers.

"Look, I'll get out of the army, start carving all those little animals I used to talk about. That'll soften me. That, and a chance to show you how much I love you. Please, Kate, give me that chance, and I promise you'll never regret it."

"Don't be ridiculous. We both know you were born to be a grunt. You couldn't stand sitting on a porch somewhere whittling hunks of wood, not for a long time anyway."

His hold on her hand loosened, his eyes wearing a look of anguish. "So where does that leave *us?*"

Kate released a massive, exaggerated sigh. "Since I can write anywhere, I guess I don't have a choice about it. I'll just have to learn to be a good camp follower."

"You saying . . . ?"

"Yeah, I'm saying it."

The torment in his gaze lightened, morphing into elation as he understood what she was telling him. "When I get out of this bed, Kate Groen, I'm going to *show* you how much I love you," he promised her, his voice husky with emotion. "Right now all I can do is tell you so. That and how beautiful you are."

"You've been telling me that for years."

"You don't like it?"

"Of course, I do. Every woman likes to be told she's beautiful, whether she is or not. But perfection can be pretty hard to live up to all the time. And if we're going to have a permanent relationship, Colonel, and I'm going to love you through your good moods, as well as your sour ones, then you've got to realize I have my own flaws, too, just like every woman."

"Not you. You're not talking about that little bump on your nose, are you? I love that bump."

"There are other flaws, plenty of them."

"Such as?"

"Well, this for one." Snatching her hand away from his, she swept her hair back from her ears with both hands. "See? Not perfection."

"What? All I see is a pair of sexy lobes."

"You're blind. My ears aren't the same size. One is smaller than the other. Why do you think I style my hair to cover them and never wear earrings that would just draw attention to them?"

He tipped his head from side to side, studying both ears in turn. "Sonofagun, the left ear *is* a little bigger than the other one. That mean you can hear better out of it?"

"You insensitive clown, you're supposed to be sympathetic about it." It was impossible for her not to laugh. It was good having the old, fun-loving Efrem back. She had missed him.

He caught her hand again, clinging to it. "Hey, don't worry about our flaws. We'll work on them."

"And what we can't change, we'll accept."

"Agreed."

"So, anything else, Colonel?"

"Yeah. You tell Sean yet you're his birth mother?"

Kate shook her head. "I've decided that can wait."

"You're right." He brought her hand to his mouth and kissed it lovingly. "It's our time."

Yes, she thought. They no longer had the need to make sacrifices for others. The future belonged to them now.

Epilogue

Present Day Alexandria, Virginia

Efrem understood her so well that he could read her every mood. Maybe not so surprising in a husband. A perceptive one, anyway. But he had been reading her from the very beginning all those years ago in Iraq.

Kate knew she would have to be very careful this morning not to reveal by either facial expression or inflection of voice the information she had sworn to withhold. It wouldn't be easy to keep such a promise, but it was imperative that Efrem not learn it. Not yet.

Kate reminded herself of the importance of this as she headed across the back lawn of their spacious, suburban house. Whatever the future held for them after today, for now it was good to be back home in Washington with Efrem posted again at the Pentagon.

What waited for her at the edge of their property was a run-down, vine-covered shack. Kate knew the neighbors didn't appreciate the structure, but Efrem wouldn't hear of it being pulled down. He had claimed, when he'd appropriated it for his workshop after they moved in, that it had character. Her response had been a flip "Well, it's certainly a character who wants to hang out in it. Just remember, you get to deal with all the neighborhood complaints."

Efrem's own reaction had been a grin. The same grin he wore now looking up from his workbench when she invaded the sanctity of the shack. That grin, along with the striking figure of the man who flashed it, never failed to tug at her heart.

"What do you think?" he asked her, proudly holding up his latest work-in-progress for her approval. Efrem had graduated from carving animals to building detailed ship models.

"As handsome as its creator, but not a very good advertisement for the U.S. Army."

"Yeah, but somehow tanks and armored vehicles aren't challenging enough."

"Never mind. You can join the Navy for your next career. But right now, Colonel, you need to get into the house, shower and change into something other than those ratty jeans."

"What's the hurry? They're not expected for hours."

"Uh-huh, but after you make yourself presentable you have a few little jobs to perform."

"I remember. Help you with lunch and the table."

"Good boy."

They strolled back to the house, Efrem's arm lovingly around her waist as he admired the flower borders. "Nice display," he complimented her. "Couldn't be a more perfect setting for a Saturday picnic on the deck."

Kate had never imagined she would have a talent for gardening. But then there were a lot of surprises married life had in one way or another brought her way, nearly all of them wonderful things she treasured every day.

Efrem stopped her when they reached the deck, gazing down at her thoughtfully. "For a happy family reunion, you look awfully pensive, Mrs. Chaudoir. Something bothering you?"

Just as she had feared, he was reading her again. She had her excuse ready. "There was an e-mail from Nadir. You can read it after you shower."

They had managed to stay in contact with most of their friends overseas. Nadir in Kabul, Jamil in Iraq, Halise in

Albania, and Leke in Kosovo. The news from them was sometimes pleasant and sometimes not so pleasant, but all of it was welcomed by the couple.

Efrem nodded soberly. "I know. Things over there in Afghanistan aren't good for them. But let's try to forget about that today."

Kate agreed, thankful that he hadn't penetrated her secret.

They were gathering all the chairs that would be needed around the long table when they heard the sound of a car in the drive. Leaving the deck, they hurried eagerly out front to greet the arrivals.

They were in time to spot their company, three adults and a baby-in-arms, piling out of a rental van that was loaded with luggage. Kate knew from a previous visit that when you traveled with an infant, even by plane, you needed a lot of gear. But it did seem to her there was more luggage than usual. The explanation for that came from her son, Sean.

"Look who we ran into at Dulles and saved from needing a cab." He jerked his thumb over his shoulder, then whipped around when no one appeared. "Hey, where are you?"

"Stuck here between two mountains of suitcases," came a muffled reply from the far back of the van. "Let me get untangled, and—Ah, made it."

A fourth adult popped out of the vehicle with a wide grin. The same grin as Efrem's. Kate never failed to be aware of how much the college age Nell resembled her father.

"I don't know why you didn't save the price of a rental and let me pick you all up at the airport," Efrem grumbled.

Sean snorted. "In that compact of yours? You've got to be kidding."

"I'll have you know it's got a very roomy trunk. And is that any way to speak to your senior officer, Corporal?"

Sean had left the army shortly after his tour of duty in Afghanistan, but he snapped to mock attention, saluting smartly. "No, sir. Sorry, sir."

"That's better."

Dissolving into laughter, the two men embraced, thumping each other on the back. The next few minutes in the driveway required a series of exchanged hugs all around, a noisy scene that commanded the attention of the neighbors on both sides.

Sean's father, Alan Secrist, was included. He was as much a member of Kate and Efrem's extended family as was Sean's petite wife, Lisa, and had been since the beginning of their annual reunions. Sadly, Marion Secrist was not among them. In the end, she had lost her battle with cancer.

Kate knew that Sean would always regard Marion as his mother. It didn't matter. He and Kate were close now, having bonded long ago after he'd learned she was his birth mother. That was all, and more, than she could have asked for.

"Here," Alan said, thrusting the baby in his arms toward Kate. "It's your turn to hold your granddaughter. I have a policy of surrendering her whenever a diaper needs changing."

Soiled diaper or not, Kate couldn't wait to get her hands on her granddaughter. Cradling the baby in her arms, she led the way into the house, the others trooping after her with their luggage.

A fresh diaper later, they collected around the table on the deck. They were in the midst of lunch, passing the baby from lap to lap, when the doorbell Kate had been expecting and listening for rang.

"Hey, we're all here, aren't we?" Nell asked. "So, who's missing, Dad?"

Efrem shrugged. "Beats me."

Kate rose from the table. "I'll get it."

Excusing herself, she left the deck and hurried through the

house to the front door. Carl Boynton stood on the step looking very regal in his dress uniform. Carl was a three-star general now and still Efrem's commanding officer at the Pentagon. He was also a good friend, although as gruff as ever.

The general wasted no time. "He ready for me?"

"I hope not."

"Well, let's get this over with," he grunted.

"Come on through. We're out back."

When Carl appeared on the deck with Kate, Efrem looked up from his plate of brats and potato salad with a puzzled expression on his face, both because of the general's arrival and his dress uniform.

"Carl, what's up?"

"Stand up, soldier. I'm here on official army business."

Efrem got slowly to his feet. The general's expression was so stern, his voice so serious that Efrem now looked a bit apprehensive. "What in the—"

"I told you this was official business, so just listen up. Efrem Chaudoir, I am stripping you of your rank. You are no longer a colonel in the U.S. Army."

There was a shocked, sober silence on both sides of the table. There had to be a bit of the ham in Carl, Kate decided, because he used that silence for the maximum dramatic effect, stretching the pause before he continued with a brisk, "As of now, soldier, you are Brigadier General Efrem Chaudoir. Congratulations."

The silence erupted into whoops of joy from every member of the family who crowded around a dazed Efrem.

Sean slapped him on the back. "Way to go!"

Sean's father pumped his hand. "Wonderful news!"

Nell kissed him on the cheek. "Awesome, Dad!"

Sean's wife kissed him on the other cheek. "Fantastic for sure!"

Beaming as she watched the scene, Kate was relieved. She felt she could relax now that she no longer had to fear she might betray the surprise.

Free at last of hugs and arm-punching, Efrem looked around, seeking her. She smiled at him across the table when their gazes met, then turned to Carl. "Excuse me. I think it's time I crowned my husband with a kiss of my own."

The family cheered and whistled when Efrem folded Kate into his arms, receiving, then returning his kiss, which on his part was for more ardent than any mere peck on the lips. And that, Kate thought, ought to really give the neighbors something to talk about.

"I'm proud of you, Brigadier General," she whispered in Efrem's ear before he released her.

Carl came around the table to shake Efrem's hand. "Don't let anyone tell you, boy, that you haven't earned and deserve this promotion."

"Join us, won't you, Carl?" Kate urged the general. "We'll have cake and coffee to celebrate."

The general shook his head. "Can't. As soon as I go home and change out of these duds, I've got a date with a set of golf clubs. But thanks for the invite. No, don't bother to show me out. I know the way." With a little wave for all of them, he started toward the door, then turned back to Efrem. "You'll get the formal letter of notification on your desk Monday morning. And, uh, you'd better start thinking about getting that star on your shoulders."

Efrem lay stretched out on his side of their bed, watching her as she got ready to join him for the night.

"You knew about this promotion ahead of time, didn't you?"

Kate paused in the act of lathering her arms with lotion to glance at him. "And what makes you think that?"

"The timing was just too perfect to be a coincidence. The family here, a picnic on the deck, a cake to celebrate. Come on, wife, I want the details."

"If you must know, I did learn about it ahead of time. Dara told me."

"Is that woman still leaking Pentagon info to you? One day she's going to get caught and fired."

"It isn't as though she's telling me the contents of top secret documents, which she doesn't have access to, anyway. You wait. You'll want Dara there when someday she hears you're going to be appointed to the Joint Chiefs of Staff."

"Huh, like that's ever going to happen. So, how did you manage to get Boynton roped into your little conspiracy?"

"With great difficulty. He wasn't pleased when I refused to tell him what little bird passed the news to me."

"I can imagine," Efrem said drily.

"It took a lot of persuading before I could get him to agree to give me forty-eight hours and no longer to put the whole thing together. He grumbled about it, but I think he was pleased that I wanted him here today to make the announcement."

"You are something, Kate Chaudoir. Hey, stop with the lotion already." He patted her side of the bed. "I want you in here with me. I plan for us to do a little private celebrating of our own."

"Are you forgetting there are people in the house?"

"So, maybe they can learn a few lessons from us."

"Efrem, you are a dirty old man."

"Yeah, he growled, a wicked gleam in his eyes as he held out his arms for her, "and you just love it."

"That I do, Brigadier General Chaudoir," she admitted softly, going into his waiting arms. "That I do."

ABOUT THE AUTHOR

Bob Rogers, writing as **Jean Barrett,** was a teacher before he left the classroom to write full-time. He is the author of twenty-three contemporary and historical romance novels for Kensington, Berkley, Dorchester and Harlequin-Silhouette. His books have been printed in numerous foreign editions throughout the world. A longtime member of Romance Writers of America, he won the national Booksellers' Best Award and twice won the national Write Touch Readers' Award. His novels have appeared on such best seller lists as Waldenbooks, B. Dalton and Book-Scan. Bob and his wife, Laura, live on Wisconsin's scenic Door Peninsula.